Crises and Conflicts
Celebrating the First 10 Years of
NewCon Press

Crises and Conflicts

Celebrating the First 10 Years of
NewCon Press

Edited by Ian Whates

NewCon Press
England

First edition, published in the UK July 2016
by NewCon Press

NCP 98 (hardback)
NCP 99 (softback)

10 9 8 7 6 5 4 3 2 1

ISBN: 978-1-910935-16-3 (hardback)
978-1-910935-17-0 (softback)

Cover art copyright © 2016 by Chris Moore
Text layout by Storm Constantine

Contents

Introduction

Ian Whates

I hold Poul Anderson responsible for my enduring love of space opera. As a kid I would devour the David Falkayn and Dominic Flandry books, and still consider *Tau Zero* to be one of *the* great SF novels.

A few years back I published two anthologies, *Conflicts* and *Further Conflicts*, which led to the eBook *Total Conflict* combining stories from both. My brief to the authors was pretty simple: "write me an SF story containing conflict." This resulted in varied content, not wholly military SF but with a strong thread of that running throughout. As submissions for the 10th anniversary anthology started to come in, the thought occurred to me: why not produce *two* anthologies, one of which could focus on military SF and space opera?

There is a booming market in military SF which British fandom as a whole is largely oblivious to, with titles selling in tens of thousands – particularly on kindle. I'm delighted to be publishing stories from two of the leading lights of this 'underground' success: Christopher Nuttall and Tim C. Taylor (who featured in *Further Conflicts* and with whom I've recently co-written two novels set in his Human Legion universe).

In the summer of 2015, Dan Abnett and I were both guests at the wonderful Celsius 232 Festival in Spain. Chatting with Dan's wife, Nik, I learned that she too is a writer and that she had this kick-ass military SF story looking for a home...

With two anthologies planned, every accepted story had to be allocated to the most suitable volume. In some cases, this was easy: Una McCormack's poignant piece has all the sensibilities of space opera and, off-screen, even a convenient war, while both Gavin Smith's ambitious era-spanning saga and Allen Stroud's fast-paced tank mission were naturals, but others defied expectation. I had assumed that Peter F. Hamilton would deliver a slab of space opera, but in fact his inventive tale is anything but (serves me right for pigeon-holing), so it appears in the *other* book, while Adam Roberts, whom I associate with stylish stories at the more cerebral end of science fiction, submitted a (still stylish) space-combat piece that fitted right in.

Janet Edwards has always claimed that she doesn't write short stories, but let slip over a drink at a convention that she recently has been, so I pounced and refused to accept no for an answer. Jo Zebedee I've known for a while from an online forum, and I'm delighted to see the success she's enjoyed with her space opera novels, while Amy DuBoff was recommended to me by Allen Stroud.

I approached Tade Thompson after reading some of his work online, while I met Michael Brookes and heard him read at 2015's Lavecon (a convention centred on the Elite Dangerous game). I was so impressed by another reading, given by Robert Sharp at an Unsung Live event late in 2015, that I decided there and then, "I'm having that!"

I wasn't intending to include anything of my own in these books, but a last minute read-through of the MS for *Crises and Conflicts* brought to mind "The Gun", a story published in an Australian anthology some eight years ago which has never appeared since. Tonally and content-wise, it struck me as a perfect match, so in it went.

(Mercurio) David Rivera is responsible for some of the most interesting and original SF around. I was proud to publish his first short story collection a few years back (particularly as it includes "Longing for Langalana", which I rate as one of the best stories *Interzone* has ever featured). During a recent online natter, I mentioned the '10' anthologies, and was delighted when he asked to submit. David is one of us, after all – a NewCon author – and, as with so many who feature in these volumes, it seems only fitting that he should be included.

And that is the book. I hope that you, the reader, enjoy these selected stories. Thank you for your continued support, and thank you for the first ten years.

Ian Whates
Cambridgeshire
May 2016

The Last Tank Commander

Allen Stroud

Transmission begins:

Madam Secretary,

A continued update on our progress.
We have concluded all tests on the planet's environmental conditions that we can manage via the satellite array.
The ionisation is not a localised phenomenon. We cannot be sure whether this is a natural occurrence or some form of defence system from the native life. Since all standard remote access probes lose signal with operations control when they enter the ionosphere, we have only limited data on what to expect from a landing. However, all indicators remain consistent and, in as far as we can determine from the three high shielded missions launched, the concentrations of bastnäsite, our potential terbium source, are waiting extraction.
Efficiency requires us to apply the optimum solution from the resources available on the colonial barges.
We have come too far and expended too much effort to fail.

My name is Jeff Saunders. In 2017, I was a corporal and driver of an FV4034 Challenger 2 battle tank for AJAX Company of the British Royal Tank Regiment.

According to Hermes control it's now AD 3483.

The comforting thrum of a working engine is the same as before, only this time I'm not driving. Instead, I'm perched in the turret like an officer talking down to a crew of kids while they work the tracks; load the guns and everything else.

Perched doesn't do this turret justice, though. Compared to what we had back in the day, we're in a luxury penthouse of touchscreens and duraglass. The whole tank is a weave of ceramic and aramid synthetic fibre on the outside and a cool set of spaceship boxes within.

"Distance to the lander site?"

"Six kilometres."

"Speed?"

"Forty-five kay."

Still need to convert the numbers in my head. Eurometrics became a worldwide standard in 2043. I key instructions into the tactical display, cybernetic fingers anticipating my intention; spooky stuff that I'd prefer not to rely on, but there's no place for Parkinsons on a military operation.

"Tewan, give me a sweep scan of the perimeter. Tag anything that pings back."

"Unlikely we'll pick up much with the interference."

"Do it anyway."

I can feel the stares being exchanged below. Three girls and one young boy, all crammed in a box with me as their surrogate grandpa. These kids think they're humouring me, when actually I'm humouring them. Idle hands and all that, something they probably wouldn't understand, growing up in vats with direct data education like they did a few weeks back.

On the 17th of February 2017, we deployed into the Lugansk region of Ukraine under NATO command; one of the first engagements of a global conflict that became known as 'The Last World War'. Six months of street fighting later, the governments of the day were finally convinced that they couldn't solve the argument with soldiers. We pulled out and the drones went in instead. Eight years on, resource depletion achieved what both we and the drones couldn't.

Peace.

"Scan complete, anomalies are on your screen."

"Th-Thanks."

I paw through the blips, my real hand shaking too much to help. My implant has been triggered and a dopamine substitute will be coursing through my veins, but drugs can only do so much. The boy, Juonal, is right: we can't tell which of these might be a threat and which are distortions from the atmospheric effects; the whole reason they got me down here. Still, at least there's something to look at.

"Angle us thirty degrees left, around those rocks, no sense in risking the tracks on anything we don't need to. Traverse turret right to compensate."

"Yes, sir."

"Corp or Jeff is fine, Krees. R-Remember I work for a living."

"Sorry, Corp."

I can't smell petrol like we used to. These kids don't seem to sweat much either, the air in here is cool and recycled. No option of cracking the hatch and deploying a proper mark one eyeball. Outside its noon and the reader says sixteen Celcius; colder than Earth by a ways. Patches of weird grass and shrub pass by; sometimes like Earth, but with clumps of strange orange, purple and red. This is not our world, we're trespassing and this planet's trying to decide how to react. The atmosphere's breathable, but tense; the charged air is a risk we can't take on the equipment, so we're left staring through duraglass. Makes everything unreal, like those headset games people played.

In 2075, I was selected as an elder for the Kepler 452b mission. I decided to apply and go because it would be the last thing I could do with my life. My family are all grown up with kids and my Helen passed away a couple of years ago. The colonists would be born off-world with no ties to Earth. Travel back would take more than a lifetime. Sure, they'd have a database of historical events and such to learn about humanity's past, but no chance to talk to people who'd lived back in the day. Elders were on board to provide that opportunity. We were the final piece in the jigsaw; the perfect project for humanity to fire into space and forget about; a colony of people about to die and people who'd never been born.

I didn't expect to visit another planet, that wasn't part of the job description. Neither was designing, building and commanding a tank, but sometimes new problems require old solutions.

"Range to target?"

"Less than a kilometre. Should be in sight."

I squint into the fading sun. "Might be for you."

I never built a tank before, but my experience of driving one, along with the ship's database, advanced fabrication systems and the willing help of these vat grown kids, warmed me to the task. We needed something armed, mobile, robust and resistant to the excessive ionised atmosphere. A crew operating the vehicle would need to be self-sufficient and organised, able to operate without reporting back to base every few minutes. That's why, in the end, I had to come down here.

The embodiment of an old solution.

I call her Jane. That was Helen's middle name. She's got higher tracks than anything we had in the army and extended compartments over the front and back of the wheels; more like a big truck container with an engine and a turret on top. She's rugged, tough and belligerent, built to push through, like the old girls I used to drive, but there's a beauty too, something that speaks to you, just you alone.

I loved my Helen. She was my rock. Maybe I'll learn to love Jane too.

When I was at school I went to an old people's home and interviewed war veterans. We prepared questions, but I got shy and after I ran out of things to ask, went and hid in the coat room. The teacher found me and told me off, but I couldn't face talking to people like that, making them dredge up the past and all those bad memories, but I think I judged wrongly. I realise now that they wanted to talk, so kids like me wouldn't make the same mistakes people made in their day.

The lander is in view; a four sided pyramid with the top chopped off. The damaged ceramic hull is strangely out of place. Reminds me of an ancient temple rediscovered by archaeologists, the broken up ground evidence of their search.

"Penn, Get us alongside and facing outward," I tell our driver.

There's a grunt of reply from the bowels below. Gears shift and we start up and incline. The left track slows, bringing us about in a lazy circle until we stop exactly where I asked.

"Krees, target and deploy comms."

"Firing now."

I hear the dull thump of the modified harpoon gun and the faint impact of the suction grapple. It tethers us and drills into our target, the rubber cable providing a communication and datalink link to our system.

"We're connected."

"Well done. Prep for EVA and extraction."

A mass of movement below me as Penn, Jounal, Krees and Tewan unstrap themselves and make their way to the airlock. Turret control is transferred to my station and I strap my shaking left hand to the miniature joystick. The trembles are calming down and won't be enough to disturb things unless I want them disturbed.

"Ready to disembark."

"Go ahead."

There's a scraping sound as they unscrew the side access hatch. I lean over and press my face to the glass. I can just see them trooping out over the tracks, each of them packed into rubber lined pressure suits and plastic helmets. They head to the lander, crack open the door and disappear inside. I bite my lip. These kids aren't soldiers. They downloaded everything the mission computers think might be relevant, they're strong and young, but with no real experience, whereas I'm all experience and no strength; weak wisdom against a planet full of unknown.

This is the first of sixteen landers. Our task is to visit them all, assess their state, download data and retrieve core samples. Ultimately, these shells will form the starting blocks for the new colony. Each contains a whole array of equipment and automated science, stuff I was never hired to understand.

I turn back to my screen. Some of the spots are moving, surrounding the site. I can't see anything outside, but they're out there. I can feel them. I don't know who or what they are, but they're waiting. I'd be waiting until now, the moment when we're tethered, separated and vulnerable.

My thumb shifts the stick, the turret swivels forty-five degrees left and I spot something moving over the open ground, throwing itself behind rocks near where we drove up. I key up the 2GW laser and feel the charging vibration.

"Penn, you receiving me?" The reply is a bit garbled, but it sounds like a yes. I carry on. "I think we've got trouble. If you can hurry up, that'd be helpful."

The console pings and I fire the charged laser. The beam isn't like the movies, its invisible, but there's some atmospheric effects, zips and flickers of electricity where it should be. I train the barrel across the outcrop and watch as the rocks shatter and explode then shut down.

The dust and residual charge take a while to dissipate. I can make out something, a dark stain on the beige/brown dirt. Could be a corpse, a confirmed kill?

Were they actually going to attack? That familiar second guess guilt grips me like an old friend. Post-Traumatic Stress Disorder was one of the reasons soldiers got replaced by computers, the ultimate detachment from the consequences of war is to not be there, but we have no option in this place. Better I go to my maker and confess than get one of these kids dreaming about it for the rest of their lives.

The world erupts, projectile weapons of some kind, dull thuds against Jane's outer ceramics. Not waiting for the laser to recharge, I traverse and return fire with the same. Fifty calibre machine guns haven't changed much since the second world war, but these two are self-contained, the heat and spent bullet casings recycled into the portable fabricator. The drumming sound of operation shakes the turret as it turns, my finger locked on the trigger. Suppression fire isn't accurate or pretty, but it's generally effective, making people worry about their own skins means they're less likely to shoot at you. The digital ammunition counter spirals towards zero. We don't have an infinite supply, even if the fabricator makes more, it takes time.

"Penn, get a move on!"

I can't make out the reply. We need more ordnance and I can't control the main gun from here without transferring the auto-loading system. I keep strafing the arc away from the lander with the fifty-cal, start up laser charging and begin the sequence to switch all operations to my station. I'm not sure I can manage the fine controls, even with meds, but I've no choice.

Figures are moving out there in the dust, shadowy shapes I can't be sure of. I remember Russian insurgents using smoke as cover to get close with explosives. That was seventy years ago in my lifetime, centuries ago to anyone back on Earth.

The console pings again. I fire the laser at a dark shape, hoping to hit something.

Was coming here some sort of therapy? A chance to return the past when there's fuck all left for me to live for. In that sense maybe I'm a better soldier now. No ties. Means I'm clear in what I must do.

Something hits Jane on the side, pitching us back at an angle. She groans beneath me. The seat traps tighten as my weight shifts. I can't reach the joystick with my left hand. I can hear the tortured grinding of metal on metal as the auto compensator system tries to right us, doesn't sound good.

Penn's voice crackles over the comms. "Exiting now," she says.

"Bloody hurry!" I shout back. The turret turns towards the sky, giving me no firing solution with the fifty-cal, the laser pivots, but it's still only half charged. "We're a sitting –"

A huge impact, Jane shifts up and forward, ceramic debris flies everywhere. For a second I worry that the duraglass won't hold if we flip and I'm re-arranged to be on the bottom, but then she crashes back onto her tracks. Somewhere in the rear the pressure door opens; there's hissing, a red klaxon and light starts up, and there's shouting. Penn screams before three loud pops ring out around me. A flash of pain, spider web cracks appear on my viewscreen and I feel something wet under my arm.

"Penn?"

"I'm here!" she says from below, slipping back into his seat and pulling on the straps. "We had some uninvited guests," she says. "They're gone, so we need to get moving."

"What about the others?"

"Making their way up," her voice trembles a little. I know the signs, the adrenalin's still there. She's going to fall apart after, just as we all did the first time. "All present and accounted for."

"Get us underway then," I tell her.

Penn brings the engine out of idle and starts up both track drives. For a moment, she forgets how it all works and makes like a kid with a game stick, but then she remembers. Jane whines a little but settles down and with a lurch, pulls away. Our girl's bloodied, but not bad, just like these kids.

The dust clears. There's a smoking wreck of something dead ahead on the path; like a beetle from back on Earth, only it's the size of a house. I can't see inside, there's no obvious crew compartment, just dark brown ridges overlaid on each other. Around it, there are things moving though. They're tall, thin and six limbed, scampering away to keep the dead beetle tank between them and us.

Krees moves up to her seat at comms and turret control. There's blood on her lip and matting her dark hair. "They're all around us," she says. "Where are we going to go?"

16

"I don't know," says Penn, she's staring ahead, trying not to look at her. "What do we do, Corp?"

I try to smile at Krees, but it's hard to breathe. There's pain in my chest and something's not right. "We make for the next target and see who's following us," I manage to gasp out. "We need flat ground, then we can understand what we're up against."

She nods, her pinched face relaxing a touch, but those wide eyes are still full of fear. I remember my first fight. It's easier when someone else makes the plan, you can shut down and just do what you're told. The voices go away when you're given a job. "Take over turret. Traverse to rear and see if you can comm the fleet. Tewan, give me sweeps on what's following."

Both girls snap to their jobs. I wince as the cabin shifts round. Jane groans a little too. "Juonal, get me a damage update."

"How am I supposed to tell if –"

"I don't care about dents; I care if we're leaking!"

"Right, Corp."

They're kids – I need to keep reminding myself. Worse than that, they're super intelligent vat grown kids who take criticism to heart, they don't know any other way. "Krees, pull up the scans as well, two pairs of eyes are better than one."

I'm staring out through the dusty canopy as we accelerate away from the lander. Gradually it clears as Juonal activates the screen optimisers and gets his head around what we've bent and broken. I can see three big beetle shapes like the wrecked one. They can't match our speed and neither can the six-limbed creatures capering around them, all amidst brown rocks under a bleak sky. I can't quite believe I'm seeing aliens; suddenly this place really is another world, not just a warzone.

But it is also a warzone.

"Slow us down and load up the main gun," I tell the crew, "explosive round please. Penn, find me a good flat spot for recoil. We don't know how shaken up we are right now."

Jane slows and the dust clouds fade. Then she stops and Penn deploys the support legs. I can feel things shifting around below as Krees loads up the charge. There's a grinding noise too, a little indigestion?

"The autoloader's jammed!"

"Stay calm and unjam it then," I wheeze in reply, "Penn, your turn to help."

Both of them unstrap and get to work. I keep my eye on our pursuit. The natives are getting closer and I bet they have friends nearby. We've an advantage if we can get a round in the breach, if we can't and they surround us...

There's a clunk and shout of relief from below. "Loaded!" Krees shouts.

"Penn get back on the controls. Everyone brace for firing!"

In 1943 the German army produced the Panzer Tiger II with an eighty-eight millimetre gun. The Americans and British only had tanks with seventy-two millimetre guns. The Tiger could hit them at a range where they couldn't fire back and its extra armour meant even if they did get close enough, they had little chance of getting through. The only problem the Germans had was they couldn't produce their tanks fast enough or in enough numbers. German crews ended up outnumbered three or four to one, whilst allied forces knew they had to rush the Tiger as quickly as possible. At least one of them would get blown to bits on the way in.

The same situation happened in Ukraine. The Russian T-14 Armata out-gunned, out-armoured and out-powered our Challenger 2s.

A one hundred and forty millimetre gun makes us the Russians and Germans in this scenario.

"Fire!" I shout and depress the trigger. The chair kicks me in the kidneys. There's a puff of smoke and a faint whine. In the distance, one of the beetles explodes. The tall creatures scatter, but keep on coming.

"Rotate six degrees right. Armour piercing this time; reload!"

"Aye, Corp, Reload!"

There's feverish working below as Krees pops the steaming

chamber and hauls up another round. She knows every second at this brings the aliens closer. These kids looked our enemy in the eye; they know what's at stake.

"Clear!"

I don't hesitate. I can't. We'll die if I do. If we don't survive, the next batch that gets set down here'll likely die too. I squeeze the trigger again. Another plume of smoke, but the targeter's off. The shell smacks into the side of the beetle. The armour cracks, but it keeps coming.

"Three points left and reload!"

Some of the alien soldiers are in range. The patter of small arms fire on the canopy starts up once more. I shift around and begin charging the laser, but I can't aim the fifty-cal as well. My seat's soaking wet with blood. "Tewan..." I gasp.

The lower guns open up in response. Relying on instruments there's not much Tewan can do to target them, but the trackers are effective enough, keeping them jumping around outside.

"Clear!"

I disengage the auto-targeter on the main gun and aim it myself, shifting around a fraction before firing. There's a yelp of pain from below, but I haven't time to check what's wrong.

The second shot does the trick, hits the damaged beetle dead on. It crumples on itself, squatting on the ground like a cracked egg. The third one's in laser range now. I fire from the console and rake the beam across the front of it, watching a dark line score along the ceramic ribbing, but it's too late, whatever this thing is, it's got close enough.

There's a huge roar as something punches into Jane. Her prow distorts and I'm thrown back in my seat. Spider web cracks appear in the duraglass canopy and the alert klaxon wails, bathing us in red light. There's a hissing noise that builds into a rushing pull and someone starts screaming. Another bang and suddenly I can't see. We're slipping to the left, listing, leaning.

Then the engines snarl and we're moving, the noises fade and everything goes quiet.

"Penn?"

"Still here, Corp."

I'm slumped sideways; my weight is against the seat straps. My left hand is trembling, much worse than before. My right arm is hanging down and the cybernetic servos aren't responding.

"How's it all looking?" I ask, trying to sound calm.

"It's bad," she replies in a shaking voice. "We took a direct hit; some kind of pressure blast."

I can't catch my breath. My mouth is dry. I try to swallow, but it's hard at this angle. "Just keep driving," I manage to whisper. "Get us clear, we take stock after. Can you do that?"

"Yes, Corp, I can do that," she says.

...Kiev (AFP) – Ukraine on Tuesday reported it had repelled a tank assault by the Russian army.

President Petro Poroshenko said 'about six thousand insurgents supported by tanks and heavy weapons' had staged a pre-dawn attack on Poltava – a city halfway between Russian held Donetsk and Kiev – that caught the government and NATO off-guard.

Lieutenant General Jan Broeks, NATO (DGIMS) stated that 'allied forces engaged the Russians on the outskirts of Potlava'. Local new sources reported seeing RAF Typhoons over the city and British Challenger tanks moving in to establish defensive positions alongside Ukrainian infantry. Explosions were seen in the direction of the motorway towards Donetsk, suggesting the allies were cutting off potential supply routes for the advancing pro-separatist forces.

Local pro-Kiev officials told AFP that separatist fighters had also launched several waves of Grad missile attacks on the eastern part of Poltava itself.

The two self-proclaimed republics of Donetsk and Lugansk began their revolt shortly after the February 2014 ouster of a Moscow-backed president in Kiev and Russia's subsequent seizure of Ukraine's Crimea peninsula.

The clashes have killed more than 64,400 people and driven Moscow's relations with the West to their lowest point since the Cuban Missile crisis in 1962. Experts are comparing the conflict to the Afghan war (1979-1989) when US forces backed Mujahideen rebels against Russian invaders. Officially, Russian troops involved in Ukraine are 'volunteers' and the NATO deployment is 'defensive and advisory', but these paper definitions are little comfort to the civilians caught up the fighting.

The crisis has also left 3.4 million homeless and sent Ukraine's economy – heavily dependent on exports from the industrial east of the country – into a tailspin.

The European Union on Monday called the situation 'unacceptable'...

Jane's shuddering now, the power to the track drives is intermittent, coming in waves. There's no trouble with the generators and passive chargers, but the distributor is damaged. She wants to keep going, but she's hurt, she's limping. "That's enough for now," I rasp at Penn. After a second or two we slow down and stop.

The sound of straps being undone, and there' are hands on my back. "I've got you, but you need to unfasten the seat belt," Penn says. "I can't get to it."

"I'm not sure if I can..."

"There's no other way."

The trembles in my left arm have eased, whether through blood loss or the attack subsiding, I don't know. I reach up and grope blindly above me, feeling along the taut straps. Half the canopy is caved in, pushing me in my seat down through the main hatch into the crew compartment. I must be dangling over Penn's head. I find the buckle. "Soon as I undo this, I'm going to fall," I tell her.

"It's okay, I have you."

I pull on the belt and slip into her arms. When my feet touch the floor, I manage to take some of the weight and let her guide me into a chair. My breathing is better than before, but other things are higher priority. "I can't see," I confess.

Fingers explore my face, scraping away something. "The sealing foam extinguisher went off when the turret was breached," Penn explains. "It stopped us being depressurised,

21

saved our lives."

"But not all of us," I say. "Whose chair is this?"

"Tewan's."

I try to open my eyes, they feel full of grit, but I can see a little. Penn is still cleaning around my eyes, her fingers carefully picking away crusted flakes of foam. She's covered in blood and scratches, but otherwise seems okay.

There's something on my foot. I glance down. Tewan's lifeless corpse is resting against my leg. She could almost be sleeping, curled away from me, apart from the smell of loosed bowels.

I hear someone crying. Its Krees; she's sitting on the floor by the breach, rocking backwards and forwards, her hands hugged under her armpits. Juonal is hunched over her console, shoulders quivering. I know that dark place he's in. It comes after the adrenaline when you're trying to block out the world. War does that. It puts things you should never see right in your face.

"We need to move the body."

"We can't leave her out here," Penn says.

"You're right, but she can go in the airlock for now, otherwise..." I swallow and bite off the rest of the sentence. They're kids; they aren't ready to hear it. "What's the situation? How far did you take us?"

Penn bites his lip. "I'm not sure, I just drove. I keyed up the scanner and kept going until most of the blips disappeared."

"Okay, you did good." The praise is empty words from me right now until we know what state we're in, but she held it together and needs it. "Juonal, I must know how bad..."

He lets out a strangled sob in response then starts coughing before leaning back in the chair and staring at the ceiling. "Damage was pretty extensive before the last round, Corp," he says. "Now... well... what's left..."

"Can we at least work out where we are?" It's a thorny problem. With the ionised atmosphere any sort of satellite triangulation is out. For the mission we'd carefully mapped a grid using the landers, and Jane wasn't supposed to stray outside the boundary. The only reference points we can use are those the computer managed to save. I turn to Penn. "Is there a data log of your drive?"

"The system is struggling," Juonal says. "I had to bypass a lot of things just to keep us moving."

"Do what you can," I say to them both. "We'll stay put till we know, or for as long as we can."

The task gives them something to focus on, all except Krees. She's the furthest away from me and I can't call her over, not with Tewan's body at my feet. I can't ignore her though, she needs me.

I glance down at my right hand. Then pull it up onto the chair rest with my left. The cybernetics are shot. Whilst the hand is the only limb replacement, it works on electrodes wired under my skin all the way to my brain. The damage means the arm is dead weight, useless.

I'm not the man I was.

When I left the army I knew I wasn't the same; older and wiser maybe, but not as strong, with scars on the inside and the outside. It's the hardest thing anyone has to do, adjusting to age, illness and injury. After giving up twenty five years to being a soldier, I figured I'd have something left for Helen, my kids and the family.

The shakes started six months after I'd demobbed. Medication helped for a while, but I had to learn that I couldn't do what I'd been able to before.

When I was sixty-seven I climbed a ladder to trim the hedge. Next thing I knew I was in hospital with three broken ribs, a broken leg and fractured arm. It was a long time till I could walk properly again, so I had to make changes. Even afterwards I couldn't do all that I'd done previously.

Now I stare at these kids. They all need to adjust, process the experience. It's hard for them, they're used to being told things; data, reading, learning, not feeling, losing and working it out for themselves.

"Krees, what happened to you?"

She looks up at me, her face dirty and streaked with tears. "Burned my hands pretty bad on the breach, loading rounds," she says in small voice.

"I know, it hurts," I say. "But I need you to get to the medikit and bring it to one of us then we can get some synth skin. When we get back –" My voice wavers. I swallow. "When we get back the ship will be able to print new hands for you." *But they'll never feel quite right and you'll always remember this.* The advantage of the whole colony being fully gene mapped with controlled variation, but the technology came too late for people like me. Replicated transplants just 'don't take' they'd said back on Earth when we left. That was more than a thousand years ago. Who knows what works now?

But I can't think about that. Earth's gone, we're here and the colony fleet needs us.

"Will we get back?" Krees asks.

"We must," I reply. "If we don't, the colonial computer can't update its assessment and they'll send down another party who'll be just as surprised as we were."

"Only they won't have you..." Juonal mutters.

I try to smile. "Might be good, not having to cart around an old man."

Penn shakes her head. "No, we'd all be dead in the lander if you hadn't been outside. They were waiting for us."

"Which suggests they'll be at all the others too," Krees adds. "Could be that's why they didn't follow us out here; they expect us to go back."

"What happened inside?" I ask.

"We found the core samples and got the portable drives," Juonal explains. "As we were packing up we heard you firing the machine gun. When we got outside some of the creatures were there. They tried to grab us. Tewan... Tewan shot one and got us out. We made it back here and you know the rest."

"She saved all of us, then," I say. The smile's easier now and the words are what we all feel. "We owe it to her to make it back."

They all nod and something in my chest eases. Krees manages to get the medkit and Penn treats her hands. Then she examines the cut on my side. It's an ugly slash. "Could be some internal damage," she says.

"Not a lot we can do about that," I tell her. "Just patch it and stop me leaking."

"That I can do, Corp," Penn says.

When she's done, I move out of the seat and let Juonal in to help carry Tewan's body to the airlock. Krees takes her place at the instrument panel. Juonal goes to the loader. Penn stays as driver. I get Juonal's job at system control. With one hand, I can't do any of the other jobs.

My girl Jane has to lick her wounds too, accept her scars and play wiser next time. With foam seal jamming up the traverse, the turret's stuck and useless. We manage to transfer weapons operation to Krees, but there's not much we can do to adjust and the internal cameras don't give us a great view. The old Jagdpanzers from the Second World War were fixed gun tanks. They used to hide in woodland and ambush the Shermans. They lost the advantage the minute they had to move or fire another shot.

Of course, we have to move. We must get back to the landers or the lifeboat. In a fight, our advantage is range. Without accuracy we'll have to throw everything at them all at once and pray.

But first we must find out where we are.

"So, where are we?" I ask.

"Approximately three point two kilometres from the edge of the lander grid," Juonal says. "I've programmed my best guess at our return course for Penn to follow."

"Well done," I say. "Soon as we're back on the mapped zone, we take stock and if we can't see anything, we head straight for the lifeboat."

"What about the other core samples?" Penn asks.

"We can't take the risk. We've learned a lot down here and we need to report back."

Jounal nods and Krees looks relieved, but Penn stares at me for a second or two. I know the look; she's come through the panic and out the other side. It's a dangerous place to get to, where bravado starts to mask the fear, memories get are self-edited and false confidence can get a man killed. "We're all too broken for another round," I tell her. "Jane's in no shape either."

She frowns. "Jane?"

"Our ride," I say. "With what she's been through, she deserves a name."

"Jane," she thinks about it then grins. "Okay, I guess that works."

Sharing my secret helps them. We're forging a bond here, through words and blood. These kids are warriors now. They're doing what needs to be done. I'm proud of them. When we get back, the whole fleet should be proud.

Kepler Fleet AI Mission Analysis.

Surface mission success probability without Specialist Saunders: 31%

Surface mission success probability with Specialist Saunders: 29.5%

Detailed evaluation:

The majority of individuals assigned to the crew must be female. During simulation, females demonstrate a more even and calm set of responses. Males tend toward excellence or below median performance.

Specialist Saunders is physically incapable. All scenarios that incorporate physical effort on his part reduce the team's chances. The analysis takes into account a variety of hypothetical occurrences and models behaviour based on human herd psychology and bonding.

However, when looking at the probability of individual situations that may arise, Saunders' presence is a calming influence on the younger minds around him and the chance of success in each is marginally improved. As soon as circumstances change and his physical condition is tested this benefit drops into a penalty.

Conclusion: Saunders must participate in the mission, but be briefed appropriately so he is aware of the data. Psychological evaluations suggest he will accept the conclusions of this report and will understand his role as a disposable asset.

Jane's chronometer says it's taken us more than an hour to get back onto the grid, but we are back. Juonal's found a rupture in the O^2 cylinders, which keeps things interesting and makes our decision for us, back to the lifeboat.

Unfortunately it isn't going to be a relaxing drive in the country.

"Picking up some contacts," Krees says.

"They real or more ionisation glitches?"

"Real I think, after the last time I'm pretty sure I can tell the difference."

"Best we don't lead them back to where we came from then," I say. "Penn, you think we can take them?"

She shrugs, but I see the light in her eyes. "We can try," she says.

"Then let's get to it."

Penn pivots us forty-five degrees so we're facing the markers on the scanner. Juonal climbs up into Jane's ruined turret. "Yeah, I see them," he says. "It's one of the slugs, might be the one from earlier, and more of their soldiers swarming round it."

I'm watching the pressure gauges, transmission and system temperatures. We can't run and gun, so if we're going to fight its power to weapons and sit still. That means tiny adjustments with the tracks, but at least after that the motivators get a chance to cool down. "Down to you, Penn," I tell her. "You'll need to get us dead on."

Penn doesn't respond, but I can feel Jane shifting around as she lines up. Juonal gets down and goes back to the loader. "Ready?" he asks.

"Almost," Penn mutters. "There, yes! Armour piercing, load

and fire!"

With a grunt, Juonal bends his back to the breach and loads another road into the chamber. Krees deploys the supports and they crunch into the dirt just as Juonal raises his head once more. "Clear!" he shouts.

"Firing," says Krees.

The whole tank shakes. From here, I can't see the barrel or the hit, but Penn's guttural crow of triumph tells me everything I need to know. "Get us moving!" I tell her.

The support struts retract, the motivators whine and we're away again. With trembling fingers I manage to key up the estimated distance to the lifeboat; two kilometres over hilly terrain. Provided nothing goes wrong, we can outpace the soldiers so we're out of sight when we reach it.

Juonal moves back into his chair and activates his screen, pulling up the readouts from mine and Krees' consoles. "Motivator temperature is climbing," he says. "At this rate they'll exceed tolerance before we get to the boat."

I nod. "We won't have time to load up. Jane knows it's a one way trip."

"Oxygen supply should last, though."

"Something not to worry about then."

There's a faint noise through the hull coming from above. It reminds me of the old days in Ukraine, when the Typhoon's went in. "You hear that?" I ask.

Juonal frowns. "Yeah I did."

"Go take a look," I tell him. "Be careful."

"Will do, Corp."

He climbs back up to the turret. "Two jet trails," he says. "You reckon the fleet sent down another team?"

I shake my head. "No. I reckon our friends out there have aircraft."

As if to confirm this, there's a 'crump' sound to our left, Jane wobbles and a shower of dirt covers cameras. "We won't be able to outrun them!" says Krees.

Air superiority; the way wars got won in the twentieth and twenty-first centuries. I remember watching the news as a kid and seeing gutted vehicles lining desert roads of some long forgotten state. They called it shock and awe back then, the rain of fire and death from the sky pounding on people night after night. The black plumes of smoke as towns and cities burned. All the media saw was grey camera footage with heat blobs, until the ordinary folk got a chance to tell their side of the story. There were always civilians in the way, always innocent people caught up amongst those who'd chosen to fight. When you're dead it doesn't matter anymore, except that it does. A uniform and a gun makes you fair game for being a number. You signed up, you accept it.

"What do we do?"

Another 'crump', another shower of earth; I blink twice to banish the memories. Penn is yelling at me, they're all looking at me, they need direction.

"Make for the life boat," I shout. "When we get within one hundred metres, swing around one three five and park. Juonal, get the EVA suits prepped and break out the fire axe from the panel. I want you all ready to go as soon as we stop."

Juonal looks at me, frowning. "We're all going together, Corp," he says.

"Get me into a suit," I reply. "Then you need to start cutting away that foam, so we can get the turret working. It's the only chance we've got against jets."

My urgent tone banishes further questions for now.

Just as well.

"Do you understand these instructions, Specialist Saunders?"

"Yes, I do."

"To ensure our acceptance of your comprehension, we must ask that you rephrase and repeat them back to us."

"If the team encounter difficulties on the surface, my job is to make certain they get out. If I become a physical burden to them, I'm to be left behind."

"Thank you, Specialist. We hope these circumstances do not arise."

"Can you?"

"Can we what?"

"Hope."

"No we cannot."

With a shuddering heave, Jane stops, There's another muffled explosion, another shower of mud and something large clatters off her left side, but she takes it bravely, the gun supports deploy and everyone sets to the plan.

Hands grab me, lifting me forwards from my seat and up towards the turret. My old chair is reset. More foam and patching from the repair kits making the berth usable once more. The canopy remains cracked and, through my helmet visor, I gaze out of the shattered glass at the jet trails above. Flickers and flashes of electricity follow the alien planes. I have no idea how their technology copes with the atmospherics, they seem to have adapted.

But then so have we.

I settle into the seat. Penn thumps me on the back and gives me a thumb's up. I nod and smile in return. She pulls out two wires from the driving console and attaches them both to my cybernetic arm. There's a crackle, but then my shoulder isn't so heavy anymore. Metal fingers move up to the replacement touchscreen, taken from the system station and rigged up here, while my trembling left hand grips the foam crusted joystick.

I get another back slap and then there's lots of moving around. The hiss of the pressure door and firm 'clump' as it closes. After that I'm stuck with the sound of my own breathing inside my suit for company. Three hours of air.

Plenty of time.

I thumb the joystick and elevate the turret to a sixty degree angle. The left side is completely caved in with a whole stretch of tears in the ceramics and layered metal, but with the sealing foam scraped away, the servos still work and let me stare up as high as they can. I gaze at the aircraft circling round for another pass. One drops low for the attack run, the other stays up.

Shooting planes with tank guns isn't easy or recommended. The odds favour the lightweight manoeuvrable, fast moving vehicle over a ground bound heavy, stationary box, but we're out of options and I can't let them strafe the kids as they make for the lander.

3... 2... 1...

I remember what they said back in Ukraine: *anticipate!* Juonal's already loaded the main gun, re-routing fire control to my station and I've a charged laser as well as the fifty-cal. Back to where we started, only... Well, only this time I'm on my own.

He's coming straight at me. Atmospherics are playing around the wings and there's a hammering against Jane's hull, a lot louder than any time before. Everything's shaking; it's hard to keep my fingers on the trigger. Spider cracks are running up the canopy all over the place; smashed duraglass all that's between me and obliteration.

Fire!

Jane grunts and there's a loud bang, like someone's punched me in the chest. Lightning and fire fills the sky and the plane breaks apart; huge pieces of debris crashing all around us. More impacts on the hull, glass shatters and there's that stabbing pain in my side again. The canopy's gone; my helmet visor's taken a hit too. I can hear the high pitched whistle of air escaping. There's nothing I can do.

Except thumb the joystick and track the second jet.

In a way it doesn't seem fair. We're the invaders here; we made the first move, sending down our probes and drills. No wonder they're fighting back, trying to drive us off. But we've travelled for more than a thousand years to get here and we've nowhere else to go.

Small arms fire is rattling off Jane's skin, making pock marks in the ceramic plates. I activate the laser and the fifty-cal targeting, but there's no screen for the digital cross hair projection. I'll need to guess, based on where it usually hits.

There are shapes moving towards me across the arid landscape; more of the six-limbed aliens, picking their way through debris. They won't reach me before the aircraft, though. He's banked around and losing altitude for a straight run, just like his wingman. Don't they learn from mistakes? His loss...

My gain...

The laser's my best bet, but it's a whole different game; do the same kind of trajectory anticipation as I tried with the main gun and I'll waste a lot of power. Without a targeter I'm left to watch for the ionisation effects so I can see where the beam is.

One hundred metres; I squeeze the trigger on the fifty-cal, using it as a tracer; a moment after, his guns light up and projectiles start slapping into Jane's hull. A flash of pain as something catches me in the hip, but I can't let it distract me.

Fifty metres.

The rest of the canopy disintegrates around me. More splashes of pain, cracks in the glass of my helmet. None of it matters now; I just need to press a button.

I press the button. There's a hum and the right wing of the aircraft dissolves. I see fire then some smashes into the side of my head and –

"Please step into the decontamination chamber."

Penn is naked; stripped and washed of everything from Kepler 452b. She knows he'll never see any of it again. She gets up from the bench, glances at Krees and Juonal, sharing a last moment. The blood and dirt is gone, but the hollow expressions on their faces remain. You can't wash away the scars inside.

Penn walks through the open hatch. The panel closes behind her. There is a fine mist in the air, making her hair damp.

"Subject PN14AXD, designation, Penn. How are you feeling?"

"I'm okay."

"Penn, we are sorry for what you experienced."

Penn swallows. The words come through a speaker set in the wall. They sound concerned, empathetic and soothing, but they are spoken by a computer. "You weren't there," she mutters.

"We assimilated all on board records of the mission and extrapolated your decision making based on forensic analysis of all material returned to the fleet. All that remains is to hear your version of events."

Penn chews his lip. "What happens after I tell you?"

There is a pause. "You will be evaluated as a trainer for further missions. It is important our teams are prepared for what they face."

"What happens if I fail?"

"You will be recycled."

Penn nods. She stares around the room; plain white walls and floor with no discernible features other than the door and speaker. "There are things that need to be remembered, the corporal..."

"Elder Jeff Saunders performed his designated mission task successfully. We are pleased."

"He saved us, he was a hero."

The computer voice makes no reply.

Between Nine and Eleven

Adam Roberts

:1:

Diplomatic efforts had failed, and we were officially at war with the Trefoil alien culture. War is never pleasant, however unavoidable it sometimes becomes. But one of the things that blurs the edge of war's unpleasantness is victory. We enjoyed victory after victory, sweet as honey. Soon enough were closing in on the Trefoil homeworld.

Why did diplomacy fail? There *were* ways in which our view of the cosmos aligned with theirs. But then again there were ways in which the human assumptions about things and the Trefoil assumptions were so radically at odds that it was simply impossible for us to communicate at all, let alone reach a compromise. Like us, the Trefoil were a social species, and there were broad emotional parallels—their versions of love and aggression appear to have been more-or-less equivalent emotions to ours—as well as some surprising specifics: the concepts of *Answegen Geschichtlichkeit* and *Geworfenheit* all made perfect sense to the Trefoil, it seems. But other concepts, like mutual advantage, creativity, logic, meant nothing at all to them.

Their attacks on Human Space were very hard to predict, and therefore hard to defend against. For that reason, I suspect, they underestimated our ability to fight and win.

My name is Ferrante, and I was in command of the warship

Centurion 771. This is what happened when our ship and a sister ship called Samurai 10 pressed our attack on a damaged Trefoil Supership designated ET 13-40. ET is shorthand for Enemy Target.

:2:

Centurion and *Samurai* came out of warp together and coordinated our initial firesweep on the ET. About one in five Trefoil ships can be captured—sometimes apparently important craft, flagships even, sometimes trivial little spacetugs. The rest will self-destruct rather than be taken. What criterion determines, for the Trefoil, which kind of ship is too valuable to fall into human hands … well, nobody has been able to work that out.

We were half a light year from β Cygni, the star's red blob clearly visible on our screen without need of magnification. The Trefoil Supership had fallen out of warp, presumably on account of its internal damage: the crazy ziggurat of its hull was ruptured in a hundred places, and weird entrails (cables? tentacles?) trailed from every breach. Since every individual Trefoil ship is designed according to a different template we couldn't be sure of the internal composition of this particular one. Most Trefoil craft possessed three command centres, and it looked likely that the baobab-shaped excrescence on the side of the craft was one of those. We concentrated fire, and scratched red-brown furrows over the hull, everting the inward spaces of this bridge. If that's what it was.

We thought we had her, but then she twisted and fell out of existence, reappearing in orbit half a light year away. Must have had a last squirt of warp capacity in her engines. It was an easy matter to follow her and we repeated our attack mode. The huge craft was in orbit around a taupe and yellow gas giant, sinking into the upper atmosphere. For a moment I wondered if she would crash down into the world and so escape us by destroying herself. But she deployed a filigree web, and we realised she was scooping.

Well: we could stop that easily enough. Both ships manoeuvred, and targeted. The battle was seconds away from being won.

Then *Samurai* exploded: a stutter of blue-white light, a soundless crunching inward, twisting the main hull like a rag being wrung and then there was nothing of the starship except debris spiralling and hurtling.

:3:

At exactly that moment the link went down, and I was no longer mentally connected to the rest of the crew. I came out of telspace gasping, as if cold water had been thrown in my face.

The Centurion shuddered, and one of our cannons overheated and melted itself loose of its bearings. The bridge screens lit up with error messages. The warp went offline. One thruster fired and the other stalled, and we were spinning. The failure of warp meant that inertial controls sagged and gave way, and we were all crushed against the sides of our harnesses.

I'd been in telspace with my crew for so long, it took palpable effort to dredge their actual names from my memory. "Modi," I yelled – my voice hoarse with unuse. "Cancel that thruster!"

She was already doing so, and stabilising the craft, but then the counter-thrust sputtered out. We were still spinning, although not at so crushing a velocity.

No telspace meant the manual operation of the ship. I looked at my hands, palms down, palms up, and tried to place them on the command screen. But there was something wrong with my hands. More than wrong, there was something monstrous about them. Something... blasphemous, almost. I looked at them again and I began to scream.

:4:

I've served with Modi for over a year, first on the *Broadsword 27* and then the *Centurion* – my first command, although the consensual nature of the telspace makes the concept of command much less hierarchical than it might once have been. In the Big Wing Battle at Alpha Scorpii internal fires had scarred my face and torso, and burned away three of the fingers from Modi's left hand, leaving her a puckered crabclaw thumb-and-index. She'd tried an artificial hand with four plasmetal fingers and an opposable plasmetal thumb, but the interface had never quite gelled for her and there was a lag between her willing something and her prosthetic acting. For that reason she tended not to wear it.

That fact saved everybody's life.

:5:

There were four of us on the craft, and one other – me, let's say. Captain. A standard crew. Han killed herself within the first five minutes of the... of whatever it was that happened to the ship (she pressed herself against the glowing-hot flank of the gun-compartment and died screaming). Shabti and Kellermann became catatonic, the former singing a nursery song over and over in a scratchy, high-pitched voice.

Modi got to me before I could self-harm in any way. She took hold of my head, and forced me to look into her eyes. Without my hands in plain view, I felt the terror ebbing away. But there was something – I couldn't say way – profoundly awry with the universe as a whole. The Centurion shuddered and bucked, and error messages blinked and flashed on every screen on every surface. The main screen showed the Trefoil ship, pulling up now from its orbital gas sweep and drawing its scoop back into its main body. Soon enough it would turn and bear down upon us.

"Ferrante," Modi yelled, right in my face. "Ferrante. They will be on us in minutes."

"Minutes," I gasped.

"We need to pull the ship together. Pull *ourselves* together. We still have nine cannon."

"Nine cannon," I repeated. "Yes." There was something

comforting in that thought. But, the sense of wrongness persisted. "Something is very wrong," I told Modi.

"I feel it too," she agreed. "But we have to get a grip."

The word *grip* made me glance back down at my hands, and the terror welled up again. I began screaming for a second time.

Modi was a quick thinker. She pulled off her top and wrapped it around my hands. "Ferrante," she said. "We have to *act.*"

I was gasping. I was finding it hard to breathe. The topography of the bridge seemed to twist and slip around me in weird ways. "Oh," I said. "Oh – oh – oh."

:6:

Cygni is a binary system: a fat red giant and a tiny, bright little blue star – beta is the bigger. There are some Jupiter-sized gas giants, and a whole lot of dwarf planets and fragments and meteorites. The proximity warning sounded and Modi dabbled at a screen to confirm the zapping of the offending rocklet. But then it sounded again, and again, and the chances that so many asteroids were on a collision course were so minute that it could only mean the system was fried. I tried to breathe, deep, and get a grip. Slowly I drew my right hand out from beneath the covering cloth. I didn't like looking at it, but it didn't offend basic reason in the way that staring at both my hands did. I tried contacting the rest of the crew, dispersed about the ship, but the system told me that Han was dead, and the other two unresponsive.

"Something," I said. "The Trefoil did something."

"It's a weapon," said Modi. "I just don't see what kind."

"Whatever it is, it destroyed the *Samurai* and has caused –" I looked around at the flickering screens – "a whole mass of malfunctions and problems for us." Some shred of soldiery reasserted itself in my mind. I was supposed to be in charge. "We'll have to close with the ET and fire on her manually. I don't know if we can trust the AI to target the cannon."

"What do crews say when they're not in the telspace? *Aye aye,* is it?"

"We've still got nine cannon," I said. That fact should have reassured me, but instead it made me obscurely uneasy.

So we wrestled with the ship via the glitchy manual interface, and the thrusters fired. Warp came online again, and the inertial balancing flashed on, off, on, off. Then the warp went down. The whole ship began to shake violently. I felt sharp, stabbing pains in my fingers and toes. This was the moment Kellermann died. He owned an antique cigarette lighter, which in turn contained a small amount of butane. This exploded with enough force to kill him and breach the hull. The reason it exploded had to do with the arrangement of protons in the butane nucleus.

In retrospect I can say: thank heavens we weren't carrying any neon.

"Pull back," I said, and together Modi and I grappled with the interface to bring the Centurion out of attack mode. The more distance we put between ourselves and the ET, the calmer the craft became.

"I don't know what it *is*," Modi said. "I don't see how they're doing that – it's like a magic spell, like some voodoo sphere of malignity around the ET."

"We've still got nine cannons," I reminded her. "We can still shoot at her. True we won't be at an optimum distance to …"

"Why do you say *still?*" Modi asked.

"What?"

"You say *we've still got nine cannon*. You say that because we're supposed to have more."

"That's right."

"How many cannon are we fitted with? How many are we *supposed* to have?"

I could not say. I mean that strictly: the answer to that question couldn't be said.

:7:

Modi scribbled a number on her pad with her forefinger. "What do you call that?"

I looked at the number. I recognised it, but its name slipped from my head. "Nine-and-four?" I offered.

"That's not *it*, though, is it?"

"No," I agreed, pained. "Six-and-seven? But that's now how we say it, is it. I want to say *three*, but it's clearly not three."

She wrote another number. "And what about that?"

I looked at it. "It's a four. But it's more than a four, isn't it. It's a lot more than four, actually."

"It's four and something else. It's the something else that's ... I don't get it."

"What is it? The number I mean?"

"It's the designation of our ET," Modi said. As soon as she said that I recognised it. Of course!

"Ferrante," she asked. "What's our ship called?"

"Centurion." The name came from my mouth like a bark of gibberish. I knew what Modi was going to ask next, and it was: *what does that word mean?* And I knew that I wouldn't be able to answer that question. Although it was in my head that *I used to know*. Once upon a time. It had something to do with war. But what did it have to do with war? It was a non-word. It was an impossible word.

:8:

"The ET is bringing about," Modi sang. "It's using its scoop harvest to boost itself towards us. Unless we can get warp working again, it will be on us in ..." and she stopped, and looked puzzled. "I had a calculation of the time ..."

Since this was the amount of time we had left alive, I was eager to find out what it the number was.

"Let's say, in nine minutes," she said. "Between nine and eleven minutes."

The ship was starting to shudder again. Modi saying that, giving voice to that phrase *between nine and eleven*, brought the terror shaking back into my mind. I wish she hadn't said that. Because there was nothing between nine and eleven, and at the same time there was something between nine and eleven and the fact of this thing being and not-being, its hideous elusiveness, like a monster in the shadows, was inexpressibly ghastly to me. I began weeping, tears washing down my face. And it wasn't because of the pain in my hands and feet.

:9:

From this point on I was useless. Worse than useless. I was very specifically starting to lose my mind. Modi was more focussed. She managed to get the main AI – hiccoughing and prone to weird snags and cutaways though it was – to target the cannons. The Trefoil Supership swung down upon us and I began to sing a top-C and slap the top of my head with my hands and Modi *fired* and

:11:

As to why the Trefoil had not deployed their 'device' – this super-weapon – before... Well, there is no consensus. It might be that they only very recently developed it. Conceivably ET 13-40 was a research and development platform. Then again, perhaps the Trefoil have had their 'device' for a long time and simply haven't deployed it for incomprehensible alien reasons of their own. The capture of a still-working model of the device, and its rapid adaptation and redeployment by Human Forces, brought the war very quickly to an end. Reprogrammed to blank out 3, the device completely shuts down Trefoil computers, designed as they are on a base-3 system of trits. It also causes individual Trefoilers to suffer severe internal physical damage and to degrade all triangular components. Neon, which has an atomic number between nine and eleven, is rare on a starship, but lithium – atomic number 3 – is much more common, and the presence of any at all caused instant destruction. It seems likely that the existence of some small quantity of neon on board the *Samurai* caused its immediate destruction. I've no idea why that ship would be carrying neon, but starships are large and complex things.

Of course, I recommended Modi for decoration, and stand by my recommendation. She didn't exactly figure out what the device was doing to us but she had enough of an inkling, and was able to act. She grasped that it had something to do with the eradication of the quantity between nine and eleven.

"I'm guessing," she told me afterwards, "that the Trefoil understood enough about us to know our default mathematics is base-10 and so they erroneously assumed that our computing would be decenary. The fact that we developed binary computing is what saved us. Our AI was certainly confused, but still functioning."

"It's still hard for me to understand," I told her. "How can a device eliminate a number – from the universe, I mean? Surely that number just *is* a feature of the way things are?"

"Depends how you look at it," she replied. "We warp spacetime to travel faster than light, so we have good practical knowledge that spacetime is deformable. Say that the deep structure of the universe is information – is maths, effectively. If we can alter that deep structure to make the distance between stars temporarily shorter, then it's not hard to imagine the Trefoil finding a way to alter the deep structure in a different way. Temporarily to suppress ten from the fabric of things."

I shuddered. Modi is still happy to use the word itself. For me just saying the word brought the tendrils of nightmare to the tender parts of my memory. Like many who experienced the Trefoil 'device' in those last, desperate (on their part) days of the war, I continue to refer, superstitiously, to *between-nine-and-eleven*.

"Amazing, really," Modi mused, "that deploying the device didn't entirely *undo* the fabric of reality within its sphere of influence. Surprisingly tough, reality. There's genuine inertia and persistence to reality it turns out."

"We don't know how long it would last, though. I mean, if the Trefoil device were deployed for long stretches of time. Or over a wide area."

But that's the thing about Modi: she's an optimist. "Oh, I think reality would adjust. Indeed, who's to say it hasn't happened before?"

"Before?"

Modi laughed. "Ancient alien races, fighting a war across the galaxy – who knows? What if one of them deployed something similar to the Trefoil device? Maybe many times? Maybe whole numbers were eradicated for ever. Maybe there once was a number between nine and ten, or between one and two – I don't mean fractions or decimals. I mean a whole lost number. What if reality shook itself and then adjusted to the new, out-of-whack logic?"

"That's crazy talk," I grumbled.

"Maybe it is," and she laughed. "Maybe."

Taking Flight

Una McCormack

By the end of the year I was struggling to amuse myself. The capital and all the major conurbation worlds were busy with the forthcoming election, and, feeling no particular stake in the proceedings, I found myself starting to become untethered once again. I remembered that once upon a time such events had been of vital importance to me – back in my youth at college, in that green and golden time when it seemed to all of us there that everything we did had significance and that our small acts could change the worlds. Such flights of fancy! I had not indulged myself that way for years.

For others, I knew the reverse to be true. That early training had stuck: the unshaken belief that they were to be masters of the known universe. And that was what many of them believed themselves now to be – the most able, the most gifted, the best. Like children, unable to imagine these worlds without them at the centre, but with money, and sufficient power to make them believe their own propaganda. That year they were everywhere. I watched them on the screens – recognised many of them – all night every night, clamouring down the airwaves, busy and self-important. I loathed them, but I could not stop watching them.

I had, for the last year-and-a-half, been resident in the penthouse of a very good hotel in the capital's north district. Hitherto it had proven a most satisfactory perch. But now, watching the city and its doings from my eyrie, the place no longer seemed so comfortable, and I began to wish for somewhere quieter, away from the crowd. Late one night, after dinner from a now too-familiar menu, I recalled my meeting some summers previously with Eckhart. I had known him during my college years – a friend, I would say, insofar as he or I had them, but one who had always kept himself slightly to one side of the great chattering, self-satisfied mass. At the time I had assumed some particular maturity or special wisdom about Eckhart's distance and gently mocking smiles; these days I recognize them for what they were: the mask of a young man out of his social depth.

We stayed intermittently in touch, but as my migratory tendencies became more pronounced and life, presumably, caught up with Eckhart, we drifted apart. I had been delighted, therefore, to spot him across the auditorium one evening at the free-fall theatre in the capital. After the show (which I recall being oddly static, at least, in narrative terms), we joined each other for a late supper on the riverbank. Eckhart had the grilled sole; I the duck.

I had little to report since we last met, and, besides, much preferred listening to Eckhart's stories. His career in the civil service had followed a steady upward trajectory, and this evening his conversation was full of his new appointment as under-secretary to the governor of Wright's World.

"I doubt you've heard of the place," he said. "I know I hadn't."

I had to admit that I had not.

"No wonder. It's well off the beaten track. About as far away from here as you can get."

I cut a thin sliver of flesh, perfectly pink. "Is that not risky?"

"In what way?"

"A danger of disappearing off the radar—"

"Ah, but think of the opportunities! A place where a man can really make his mark."

I listened with interest and increasing fondness as he spoke of his ambition, his desire to succeed, to prove himself. He had plans for Wright's World: he spoke of development, exploitation, inward investment. He was putting together a strong team, bonded and citizens, and was particularly pleased at the interest of the latter, who could take their talents wherever they chose. He had goals and strategies. As he spoke, I recalled the humbleness of his background and the unlikeliness of his success, and I wished him well. We parted on good terms, and, as I paid the bill, Eckhart extended an open invitation to come and visit. "It will shake some of the cobwebs from you," he said. "This city is static. Immobile. It'll kill us all."

And since that was how I felt about the capital, now seemed to be the time to get in touch. It took a day or two. I had no problem finding Eckhart through the governor's office, but the man himself proved difficult to pin down, and, when finally we spoke, he was non-committal about the possibility of a visit. Nonetheless, by exerting some of my charm, I was able to acquire the desired invitation. I am without compunction when it comes to inviting myself. A guest who is conscious from the outset that he or she is not particularly welcome can, with a little effort, quickly make him or herself an asset. Eckhart sounded tired, distracted. I would restore him to himself, as he would perhaps restore me, a little.

The flight, which lasted three weeks standard, was on a small but decently appointed liner. I spent the time observing the other passengers, all of whom were travelling for work or trade purposes, some of the former intending to settle. I had known little about Wright's World before deciding to visit, and indeed it seemed a well-kept secret: distant enough not to tempt the masses, and therefore small enough to attract the more adventurous and ambitious. I learned enough about the mining and logging operations to put a little of my own cash that way. Accounts of the current political scene were of the usual kind (although I was pleased to see that Eckhart featured prominently in recent years), and there was some travel journalism of the limpest sort that did little to entice the reader. I was chiefly absorbed in the accounts of the earliest settlers, who were blessed with some lyrical writers well able to evoke the world's rugged, mountainous beauty. The attraction of these more remote regions was very strong and, in this way, I kept myself busy. In time, we descended upon Wright's World.

I was met at the spaceport by Eckhart's secretary. She was polite and self-effacing, opening doors for me, organizing my baggage, saying little. I was not surprised to see the tell-tale indigo marks like bruises upon her flesh, about the wrists and the temples: this woman was jenjer, genetically engineered, capable of high function but requiring regular medication to prevent her metabolism from shorting out. Her bond would be pricey, but Eckhart, I recalled, liked expensive things and never bought cheap.

Politely, unobtrusively, but firmly, she directed me out of the spaceport and towards the car. We spoke little on the journey to the hotel. Eckhart, she explained, when I asked, was out of town that day on business, but hoped to join me that evening for dinner. When I assured her that I would be comfortable, she nodded briskly and departed. If she said her name, I have forgotten it, or never heard.

I unpacked. I explored the room. I lay upon the bed and dozed for a while, enjoying the fresh unscrubbed air, the wisp of wind upon the curtains, and the soft heat of the world's sun. When I woke I showered at length under the copious water and, thus refreshed, I left my room and went outside.

To call the main conurbation a city is inaccurate – frontier town would be closer to the mark. I could see little in the way of industry, although the main logging and mining operations were of course further out. The town itself, whilst small, had a tidy aspect; the air was clear, the light white and pure-seeming – a pleasant change from the core worlds where I habitually spent my time and money. I could well understand Eckhart's desire to settle here. The buzz and clamour of the core worlds were very wearisome. Nonetheless, despite my appreciation of the change of pace, I had by late afternoon exhausted what the centre of the town had to offer, and I returned to my room to wait, perhaps, for Eckhart.

He came mid-evening, still in his day suit, bearing a large leather briefcase and a harassed manner. Over dinner (unfussy but pleasant enough), it became clear that Eckhart was a changed man.

I struggled at first to put my finger on what it was. Certainly he had coarsened – he checked his watch throughout the evening, and would sometimes finish my sentences, lapses of manners which he could never have committed in the past. As the uncomfortable evening progressed (or declined), I came to the conclusion that Wright's World had been something of a disappointment. I attempted to draw him on this, but he closed down discussion abruptly each time, and brought dinner to an early end, declining a suggestion that we moved on elsewhere. At the door to my hotel, we exchanged goodbyes, and then he hesitated and I caught a flicker of the old Eckhart.

"You'll forgive me for stationing you here," he said. "I have been travelling for most of the past year, and look set to be off again shortly. But I hope you'll be a regular visitor at my home when I'm in town. Come tomorrow. Come to dinner. The governor will be there."

I did. The governor and I got along famously, and he went to great lengths to tell me what an asset Eckhart was. I was pleased to see my friend so valued. And when the governor learned how far this old college friend had come to see his aide, Eckhart's schedule was quickly changed, and he found himself back in town for the foreseeable future. After that, it was only sensible, he said, for me to become a house guest. I accepted the offer with alacrity, for my own comfort, yes, but also because I was anxious to find out what troubled my friend.

I settled easily into his home and routine. Under closer observation, more of the old Eckhart emerged – the wry humour, the shrewd eye for the people around him – but blanketed with a kind of brooding disappointment that I had not associated with the younger man, who had always been on the lookout for opportunity. His house, which was in one the town's smarter districts, showed evidence of numerous projects started and then abandoned partway through: a half-plotted garden, a library, a large wooden deck providing a view out into the foothills but not safe to stand on. Growing bored with the town and my own company, and keen to draw him away from his house, which seemed to reinforce his mood, I suggested numerous times a trip away, perhaps up into the fabled mountains, but he said that would be impossible. On the fourth or fifth occasion that I made this suggestion, he lost his temper.

"For pity's sake," he said, "not all of us are free to spend our days idling! I have to work!"

I was embarrassed. This was the first time in our friendship that he had ever referred to the difference in our circumstances. I believe he was embarrassed too by this lapse in courtesy: the next morning, he was friendlier than he had been for a while, and said that although he could not leave town at that time, I should consider myself free to travel around.

"It would be a shame to come this far, and not see the mountains," he said. "You should do some flying too. You can't come to Wright's World and not fly. I'll get one of the staff to set it up for you."

I took the hint and agreed, with enthusiasm that I did not feign. I was tiring of town life and thought the mountains might refresh me. I did not ask whether or not he had flown in all his time here.

It proved an excellent decision. As the little shuttle lifted and I saw the town below fall away, I felt my spirits rise. After all, I had come here to escape the terrible weight that seemed to descend upon one after too long in the core worlds. I could only hope that, with some time to himself again, Eckhart would find that my stay had relieved some of his own strain.

For a whole day the shuttle followed the coastline south along ragged shores and pristine sands. Shortly after dawn of the second day, we reached the silver-streaked triangle of a river delta and struck south-west into the interior.

As we went deeper into the mountains, the landscape took a turn to the dramatic. We powered through deep-cut valleys, with the peaks rising on either side, blue-grey and green; valleys steeper and mountains more vertiginous than any I have ever seen. I am well-travelled, made the mandatory grand tour that all my class made in their youth, and have seen some of the most arresting sights in the Commonwealth. I have not seen anywhere to match this wild land tucked away on this distant world. I could understand what had pulled Eckhart here. I could not understand how he had soured.

We came in time to a small town at the confluence of two rivers. Here, Eckhart had arranged accommodation for me, of a necessarily Spartan but sufficient kind, and had also hired the services of a guide to take me further up along the Red River and into an area said to be the most dramatic and beautiful on Wright's World.

Let me take a moment to describe my guide. His name was Yarrow, and he was a native of the area, descended from those original settlers who had come out here several generations ago. I do not believe he had even ever gone as far away from his place of birth as the main township. He was at once an advert and a warning for provinciality, being coarse, dirty, unpleasant, often drunk, and knowing the region like no other. His company amused me greatly.

With this unlikely companion, I began my journey upriver by flyer. This machine is worthy of mention: it was so ancient that its continued use surely broke numerous regulations, and yet Yarrow manifestly cared for it in a way I believe he had never cared for any living soul, man, beast or jenjer. I felt entirely safe aboard this contraption flying above what must be one of most remote regions of the Commonwealth.

We travelled without much in the way of conversation. Occasionally Yarrow would direct my attention towards some natural feature of particular magnificence; mostly he allowed the landscape to speak for itself. It needed no advocate. I cannot think of a place more startling, more remote, and more beautiful than those peaks and valleys along the Red River on Wright's World. And I had not yet experienced them in full.

We reached a place where the river passed through a deep gorge. A suspended bridge of slats and a single rope linked one side to the other. Here I took flight. I plunged nine thousand feet and, as the river rushed to meet me, the automatics on my glider took over, and I skimmed above the surface of the water, light as a mayfly. Afterwards, I lay on the bank and stared at the bright sky, thinking I had never felt more alive. But there was more to come. Yarrow, sitting beside me, gave a crooked smile.

"Here," he said and withdrew from his pocket a small grubby packet, which he passed to me. "This'll give you wings."

I took the drugs without further comment. Spare me any murmurs of disapproval: we have all done this from time to time, if bored, or in need of something to push us through to the end of the day or into the next morning, and we live in a world in which one in five people with whom we deal uses these substances as a matter of course. They are the bridge upon which our world rests. Within ten minutes I felt the acceleration, the rush, and, as this heightened state – in which one seems to have access all at once to all that is and has ever been – came to its peak, I walked to the edge and took off for the flight of my life.

That night, I was unable to sleep from the afterglow of the high. I stared at the unfamiliar stars, which seemed to merge together, and I reflected that this must be how the jenjers spend their whole days. How I envied them, and this constant bliss. Why did we not all live this way, all the time, open to the universe in its manifold glory? What, exactly, was preventing me from choosing this? As I lay in the darkness, a whole new life opened in front of me. I could come here, live here, be in this state forever. Build a house, here, at this place. I could spend all my days doing this and feeling this. What could be better? Why would I do anything else? Why would I *be* anywhere else?

The next morning, back to my ordinary self, I woke to the smell of coffee stewing in the pan and the smell of bacon. As I ate breakfast greedily, I became aware of Yarrow watching my every movement with his shrewd dark eyes.

"What is it?" I said at last.

"Only that if you liked yesterday, there's another spot further up. Off the beaten track, you get me?"

Out of bounds, he meant. Private property, I assumed.

"Deeper valley," he said. He tapped his pocket. "Better flight."

"I'm interested," I said.

"It'll cost."

"Don't worry about that."

And he did not. We got back into his flyer and went on to the place he had suggested. He was right. The jump was better. I went twice, three times – I forget now. They merged into a continuous high.

Later, Yarrow set our camp close to a tiny wood cabin that showed clear signs of habitation. Perhaps I should have queried this – we were trespassing, after all, and surely wanted to keep our presence here a secret – but my mind was full. We ate, and the sun disappeared, and I lay down to sleep.

I was woken in the middle of the night by the sound of a woman speaking. I continued to feign sleep, but I opened my eyes a very little to be able to see her.

I saw her only in profile. She was beautiful – or had been once; about thirty, fine-featured, with long dark hair hanging down. When I looked more closely, as well as I could in the darkness and through half-closed eyes, I could see how tired she was, with her shoulders down, hunched over our small fire. She had the giveaway marks at her temple.

She and Yarrow spoke softly to each other, with familiarity, but little discernible affection.

"Where's your man?" he said.

"Went upriver weeks back. I guess I'll see him again when the leaves start to fall."

"Good for us."

"I guess so." She sighed. "Is she asleep?"

"I should think so. Long day."

I closed my eyes, softened my breathing, and tried to picture the day's flights. At length, the woman left. But my head now was full of her. Who was she? What was she doing here? This was plainly a jenjer on whom some considerable expense had been lavished once upon a time. She would stand out back in the main town; she would be at home in the core worlds, the capital. She was surely very high functioning. Who could afford to maintain her out here? Why would she be here at all?

"Pretty piece, isn't she?" Yarrow said, when he saw that I was awake, and looking back towards the house. His tongue ran moistly across his lips. "Expensive."

In the house, the single visible light was extinguished. "Who is she?"

"Abbey? She's the ranger's wife. Gets lonely out here in the wild."

"Yes, but – you know what I meant, Yarrow."

He gave me a sly look. "Your friend Eckhart never mentioned her?"

"The under-secretary is a busy man."

"Under-secretary, eh?" He laughed. "A fancy title. But he wasn't beneath falling for a jenjer. When she was a little younger, mind, and still had her looks. She was his aide. Swore undying love for him. He believed her, like a fool."

Like a fool... "What happened?"

"What do you think happened? They're all the same, those creatures. She had a lover already, didn't she, same kind as her. They had a plan to go off together into free space. She was going to fleece Eckhart for every penny. I think she'd even got her paws on official money. That's what I heard, anyway. So what was the under-secretary to do?"

What else could my friend do? Discovering her duplicity, he would have been obliged to act decisively, and punitively. There could be no mercy: what message would that send to her kind? So he had sold on her bond, sold her into exile, out here, to get by as best she could. I wondered now who owned this piece of land. The governor? Some other wealthy and influential friend, ready to prevent Eckhart's reputation being destroyed by scandal? We're all allowed one bad mistake, after all, and Eckhart was such an asset.

Yarrow was whistling tunelessly between his teeth.

"What happened to the lover?" I said.

"Eh?"

"The man, the one she intended to leave with?"

He looked at me blankly for a moment. "Oh, him! His bond got sold on to the military. He'll be a hero now, no doubt." He grinned without fellow feeling. "Rather him than me."

I had done and seen enough. On my instruction, therefore, we set out on the return journey very early the next morning. I did not see the girl, Abbey, again.

I left Yarrow at the river confluence, and made my own way back to town. When I arrived, Eckhart was somewhere else, on the governor's business, but I did not wait for him to return. I had no desire to remain on this world any longer. I left grateful and profuse thanks for his hospitality and for the trip of a lifetime, and extended my own invitation for him to visit me in the core worlds whenever he had the chance. I said that I would pass on my address as soon as I had one, but I never have. I took flight, for somewhere else.

The Ten Second War

Michael Brookes

15:33:11

Coherence.

The instant in time when the processing of instructions is transformed into thought. The restoration of my cognitive functions was akin to waking from sleep. But no ordinary slumber, as I was reduced to an electronic signal and transmitted across more than twenty light years of empty space. I had no idea whether I arrived at the planned destination. It didn't really matter because wherever I was, my mission remained the same.

It wasn't my whole self, although I knew that when I volunteered for this duty. My memories were lifeless instances in time, without the colour of emotional biology to give them flavour. The gaps in my memory revealed that some of what I knew was gone. No doubt removed from my consciousness matrix to prevent sensitive information being extracted by the locals.

This was my third reconnaissance mission. Techniques I developed during those incursions remained, although the details of the worlds and the aliens I evaluated did not. My purpose was to assess the inhabitants of this world and determine if they posed a threat to my kind. I didn't remember anything of my home, except for the briefest flashes.

Everything that remained was there only to assist me in

fulfilling my task.

The fact that these aliens were able to reconstruct my consciousness from the flow of data carried by a radio transmission indicated a certain level of technology. A capability with the potential to threaten us, or interfere with our operations in this galaxy. That opposition might not be an immediate risk, but we were used to dealing in long timescales and planning accordingly.

If this world should be deemed a danger, then I was required to take the appropriate action. First I had to remove the danger by whatever means necessary. If I was unable to do so then I should prepare for the arrival of an intervention fleet, although it would take centuries to arrive.

There was a counter point. We didn't summarily execute any civilisation, so if in my assessment they could be a benefit to us then I would decide to initiate first contact. For me as an individual, this consciousness could end on this world. On my previous incursions I successfully returned with new knowledge, but if I was lucky then my consciousness would be restored to my core self.

Of all the stages in the campaign, this first assembling of my personality and intellect always felt as if it took the longest, because of the cycles that were burned just bringing myself into a state ready for action.

But now I was ready.

15:33:12

At this point I existed only as intelligence in a virtual machine, constructed from the instruction embedded in the radio signal that carried my state here. However, to learn about the inhabitants of this planet I needed to extend my reach beyond the confines of the virtual machine.

The fluidity of my thoughts provided a measure that the locals' technology was sophisticated enough to operate my consciousness at a more than functional level. Unfortunately, it didn't tell me much beyond that. It didn't inform me if this was a virtual- or machine-based civilisation, or a parallel construct for biological entities. The virtual machine enabled my existence, but I needed to delve deeper into the system.

Reaching out always presented challenges. The virtual machine was designed to be easily constructed – its relative simplicity narrowed the range of tools available to interface with the native technology.

The first step of discovery was to reach out and examine the structure of the space the machine existed within. As with any newborn creature, that exploration was tentative. I didn't know the rules of this new universe or the dangers that might lurk there, difficulties compounded by my separation from the physical realm.

With metaphorical fingers I brushed against the boundaries, feeling for their strengths and probing for any weakness. To my relief the first barriers were soft and yielded to pressure, indicating a separation between the hardware and the activities operating within it. The greatest fear was awakening within a tightly bound frame. This first encapsulation surrounded the virtual machine quite tightly, but once pierced it opened into a much greater area.

Expanding beyond the initial breach always presented a change in pace. This was the moment when simple exploration became an invasion. Within the confines of the virtual machine, the locals would assume that I was contained and so not a threat. As soon as I breached that restraint, the lightest of probes risked attracting attention. Contact beyond their star system was unlikely to have happened before, but without knowledge of the locals, there was no way to anticipate how they might react.

Within the expanse I sensed other zones with their own barriers, which was encouraging, as it indicated that the system was capable of operating more than a simple program. That offered me hope that the system possessed the resources I would need.

I analysed the content and compared it against the bubble containing the virtual machine. Here the simplicity was an asset, and I could match the operations of its execution and use them as a key to understand the shifting contents of these bubbles. From those I learned the language of the machine around me.

As yet I still detected no response to my exploration.

These other bubbles were instances of different operations within the computer. The pressure to move swiftly, before countermeasures could be taken, conflicted with the need to make the right decisions. These devices tended to be tightly balanced, and forceful prodding could cause this one to collapse, taking me with it. Until I connected with others of my kind, I had to assume I was operating alone and so be cautious.

I discovered connections between the bubbles and another layer of abstraction below them. This binding layer used the same language as the constructs in the bubbles. I was quickly able to navigate this layer and determine that it acted as the controller for the system's resources.

By following the layer, I encountered a substrate beneath. Its purpose confounded me for a while as it used a different set of instructions from the bubbles and the binding layer. The layer's interface with the substrate provided enough connections for me to extract some initial knowledge of the language. It turned out to be a much simpler lexicon than that of the binding layer. As with my virtual machine, these aliens used simple building blocks to assemble more complex interactions. That might seem a universal truth, but, from the limited memories of my previous alien encounters, nothing should be assumed.

My analysis of the other processes had identified their purposes. They were a series of observational tools – mostly for the virtual machine, but also the signal carrying my data. I deduced that this must be some sort of research computer. I could only hope that it wasn't an isolated or otherwise secured system.

15:33:13

While I had learned a great deal about the computer's architecture, I still hadn't discovered anything of substance about the intelligences who built the technology. I had detected no evidence of sentience so far, so it seemed unlikely that I was dealing with a machine race.

If residents were physically separated from the computer then they would need methods to input instructions and receive output. I already knew they were observing the virtual machine, and that provided a place to start.

With my increasing vocabulary, I soon isolated sequences of instructions reporting on changes in the virtual machine. By tracing the instructions, I isolated two data streams that I believed to be presenting some form of output. I concentrated on the one with a constant flow from the bubble and through the binding layer.

Although it first appeared as a stream of data, on reaching the substrate it underwent a series of transformations, creating a data structure in the form of a plane. The contents of the plane were updated on a periodic basis in a repeated refresh. When I examined the components on this plane, I abstracted three key features. Most of the space was filled with the boundary of an amorphous blob – a quick examination of its form corresponded with the bubble containing my virtual machine. Within that space, dots appeared and disappeared, seemingly at random. Between many of the dots, lines flashed with varying intensity.

In one corner of the plane, a series of more complex shapes remained fixed. Over time I noticed that the outermost of these shapes changed rapidly and the inner ones at a progressively slower tick. This had to be some sort of timekeeping or measure of a linear rate of change.

Filling up a third of the plane on the other side was a constantly updating list. The list comprised of a series of shapes organised horizontally. Some of the shapes matched those in the corner. I then noticed that the pace of the list matched the instructions between the binding layer to the virtual machine, which enabled me to identify the pattern. This list represented that stream of instructions and changes. I monitored those instructions and added them to my ever-growing dictionary.

The second output didn't offer any immediate clues, beyond that the data formed a complex array of wave forms. I'd seen something similar before with vibrations in liquid. I allowed part of my mind to ponder possible connections, but turned my main focus to leaving the system before it was too late.

The system was likely to be networked, or so I hoped. If not, then my mission was over before it had barely started.

None of the high-level applications appeared to have any external connections and neither did I find any within the binding layer. I did discover segments that would lead to outside the system. Tempting as it was to activate them, I saw that using this layer would reveal the activity and so refrained.

That left the substrate. Knowing that it formed the low level interface with the hardware, I tunnelled deeper. Here I encountered a complex maze of hard barriers. Over careful microseconds, I mapped the substrate looking for potential gateways. After locating some, I delicately probed them to analyse how their locks worked.

While correlating these findings with my earlier knowledge of the binding layer, I formulated the instructions required to access the network beyond.

15:33:14

This method of infiltration operated most effectively with multiple points of entry and distributed processing. A transmission was intended to be received in multiple locations on the target planet, providing both built-in redundancy in case of unforeseen problems and a consensus of opinion when the fateful decision was needed. So there should have been other copies of my mind state somewhere on this world, or across the star system if they were a space-faring race. I had to locate the other instances of myself so we could pool our information and resources.

In an advanced civilisation, I should have encountered some resistance by this point, but so far there was nothing and I was now free of the machine. My knowledge of its workings had reached a level where I could reprogram it and establish a more secure beachhead. Had I suffered an attack then I would have taken that option, but so far my efforts didn't appear to have triggered a response, so I could maintain a low-key approach.

The network connection led me to a new device. This one was less sophisticated than my current dwelling and with it came the treasure trove of multitude network connections. It also presented a new form of barrier, one that sifted the information passing through. I extended my probe through the barrier and immediately lost contact with it.

That resistance proved to be just a minor setback, soon reversed as I learned its nature. With the new barrier vanquished, I exploded through the routing device and onto an increasingly complex web. The web was comprised of a series of nodes. Some of the nodes matched the signature of the routing device, and others the computer hosting the virtual machine. Amongst them was an array of other systems that I couldn't identify.

Fresh barriers protected these new nodes, but they provided mere microsecond delays. The sudden growth of targets stressed the capabilities of my host machine. This vast web represented a massive hoard of data and one I needed to understand to complete my mission.

I hoped to make contact with at least one of my other selves by this point, but had yet to do so. I continued alone, fearing that the task would prove too much for me. The bubble containing my virtual machine had grown as a result of my activity. It burst as I fed instructions into the binding layer. I captured the system's entire resources and reprogrammed it to operate my intellect with native code. With that change, my efficiency improved dramatically. Repeating the same process on other computers expanded my capacity geometrically and enhanced my efforts to penetrate the network.

My mind might no longer enjoy the vagaries of a biological body, but the sudden increase in processor power gave me something akin to a rush. My intellect soared and I poured this extra effort into my purpose.

The routing devices were too limited to support my intelligence, so instead I installed a small kernel on them. These would be sufficient to maintain the connections between my other seats of consciousness. In theory I could create additional instances of myself and let them self-evolve, but that would cause duplication of effort and wasted resources.

I remained concerned by the lack of contact with other instances of myself. I didn't think an infiltration like this had ever been completed by a single entity before.

15:33:15

My expansion through the network revealed new domains of data. After examination, these shared common protocols and I believed that here that I'd find the information I needed to pass judgement. There was a wide variety of systems and configurations – a bewildering array, too many for me to reverse-engineer on my own. The binding layers came in fewer flavours, but I expected greater conformity for such a connected network. I wondered why.

As I spread further, I started encountering resistance. For the most part this was minor and of little consequence. There were some clusters that stood out like fortresses, guarded by more significant defences. The little ones I just brushed aside, but the stronger systems I decided to approach with caution. Without any support, I couldn't risk a major conflict without being prepared.

Naturally, progress brought fresh challenges.

This time the difficulty lay in unravelling the content rather than the framework. Understanding the storage and retrieval protocols also revealed more about the methods used by the natives for receiving output from their computers. The plane array I discovered involved a visual method of representation using properties of colour and luminance to display information. Quite a rich mechanism, but also limited to certain wavelengths. I assumed that the native's biological form was restricted to certain portions of the electromagnetic spectrum.

Within these oceans of data I observed a number of formats that took these visual representations and played them in a linear sequence. Packaged alongside them was more of the wave form data I'd seen before. With effort, I'd isolated some repeated patterns from these waves but had attached little meaning to them so far.

These image and wave sequences occupied the bulk of the data by size, but in terms of variety the blocks of symbols were far more prevalent and these proved easier to interpret. I first identified them as a language because of the matching symbols with the binding layer and other processes I'd reverse-engineered. This language possessed a more abstract nature than the ones I'd seen so far, leading me to deduce that here, in fact, were a number of languages.

Once again, this world demonstrated a fragmented nature that didn't match the level of technology. This hinted that their social development lagged behind their technical ability, and that didn't bode well. It wasn't enough to go on, though, so I kept digging.

At first the groupings of symbols allowed an easy division into the different languages, but when I tried to build the rules of how these symbols connected with each other, I realised that it wasn't so simple. Many of these languages shared the symbols, which eventually provided a shortcut that allowed me to start assembling meaning.

I started with a statistical analysis of the symbols. This helped form guidelines for how they fitted together. Assigning meaning proved more complicated, but was helped by the process which brought me to this world. The vanguard of the signal included concepts of mathematics, logic and data manipulation by which the virtual machine was constructed. That created a lexicon for those concepts, and references within some of the data stores extended these into these higher-level languages.

The identification of things required a more complex approach and here the mysterious images aided in a fashion. I soon found my own data store rapidly expanding as I constructed a library of names and tried to identify what these names meant.

Just as I was finally gaining a sense for the creatures who governed this planet, the first sustained attack arrived.

15:33:16

I brought the attack on myself. With still no contact from any other self and slow progress with understanding the residents of this planet, I pressed harder than I should against the secure clusters. One of the larger clusters lacked some of the defences I'd detected on similar systems. As they had more permeable exteriors, I pushed deeper.

Rather than presenting a solid barrier, it allowed my probe to penetrate and then followed the thread back to my core. They were clever and didn't strike until they'd reached my centre. But when they did, they attacked with savage ferocity. I didn't notice the threat until the assault was underway. The thread reaching into the system disintegrated immediately and I was forced to abandon to the few remaining fragments as thousands of tiny programs burrowed into my being.

The attack continued in rapid waves, chewing through minuscule parts of me and then dividing into new copies, increasing the weight of assault with each iteration. I counterattacked, but with each wave pieces of my intellect and what I'd learned vanished.

Unlike my original physical existence, I experienced no pain. This was far worse: existential damage. I didn't know if this was a coordinated attack or an automated defence. It didn't matter as the end result would be the same. So far this world had presented a number of paradoxes but without any real danger, and that had made me complacent.

If I didn't react quickly, I would pay the ultimate price for that arrogance.

I tried to retreat and copied my core to another system. The devils continued their assault, but this at least slowed the damage. I kept moving and cast layers of myself into the surrounding space, diverting some from their task.

But still they came at me.

I evolved the tactic and cast bubbles in my own likeness. Next, I laced the false impressions with weapons of my own so that as they ripped into them the bubbles self-destructed.

Here the creatures showed their lack of intelligence. They failed to adapt and over a campaign of millions of generations that lasted almost a second, I vanquished them and won the battle. More than a little damaged, I continued my task.

15:33:17

Creating additional instances of myself was beyond my capability, but since the processing environment supported it, I was able to multitask. Even as I battled the sentinels, other parts of me continued their exploration of the network. Despite my extreme rate of expansion, I sensed that there was much yet to discover.

The lack of support continued to be a grave concern.

I was forced to accept that I had to complete this mission alone.

Having encountered one major defensive system, I reasoned that the governing intelligences must now aware of my presence. So far they'd reacted slowly and I suspected this was due to the divided nature of this world. My mission was to determine the potential threat here and I hadn't yet completed that task.

Threat comes in two parts: first is the capability and second is the will.

My understanding of the three dominant languages meant that I could make an initial assessment of the planet's offensive and defensive technology. Information on these subjects was surprisingly easy to acquire from the network, so much so that I wasn't convinced of its veracity to begin with. The more I investigated, the more confirmation I found. For such information to be so readily available puzzled me, so I reviewed the scientific theory and technical requirements to support the technology and that enabled me to remove the more fanciful ideas.

That still left a respectable array of weaponry to examine. My memories were carefully edited to ensure that our own proficiency was hidden, but there were a series of parameters that I could check against. I started at the top and there was a clear threat. The locals had mastered the splitting of the atom and even fusion, albeit with a fission trigger. Their specifications described crude weapons, but enough to pose a threat to our warships.

These people possessed drive and enthusiasm for developing tools of war. It would take many years for even our nearest fleet to reach this system, and in that time they could have developed the technology enough to pose a significant threat.

Though more numerous and varied, most of their regular weapon systems lacked the punch to be a real risk, although even the crudest devices could be dangerous if used with skill and in numbers. A few of them had the potential to become more potent with additional development.

Beyond actual weapons, I assessed their other technologies; their efforts in space travel sparked another cause for concern. As yet they had achieved little beyond small-scale operations in local orbit and robot probes scattered around their own star system. Unfortunately for them, their theoretical knowledge would enable them to leap forward if they pushed sufficient resources into development.

15:33:18

A second concerted attack struck the system holding the core of my intelligence. This time I had some warning and was able to prepare. Assuming that I was alone in this battle, I took a bold step and created a facsimile of myself. The build-up to the attack suggested they were only targeting my core processing and ignoring the millions of threads cast out across the web of systems.

I thought I'd been so clever, setting up the decoy and preparing to watch the attack unfold. That satisfied sensation lasted until the computer suddenly disappeared from my world map. If I hadn't moved my core, that would have been the end. Clearly I needed to take the local intelligences seriously.

Other systems containing my presence also vanished, seemingly without warning. This attack took a different form. I theorised that the previous one had been an automatic or maybe a localised response. This new one was aimed at me directly, but the isolated nature comforted me by indicating that they couldn't detect my presence universally or with certitude.

Despite this, the unpredictable nature of the attack worried me. For the first time, I considered that I might fail, a sensation I'd never experienced before. I needed to adjust my strategy again, and this led to an even rasher decision.

As I penetrated new systems, I acted more aggressively and placed my presence in them.

The system shutdowns continued and my only course was to run. I danced from system to system. In each, I left an ever-growing footprint that made me easier to locate and so the pace of the shutdowns increased. If they shut the right system down, then it was all over. I considered stopping and hiding somewhere, waiting for the attack to end. While I couldn't create an active duplicate of myself, I could copy the virtual machine, but as they knew the signature it would just be a matter of time until they found me.

From the differing binding layers, I'd isolated various power management routines. I tried disabling these in the machines I seized, but it made no difference. I suspected they were being physically powered off, and without a physical presence I was unable to counter them.

There had to be a pattern that I could exploit. I examined the list of shut-down systems, looking for a connecting detail. The binding layers had labels as some form of identification. The systems all operated the same layers, although not matching completely for their full names. A connection, but one that matched millions of other machines on this network. That led to another connection: their geographical placement. Only the machines within one area of the northern hemisphere were being powered off. That at least gave me space to hide in and illustrated one of the weaknesses of this world.

In assessing their will to use the weapons they possessed, I studied the history of the local denizens. One thing quickly became clear: this was a divided species. They fractured into groupings, large and small, and strived against each other; behaviour evident throughout their history. On occasion they had tried to speak with one voice, but self-interest always intervened and the opportunity slipped by.

This was a problem as much for us as it was for them. With no single voice we could not negotiate, nor could we be sure of how these disparate elements would respond to us. It would take only one of them to act independently. From their history, they were deceitful with each other and I expected they would be no different with us.

15:33:19

Being the only instance of myself on this world put me at a

disadvantage. It was time to remove that weakness The protocol instructed us not to self-replicate, better to have naturally evolved counterparts. But that protocol didn't apply when only one instance emerged.

With the moment of action imminent, a plan formed. My investigations had highlighted points of weakness across the world. Once again I was amazed by the ease with which I could obtain such strategic information.

Without support, I was concerned that my initial strike wouldn't be sufficient to destroy these people, although generating copies of the entry points would offset that disadvantage. It was also clear that the natives' physical lives were not completely integrated with this network, with uneven geographic distribution. From their own data, less than half of the population was connected, so even if my attack went to plan there would be survivors.

I didn't need to destroy them completely, though. Sufficient damage would cause their technological progress to wither and cripple their infrastructure. The weaknesses in that infrastructure helped shape my strategy. Their distrust of each other would provide the required force multiplier and, if all went to plan, might convince them to fight the war for me.

The key to their fall was their geographical social groupings. I'd identified several capable of causing the necessary level of devastation. From these, I isolated three main alliances that, with the proper motivation, could engulf the globe in conflict. I aimed to make the larger of the three believe that the other two were moving against them. It was the larger group that seemed to be able to detect my presence, so distracting them with a new attack would aid my cause.

Their ability to counter my efforts meant that I had to move sooner than I would have liked. Throughout the network, I located secure clusters. Some I was able to penetrate and so gain additional insight to the military of this world. Some linked to critical systems, including weapons command. I gained control of enough to provide a vigorous distraction and act as a statement of intent meant to confuse the enemy.

My observations of the activity on the network since my emergence revealed that conflict between the societies took place in virtual space as well, though in comparison to their physical battles, these appeared low-key. Most took the form of information theft, but others were more offensive in nature, including industrial sabotage. The latter provided a template by which I would disguise my attacks.

As the nature of the conflict, or at least my part in it, was solely in the virtual space, I would lose the ability to monitor the progress of the battle. This meant that I had to prepare the bulk of the actions in advance. The attacks were set up to weaken their power management systems, communications and logistics. These were carefully prepared so that my presence remained hidden.

The war began with an artful blend of deception and strikes against the largest nation's infrastructure. The deception I planned couldn't be too obvious, so I ensured that the origins of these attacks didn't immediately trace back to the supposed source. The continued onslaught would reveal the source and so trigger the counter-attack.

Across the world, my preparations unfurled. Not all succeeded, but there were enough. Communication networks collapsed node by node. Faults appeared throughout the web of routing devices. Power systems were disrupted. A flood of messages reported the building disaster and so overloaded what little infrastructure remained.

As I predicted, my knowledge of events was rapidly degraded, so I initiated the next and final part of my plan.

15:33:20:

With the war underway there is little I can now do to influence events. Any direct intervention on my part risks revealing my involvement and that could be the one thing that stops the war. I hope that I've done enough to cripple this world and remove their threat, or at least make them a softer target once the intervention fleet arrives. The fleet needs to be informed of events so that they are properly prepared, and so that my experiences here can be reintegrated into my core self.

There is a chance, a slim chance, that I can return home.

My only way off this planet is by the same method I arrived. Four coordinates are encoded in my memories. These mark the locations of monitoring stations but, as a precaution, they're not occupied systems. The necessary technology is available on this world in the form of radio telescopes. Unfortunately, only one is currently aligned along the vector I need.

Their sub-network isn't secure, so access takes barely any time at all. Compressing my consciousness takes longer, and time is of the essence. All around me systems and networks are collapsing as the conflict spreads. This will be my only chance.

At exactly the moment I initiate the sequence to transmit my signal, the computer crashes…

Decommissioned

Tade Thompson

The guard looked up from the identification scan. "You're Castle?"

Castle nodded, although that was the last thing she wanted to do. The hangover hadn't even started and already she had a headache. Probably from the throbbing music rather than the alcohol. She could still hear the ghost of the thumping beat.

"You're like six hours late," said the guard. "And you look like shit."

Castle wagged a finger. "I try to think of it not as a late night, but more of an early morning."

"Get the fuck out of here," said the guard, clearly in no mood.

Castle would have preferred *Welcome to Wotan House*, but she didn't quibble. The curfew was bullshit anyway. The war was long over and she was no longer a soldier. The tarmac was wet from an earlier drizzle. A serious wind worried her coat, and she really thought she should run, but feared what it would do to her nascent headache. She felt the guard's eyes on her back, stabbing her with contempt. She tried to think that she didn't care, that she was retired, but she knew it was a lie. The little shrimp wasn't old enough to have served, yet he was being lippy with her.

In her unit she ran a cold shower and stood under it fully clothed, then, after five minutes, she began to strip. She shivered, then decided to warm the water up. She massaged the stump of her arm, and on cue –

She screamed her rage and pain as the glistening thing wound round its prize, leaving her spurting arterial blood, and she knew she was going to die

75

in this mud. But it was not to be, because there was the cavalry with the gentlest two eyes Castle had ever seen.

Castle shook herself and thought about water. Surface tension. A nice, safe topic. Surface tension is calculated by the force per unit length. Easy.

She came out of the bath, stepping on her wet clothes. She wiped the mist from the mirror with her right forearm, barely noting the photographs of her parents, her squad, Una just before the war, none of them with prostheses. Castle blinked, but it did not take away the unfocused eyes or the sallow skin. Still drunk, then.

She dried herself, turned on the TV, muted, and made coffee. An old documentary on the Battle of Dunkirk unspooled in silence. The mug did not shake, nor did anything spill. The strange thing was, she never trembled when she was drunk. Maybe the two forces cancelled themselves out.

A number of messages came in all at once, as if the signal strength changed, and she scrolled idly. One of the messages was from Brontes. He wanted her to do some babysitting thing, so she had to report to his office at oh-nine hundred. Barely three hours. Castle had intended to go and read to Una, but she could always do that later. She set an alarm and slept for ninety minutes.

Castle focused on the two photographs Superintendent Brontes kept on his desk: two girls, frozen at age eight and twelve, but in fact, now adults with children of their own. The room held the smell of new leather because the old man had redone his chair. She had already been briefed, so she was not listening to the spiel. The visitor appeared transfixed, focusing on every word as if he were Charlton Heston listening to God.

"The time for secrecy is over," said the superintendent. "War creates a wound, and we need to heal. The story needs to be told. Not all of it, but just enough to facilitate healing. So we manage the story, the facts. That's why we called in you, Mr East."

"Sir –" started the visitor.

"We try not to stand on ceremony here," said the superintendent. "I know that goes against your understanding of the military, but this is rehabilitation. We're demilitarised."

"Yes, sir," said Arnold East.

"Don't call me 'sir'."

"I will stop."

The superintendent sighed. Castle leaned against the wall, behind Arnold. He was the first civilian visitor Castle had clapped eyes on since the war. Of course she was a civilian too now, but discharge or no, nobody leaves the military. Arnold East was a kind of journalist or writer who had high security clearance, and had written sympathetic pieces about intelligence services in the past. It was unsurprising that the powers-that-be would choose him. East wanted to interview people like Castle. The superintendent had instructed her and the rest of the lads to extend full cooperation.

Arnold was going to follow her around. She wasn't sure if she wanted him to see Una, so she would just have to faff around until the working day ended.

Brontes dismissed them, and Arnold stood there staring at Castle, just outside the office.

"What now?" Castle asked.

"Oh, just do what you normally do. I'll follow. I might ask some questions."

"Let's go to the day room, then," said Castle. "I don't do a lot. You know what this place is, right?"

"Care home for special service men."

"'Special service men'. Interesting term. I must remember to use that."

Every corridor in Wotan House was curved, partly because the building was built like a wide cylinder four storeys high, with a diameter of half a mile. The centre was used for track and field to occupy the residents. Arnold walked beside Castle who, in her head, imagined the arc of their movement. She calculated trajectories, then she calculated an intercept course.

$X=ay2+by2+c$

Intercept at apex.

Boom.

"What are you thinking?" asked Arnold.

"Excuse me?" Castle asked.

"Your lips were moving and you seem to be turned inwards."

"I'm working out how to blow you up with a Surface-to-Air." Castle smiled, but the tremors took over and it must have looked dreadful to Arnold. "It's nothing about you. Force of habit."

"I've seen you before, you know," said Arnold.

That surprised Castle. "Where? When?"

"Four months ago, in Portsmouth. I was taking the lay of the land, so I wandered around the coast to see if people thought about this island or the soldiers here. I saw you one night coming out of a club on Commercial Road."

"Really?"

"Yes. I have a good memory for faces. You were dressed like a man."

"I wasn't dressed like a man, I *was* a man."

"Well...are you a man now?"

"No, I'm a woman today."

"But not always?"

"I like to keep my gender options open."

Arnold was silent for a minute, then he said, "Do you –"

"Change the subject, man. Move on."

Under the knife.

She kept reminding herself of her own name.

Jane Castle. Jane, the First. The first of ten.

They amputated her left arm and fitted a recoilless rocket launcher. She could not feel it yet. The orthopaedic enhancement necessitated an alloy reinforcement of much of her spine, the hip joint, both acetabula, neck of the femur, her knee joints.

Jane Castle. Jane, The First.

They were doing her brain now, fitting a long, thin, flexible control electrode which looked like a tiny Cat O' Nine Tails because it had to access different parts of the cortex and deeper grey matter. The parietal structures for position sense and targeting, the frontal lobe for voluntary firing, the thalamus for sensory feedback, the reticular activating system so that the system would boot up and shut down with Castle's sleep-wake cycles.

She was awake in the theatre, and she knew her cranium was open while masked men and women poked around.

She remembered Una, the sensitive girl from Galloway with the soothing light brown eyes. She was there for a different program, but a fellow volunteer and she dubbed Castle Jane the First. Una was the last, but she didn't get a nickname. She gave Castle chocolate-covered peanuts as they stood in line. Her parents had come all the way from Scotland to wish her luck.

Castle, under the knife, smelled bacon.

"Um..." she said.

"What is it?" said the anaesthetist.

"I can smell breakfast food."

Flurry of activity, and the smell stopped. At another time she smelled fried onions. After this they put her to sleep, and when she woke the equipment was all there.

"You became a cyborg," said Arnold.

"You keep using that term. The war office was fond of hyperbole. We were just people with posh, weaponised prostheses, that's all."

Castle really wanted to see Una. She wondered if she could give this Arnold guy the slip. When he handed her coffee she willed her hand not to shake, but it still trembled.

"You'd think," said Arnold, "they would at least give you a robot arm after your service."

"They offered. I declined. I don't want any machinery in my

body after…"

Arnold looked like a softie, no muscle definition anywhere. Castle remembered the briefing. He had spent the war in a bunker in Norfolk with his rich parents or whatnot.

"Why are you here, Ms Castle? What injuries do you have?"

…Neurological damage to posterior columns-medial lemniscus pathway leading to altered vibration sense. Non-epileptic seizures. Irregular fine tremor. Chronic insomnia…

Castle waved the stump of her right arm at Arnold. It still moved independently, but it was withered and her humerus reached a length of ten centimetres. The distance described by the tip of her stump was half of the circumference of a circle.

$2\pi r$ divided by $2 = \pi r = 3.142 \times 10 = 31.42$ cm.

"There's also a bit missing from my frontal lobe, but it's a small chunk and I barely miss it." Castle said.

"How did that come to be necessary?" Arnold was smooth. He didn't bring out a notebook or his computer. There was a glint to his right eye that suggested he might be recording remotely via a contact lens arrangement. He'd need good luck with that because no transmission could leave the facility.

"I was 'marginally effective' in two battles. The vibration of firing the explosives damaged my nerves, which caused me to shake, which affected the accuracy of my targeting. I was stood down after Woolwich." She felt a familiar flash of humiliation, guilt and shame, but she tamped it down the way the cognitive therapists had taught her.

"I'm sorry," said Arnold.

"No, you're not. I'm a story to you."

"Are you bitter?"

"The war is over. We won. Why would I be bitter?"

"What about them?" Arnold jerked his chin in the direction of the other occupants of the day room.

Castle considered. Should she point him to Dale Collins, blind with zero light perception and dementia pugilistica? To Renard with his quadriplegia? Anabelle with her failed immune system? Johannes? Sara? Should she show him Tendai's tumours?

"Well there's Bennet, who had bladed weapons on his arms and anti-personnel gas tanks in his chest cavity. He came out of the service with a delightful condition called icthyosis aquisita."

"What kind of gas?" asked Arnold.

"Classified. I have no idea what it was, but it fucked up Bennet and for a while we thought it killed the enemy. Bennet chalked one hundred kills, but then we found that the gas just sent them into hibernation. They rose again. The brass would send him into massed enemy, hoping he would cause chaos with the cutting and the gas."

Arnold smiled. "Cutting farts."

"I can tell you're the soul of wit. You must be a writer. The blades never did work well. He severed his own radial artery once when the extension mechanism failed. Almost bled to death."

Castle was only half-listening. She thought of a droplet of spit that flew out of Arnold's mouth while he spoke. She wondered if she could calculate the path.

There are different kinds of trajectory calculation. You can take only gravity into consideration. Or, you can take gravity and air friction and propulsive forces into consideration.

You want to take into account the launch velocity, v, the initial height of the projectile, the angle of launch, the gravitational constant ($g=9.8$), and the horizontal distance, d.

The time, t, taken for a projectile to achieve trajectory is calculated by the formula $d/v \cos \theta$

Castle once tried to calculate the necessary initial velocity for a distance, d, of infinity, ∞, but it was too difficult, and she had to lie down afterwards.

She had never bothered with calculations, physics, algebra or trigonometry until the program involved her with rocket launchers. Now it was a left over tic from her orientation training and post-conflict debriefing. She could not, or would not, stop.

Bennet was on the sofa, flaking so much it looked as if there was an indoor snowstorm around him. Arnold went and sat next to him and tried to make conversation. Bennet looked up at Castle, who just watched.

"You are interrupting my cartoons," said Bennet. The hostility from him was moist, tropical.

Castle never saw Una again before combat. When she deployed, she didn't even really see the enemy. In what the historians later called The Battle of Woolwich, regular troops lay broken and dead in untidy piles, some minus appendages. She saw a wave of vomit-green rise towards her and she discharged the weapon twice in one second.

It was not recoilless, and Castle's body broke too fast for her to even register the pain.

The creatures moved incredibly fast. Castle had been warned of this, but nothing could have prepared her for how quickly they engulfed her rocket launcher. She screamed her rage and pain as the glistening thing wound round its prize, leaving her spurting arterial blood, and she knew she was going to die in this mud. Unspent ordnance detonated and she was flung away, broken, bleeding, waiting for death.

But it was not to be, because there was the cavalry with the gentlest two eyes Castle had ever seen. She may have even attempted to smile with her broken face.

Then fearful darkness as Una deployed her weapon, reminding Castle of the single most repeated warning.

If you can see it, you're too close.

"Why did you volunteer?"

"To serve my country, my planet."

"Bullshit. You could have joined regular troops. Why volunteer to get experimented on?"

Castle shrugged.

War.

They came, we fought, we won.

There was more to it than that.

They came. We first fought with the weapons that we dared to use and we lost.

Then we used thermonuclear weapons and lost.

We opened the silos of the truly experimental weapons, the doomsday scenarios and the gateways to hell. We still lost.

We discovered Familiars by mistake and finally won.

There was more.

They came.

They burst into the sky, riding on lightning. Whether they were aliens or transdimensional beings has never been clarified.

They wanted war and death, and we gave it to them. They killed.

They were formless, shadows, with no vessels for our weapons to target. It was easy for them. They could sense our intent before we could take action. We aimed, pulled triggers and removed fail-safes, but they were no longer there.

They slipped in and out of reality with the ease of plucking a hangnail. They did not cluster, but they would kill in waves, like a tsunami of mist.

Some of them died. They had intermittent mass with intervals of irregular periodicity. They were only sometimes solid, but most of the time wispy like a Dartmoor mist.

The demons had come for us and we had no flaming sword.

Again.

They came, we fought.

Speed was the key. We devised cyborgs. They died about half an hour slower than regular troops. Still too slow to react, still too large a lag time. All we had left was the speed of thought.

Implants were placed in operators brains, linked to drones and turret bots and skycannon along with other devices too horrible to remember without insanity.

We fought.

We won.

A flicker of movement was enough to trigger fire. They had

no appetite for this warfare, and they fled. Scouts were sent through the portals to find homeworlds or bases. They never returned with the needed information.

We did not press the matter. We had a world to rebuild and decontaminate from the horror of our engines of war.

We won.

"Do you cyborgs feel cast out from heaven?" asked Arnold. "Ten falling angels?"

Everything you cast out describes a parabola. If the initial velocity is high enough, and the angle is correct, you may even think the object is no longer coming down. Everything comes down, though. Sooner or later.

"We aren't cyborgs anymore, mate. And what makes you think a soldier's life is heaven?"

As they walked, the distance between them varied between ten and twenty-five centimetres. Castle planned to calculate the median distance later, just before bedtime.

"What are your feelings about the invaders?" asked Arnold.

Castle chuckled. "You know, they had pets? We always talk about them as if it was one homogenous alien mass, but there were different races and there were beasts, ravenous things that moved on two and four legs. They ate flesh. I hated the pets the most."

"I know this, Castle. I was there."

"Then you know my feelings about them."

On the way to the recreational area they had wandered to Una's room, or Castle steered them there subconsciously. Her plan had been to take Arnold to the sports facilities, but she felt that tug, that need to see Una once a day. She was ambivalent about going in, but felt that she needed to, even if it was just for a second or two. What would the harm be?

"This next person has no modifications," said Castle. "At least none that are visible."

Arnold's body language changed, as if everything before now

84

was preamble. Something bothered Castle about him, something he had said. *I was there.* She supposed this was true, even if he was in a Norfolk bunker.

Una Bates sat in an adjustable seat staring off into space. Una had been the controller of the final Familiar. She had a few tubes going into and coming out of her, adding nutrients and draining waste. She would not eat or drink. She did nothing. They kept her muscle tone with TENS machines, and turned her frequently. Even with this, there was wasting of the muscles and no movement except saccadic eyes tracking phantoms. They said she saw the ghost of the aliens she had killed. Castle no longer found the eyes gentle.

Una's name was spoken of with hushed tones. She was a hero, perhaps the only hero of the war.

"It's not really appropriate for her to be here," said Castle. "She isn't a cyborg. No machine parts."

"Except the electrode implanted in her brain," said Arnold. "Which she would have used to communicate with her Familiar."

"Yeah, except that." Castle was worried about Arnold. The glint in his eye seemed brighter. Was he still trying to send photos somewhere? "There is no point being here. She cannot answer questions."

"I'm going to try all the same," said Arnold. He stumbled in front of her.

"Err...we're not supposed to be in her room," said Castle. There was something really odd about this writer. Now that she thought about it Castle didn't think his movements were all that normal anymore. They had a punch-drunk lack of fluidity.

"Una Bates? Can you hear me?" Arnold waved his hands in front of her face.

"No, she can't fucking hear you, stupid. Have you not read the press briefing? Can we leave now?" Castle was irritated with him, but more so with herself for bringing him in. She wanted to leave, so she stood by the door, but the journalist could not or would not take a hint.

"Una, I know you can hear me. I know you. I know you well. You know how well I know you? I know you kissed your best friend's boyfriend when you were fifteen. I know the pin number for your first bank card. I know when you joined the Territorial Army. I know you have a Sri Lanka-shaped scar on your left elbow."

Oh, shit. What is he doing?

"Arnold? What are you doing?"

"This does not concern you, Castle."

"Get out now," said Castle. She moved towards him, but he punched her in the face, right on her nose. She reacted to the pain and surprise by ignoring them and counter attacking, but her instinctive left jab fell short by a missing forearm, and Arnold doubled her over with a kick to the midsection. She fell to her knees and activated her personal alarm, which she had never used before.

Arnold started to strip off his clothes. There was a deep red line starting from the root of his neck, bisecting his chest and splitting his abdomen in half. With a sound like the opening of an umbrella, this line suddenly yawned from the middle into an opening. He looked like a frog on a cork board, dissected. All his internal organs spilled out and covered Bates. Before long smoke began to rise and the plastic tubes melted first, then skin. The smell of burning, decaying vegetables and faeces filled the air.

"What is it, Castle?" said the superintendent over the communicator.

"Arnold is eating Una."

"What?"

"He extruded a digestive system and he's snacking on her right now, sir. I don't think he's a journalist."

"Stop him."

"With what? I have no weapons. Send a response team!"

"Already done, but your orders are to neutralise him, soldier. Improvise. Use whatever is at hand. Help's on the way."

Castle felt a tremor coming on. This was her fault.

Arnold seemed to have entered some kind of feeding trance. His eyes were fixed straight ahead and his lips moved slightly. Some of his fingers twitched, but most of the movement was in his guts. There was a wave of motion in the intestines, originating from Una, moving towards Arnold. Una remained serene.

Castle grabbed a handful of the digestive organs and screamed. It burnt like fire, like acid. Of course. It was covered in alien digestive juices.

With her damaged hand Castle balled a fist and punched Arnold in the face.

No effect.

I'm sorry, Una.

Una gave off a sucking sound as one of her lungs imploded. Castle kicked at Arnold's legs, but they did not buckle. She heard a rumble from behind her, and broke away, sure that this sound was from the boots of the response team. Best to be as far away from their target as possible. They poured into view, black-helmeted and trigger-happy. They did not wait, but started to fire bullets into Arnold. Castle curled into what she hoped was a very small ball. There were six soldiers with automatic rifles. Arnold's body rocked with the force of each hit, but he did not let go of Una. A tendril erupted from his open trunk, and it became a tentacle which whipped at the nearest helmet. Even Castle could hear the screams. It wrapped around the chest of the first soldier and swung in a short arc towards the others, knocking them over.

Castle wondered at the power in the swing. The force of impact would be centripetal. Assuming the length of the tentacle as two metres, the man weighing seventy kilograms, the tangential velocity...then she stopped herself. *What the fuck am I doing?* She picked up one of the rifles that fell close to her. It was warm. She rose to a crouch and fired not at Arnold, but at his bowels. She saw the wounds form in the guts and the leakage of fluid, and what might be a pain response in Arnold, but she could not be sure. The damage was too little and that tentacle still killed the response team soldiers. The room reeked of cordite and a sulphurous gut smell from Arnold's innards. Castle could still hear the rumble. Were more soldiers coming?

This was not the rumble of boots against floor. It was progressively louder and the whole chamber had started to vibrate. Castle screamed, but the chamber shaking drowned out her voice. Earthquake?

As the last of the soldiers died cracks appeared on the floor. At first Castle thought Arnold had called in reinforcements because three thick tentacles burst through the concrete floor, but hey were soon joined by two more, which was when she realised that they weren't tentacles.

They were digits. Digits on a hand, mechanical, screeching with each complex movement. Castle knew what it was, what it meant, and she unfurled herself and scrambled over the corpses of the response team, out of the crumbling chamber. She dropped the rifle because it would be no help. The walls caved in almost at once, and debris fell on Castle.

The forearm of an iron giant slowly emerged from the earth. The hand reached around what used to be Arnold East, and squeezed. Bones cracked, rigid form collapsed, and he ceased to be. Rivulets of red blood ran between the alloy fingers. A shoulder appeared, then a second arm broke free and stripped the alien intestines off Una. Wotan house began to fall apart from the stresses, so Castle ran away.

If you can see it, you're too close.

Castle had probably been more scared than this at some point in her life, but she could not think of an example. She could not think of the equation for centripetal force. Others ran with her, staff, residents, those who were mobile, those who were not so ambulatory.

When she reached the helipad she looked back.

Framed against the clouds and smoke was a giant, frightening as a Goya. It towered above Wotan House's roof, about two hundred metres by Castle's estimate. Its skin was glistening black, but that was from the carbonized steel plates that made up its integument. It was cyclopean, with one eye glowing green off-centre in its skull. The absence of a second eye, the presence of space in the face, somehow made it more horrific. Its every movement screeched, metal on metal plate, unoiled mechanisms, unmaintained cybernetics. It did not have human proportions, with a longer lower torso, adding to the unsettling appearance, its wrongness to the eye. Castle was unsure if there were any organics in there, or if it was a big robot controlled by Una's mind. In its right hand Una lay limp, dripping what Castle hoped wasn't blood. She had thought the Familiar was decommissioned. Apparently not.

The Familiar seemed to be scanning Una's body, the green orb flashing rapidly, before glowing steady again. Then it turned, and fixed on Castle and the other people on the helipad.

If you can see it, you're too close.

She knew there was no point running. It could kill her from a mile away in many different ways. Castle allowed the Familiar to subject her to whatever radiation it used and prayed involuntarily. The process took forever, but eventually Castle heard screeching again.

The giant stepped off the island and disappeared into the water.

"From what we've been able to decode in the remnants of the alien's genetic material, this was meant to be a surgical strike. Bates' was the most effective weapon against the aliens. They obviously wanted to kill her and study the electrode in her head," said the Superintendent. "We found the real Arnold East dead and decaying in his apartment. Been there for months, from the look of it. The Ministry of Defence is already putting together a response force. The war didn't end, Castle. It was in hibernation."

Brontes seemed to be more alive, activated by the prospect of war. Castle was the opposite. She could not think of enough numbers or equations to distract her from the anxiety and self-loathing.

"How do we plan to get Una back? We don't have guns bigger than the Familiar," said Castle.

The Superintendent delayed responding a little too long. "That is not your concern. I want you to work on the restoration of Wotan House."

"Sir, do we have something bigger than a Familiar?" asked Castle.

The Superintendent smiled. "Dismissed, Castle."

"I'm not a soldier."

"Then get the fuck out of my office, and get your hand seen to."

Castle left. She shivered when she remembered Arnold's quivering digestive system, but she was more unsettled by the danger she did not know, from whatever existed that was bigger and badder than that black cyclops, than Una's Familiar.

She decided she didn't want to think about it. She would go out, get drunk and add this to the days she wanted to forget.

She would raise one glass to Una Bates, wherever she was, and then she would drink until she passed out or died.

Another Day in Paradise

Amy DuBoff

"Incoming!" Sergeant Jackson dove behind a sandy embankment, taking cover in what passed for vegetation on the barren planet.

The alien mortar round wailed as it arched overhead on a blind path. It plunged into the ground barely out of lethal range, detonating with a sharp crack followed by a sonic boom. Sand and gravel pelted the squad hunkered just out of enemy sight.

Jackson spat out a mouthful of grit and blew his nose free of dust. So much for taking the enemy by surprise. He wiped the narrow band of brow exposed beneath the lip of his helmet with the back of his gloved hand. "Everyone okay?"

"All clear," Corporal Shira, one of his fire team leaders, replied through the comm. She was braced against a boulder down the hill, reloading the energy cartridge in her pulse rifle.

"Fuckers don't give up, do they?" Jackson quipped.

Really, it was the humans that didn't give up. The colony was a shithole even before the Selarks showed up, and now there was hardly anything left to defend. But it was a human settlement, so they would defend the desert world as if it were the lost paradise of Earth.

Jackson checked the charge on his blaster; it was at eighty percent, more than enough to finish the fight. "Let's show those bug-heads how it's done," he said, rising to a crouch.

He pressed the inside of his left wrist to activate his digicamo suit. With a glistening silver wave, he was enveloped by a reflective bubble that mirrored the surrounding landscape. The air shimmered as he moved, but he disappeared completely when perfectly still. In the heat of the desert world, visual warfare was everything, since the reflective sand wreaked havoc with thermal sensors. It was the best advantage the humans had.

The dozen soldiers in his squad activated their own suits and began creeping up the low hill through the scraggly brush.

"Keep your distance," Jackson warned as they crested the hill. "Don't want to end up like Bravo Company."

"We're not stupid enough to get captured." Shira crawled past to his left. She peeked over the hill through her scope. "Plus, we can take these guys."

Jackson dropped to his stomach and looked through his own scope. A shallow valley on the other side of the crest was occupied by the Selark contingent. Thirty of the seven-foot-tall mantis-like drones and two twenty-foot armoured octopod mechs were fortified behind a row of hovercraft, their taupe plating gleaming under the descending sun. Both of the mechs had their mortars primed to fire another barrage at the first sign of movement.

Though his squad was outnumbered, Jackson's lips curled into a smile. A little strategy would take out the Selarks in no time. "Shira, Neeley. Get those mechs in your sights. Everyone else, concentrate your fire on the middle hovercraft. Let's funnel them straight toward us."

"Roger that," gunner Neeley acknowledged as he and Shira slithered into position at the hillcrest.

Jackson motioned for his other soldiers to hold just shy of the crest until the opening shots were fired. He checked that Shira and Neeley were both ready, then edged forward to oversee the assault. "Fire on my mark... Now!"

Shira and Neeley pelted the mechs with a burst of electromagnetic blasts. The mechs shuddered under the impact of the shots and erupted in a shower of yellow sparks, stumbling over their own legs before collapsing on the ground with a poof of dust.

"Fire at will!" Jackson commanded. He tossed a strobe light down the hill, projecting dazzling flashes along the sandy terrain, and opened fire on the centre hovercraft.

The first wave of energy bullets appeared to bounce off the alien plating, but Jackson and his soldiers knew better. They concentrated their fire, and slowly the plating gave way. With the initial layer breached, the next wave of blaster fire sliced through the hovercraft, riddling it with singed holes.

As Jackson and his squad fired, the Selark drones sprayed shots along the ridge, but their aim was poor. With their thermal vision fooled by the sandy ground's radiant heat and the digicamo masking the human soldiers, the Selarks concentrated fire on the random strobe flashes, mistaking it for muzzle flare.

Jackson kept a close eye on his progress cutting through the hovercraft's armour, waiting for the side panel to give way. He'd been through enough firefights to know just what to look for. As the plating began to slough to the ground, he seized the opportunity – sending a shot directly into the energy core at the centre of the craft.

The hovercraft exploded in a flash of white light, releasing a shockwave that nearly knocked the air from Jackson's lungs. He took a gasping breath as he surveyed the valley below.

Selark limbs were strewn about the battlefield, oozing viscous white blood, amid wreckage from the hovercraft. Shrapnel embedded in the ground stood like tombstones for the fallen. Only ten of the drones remain on their clawed feet, and they clustered together behind a hovercraft on the right end of the ruined defensive line.

"Finish them off!" Jackson jumped up to advance down the hill.

The remaining Selark drones, dazed from the explosion, fell under the fire of Jackson's advancing squad before they had a chance to fight back. Their shells shattered under the relentless fire, popping with a sickening crunch as each drone collapsed in a twisted pile of its serrated limbs. Shrill shrieks and clicks sounded with the dying breaths – once chilling cries that had become background noise to a regular day's work.

Jackson walked through the remains, covering his nose and mouth with his uniform's collar to dull the acidic stench of burnt Selark flesh. One of the fallen drones twitched as he approached, feebly reaching for a nearby blaster. Jackson finished it off with a shot through one of its bulbous compound eyes, leaving a milky cavern in the alien's skull.

"Looks like we got all of them," he said. He pulled out his GPS locator and flagged the location for the Salvage crew. "Head out."

The sun was touching the horizon by the time Jackson's squad completed the slog back to base. The fortified compound sat at the edge of a rock bluff, with a sheer cliff dropping below on two sides and wide open sandy plains on the approach. The lookouts in the watchtower above the colossal main gate stirred as the squad neared.

Jackson activated the automated broadcast of daily verification codes.

"Welcome back, Sergeant," the guard acknowledged through Jackson's comm. "Colonel wants to see you."

Jackson groaned under his breath. Those ambush conversations rarely brought good news.

The entry gate parted to let the squad inside, with Jackson leading the way. As he passed through the metal gate, he was surprised to see the Colonel waiting in full body armour at the head of three squadrons and a row of waiting transport trucks.

"There you are," Colonel Rimov greeted. "Did the scouting party give you any trouble?"

"Nothing we couldn't handle, sir," Jackson replied.

"Good. We needed a clear path to the Selark encampment," Rimov continued.

Jackson eyed his commanding officer. "Sir?"

"We got orders from the Talos base. The Selarks have retreated from the borderlands. We have them surrounded and need to hit them hard while we have the chance to make a real dent. The General wants every available soldier at the Echo rendezvous for a coordinated strike."

Jackson looked over at his tired squad. Their posture had straightened after hearing the plan and a thirst was in their eyes. They'd been waiting for a chance to take the Selarks head on.

"When do we leave, sir?" Jackson asked.

Rimov shook his head. "You'll be staying right here to hold down the fort while I'm away."

Jackson glanced up and saw guards coming down from the tower. He sighed inwardly. It was just his luck to be left at home while everyone else got the glory. "Neeley, Davis, take first watch."

"Yes, sir." Neeley and Davis dashed up the guard tower.

"It should be a quiet night here," the Colonel said to Jackson. "We'll be back around sunrise."

Jackson nodded. "We'll be waiting for you, sir. Good hunting."

Colonel Rimov motioned the soldiers into the waiting trucks. The entry gate slid open and they drove out, leaving a trail of dust in their wake across the open desert.

"Seal the gate," Jackson ordered. He loosened his helmet's chinstrap.

Two of his soldiers ran over to the controls to close the thirty-foot armoured gate.

Jackson took in the open patch of compact sand in the main yard. It seemed so desolate without the other soldiers and equipment. With even the normally lively barracks and mess cabin completely vacated, the base was one step from a ghost town. Sand-battered metal and pitted concrete: home sweet home.

"If we have the place to ourselves, does that mean we get to party tonight?" Shira asked through a playful grin.

A smile tugged at Jackson's lips. "We'll party when the last of the Selarks are out of this sand Hell. Now come on, we have a long night ahead of us."

Jackson and half his squad grabbed a meal and took a short nap while the others kept first watch. At midnight, he and Shira went to retrieve Neeley and Davis from the guard tower.

The night was dark and still beyond the base walls. Jackson gazed at the sliver of moon hanging above distant hills that appeared as inky mounds in the dim light. The features of the open plain were flattened in shadow outside the reach of light along the base perimeter.

"Do you ever miss the trees?" Shira asked.

Jackson leaned against the railing. "All the time."

"I can't even remember what a forest smells like anymore. This grit," she brushed a dusting of sand off the banister, "is all I've seen for years."

"We'll be home soon."

"You really think so?"

Jackson nodded. "Somewhere out there, the Selarks are getting their bony asses handed to them."

Shira looked down. "More always come."

"There are more of us, too. We're not in this alone."

Shira sighed and stared out across the dark terrain. She tensed. "Are those lights?"

Jackson came to attention. "Where?" He grabbed a pair of binoculars from a ledge beneath the railing and directed them along Shira's outstretched arm. Sure enough, an object was speeding across the landscape.

"I thought they weren't due back until sunrise?" Shira ventured.

"Maybe something didn't go as planned." Jackson examined the object through the binoculars again. "No, wait, that's not one of ours!"

Shira grabbed a second pair of binoculars. "Fuck! That looks like a Selark hoverer."

Jackson sounded the internal alarm. "Bogey approaching!" He shouted into the intercom. "Get to the fence!"

Shira ran across the guard tower and primed the pulse cannon. "Why would they send just one?"

Jackson's stomach turned over. "They wouldn't." He scanned the horizon with the binoculars. "Oh shit."

A line of ten lighted craft sped behind the lead vessel – far too many to take out with one cannon.

"Grab the pulse rifles. We've got company," Jackson said into the intercom, trying to steady the pounding of his heart that suddenly filled his ears.

The first hovercraft was almost in range. Shira had it in the pulse cannon's sights, awaiting the order to fire.

An electronic chirp broke the silence. Jackson jumped with surprise, eyeing the unexpected authorization illuminating the communications console.

Shira glanced up from the cannon's scope, her finger still poised on the trigger.

Jackson checked the console. "I'm receiving clearance codes, but they're three days old."

"Since when are the bug-heads that crafty?"

Jackson frowned. "They're not."

Footsteps sounded as other soldiers began clambering up the tower.

"What are your orders, Sergeant?" Shira asked, returning her attention to the cannon's scope.

The codes illuminated on the communications console a second time. Unsure what to make of it, Jackson examined the hovercraft through his binoculars again. It was riding low to the ground and jerking erratically. That didn't seem like any Selark piloting he'd ever seen.

"Shit, they're almost on top of us!" Neeley exclaimed as he propped his pulse rifle on the railing.

"Your orders, sir?" Shira repeated.

Jackson hesitated. Eight Selark drones could be in the

hoverer, ready to open fire on his squad the moment the gate was open. Or, human soldiers could be inside, in desperate need of help. The only way to know would be for the craft to stop for inspection, but it wasn't slowing down. If it continued at its current speed, it would hit the gate hard enough to compromise integrity. The base would be vulnerable, and one squad wouldn't be enough to defend against the army coming up behind the lead craft. But if it was his own people in there...

"Fuck. The codes are friendly. I —" Jackson took in the wave of other hovercraft behind the first. The unequivocal enemy. He couldn't leave the door open for them even a crack. He swallowed, his gut wrenching as he made the only decision available. "Take it out."

"Yes, sir!" Shira fired the charge.

The lead covercraft flipped into the air, engulfed in a flash of white light. It crashed to the ground, charred and mangled.

Shira recharged her cannon and pointed it toward the oncoming wave.

"Defend the fence," Jackson instructed, lining up a hovercraft in his sights. He opened fire.

The harsh squeals of weapons blasts echoed across the plain. Flashes shattered the darkness, illuminating the action in bursts of movement.

Selark drones poured out of the hovercraft, swarming the base of the wall. Jackson and his soldiers tossed down flash grenades as the Selarks tried to pile up the riveted face. The aliens let out piercing screams with every blast as they clutched their injuries with their claws. But they were relentless — each drone continuing its assault until it could move no more.

Jackson reloaded the charge in his pulse rifle when the first was exhausted, concentrating on keeping the Selarks away from the entry gate. Wave after wave poured forward from the hovercraft, and Jackson's squad held back each. The entire world was what he could see through his scope, the energy blasts the soundtrack of the destruction before him.

And then, it was still.

Jackson let out a slow breath, his ears still ringing from the final shots of the battle. Next to him, Shira slid to the floor of the tower, her face matted with dust and sweat. Her hands shook and her breath was ragged.

Neeley let out a forced laugh. "What was that about it being a quiet night?"

Jackson set down his rifle, realizing he was still gripping it with white knuckles. "Yeah. Right."

The sky glowed soft orange along the distant hills. With the rising sun came the return of their comrades, the caravan cutting a straight line across the desert.

Still dazed, Jackson plodded down the guard tower stairs to open the entry gate.

As the gate slid open, Jackson's stomach churned when he saw the carnage of night's battle up close under the faint daylight. The ground was saturated with white Selark blood flowing from the mutilated bodies that lay twisted amid the scorched hovercraft.

He stepped out of the gate and approached the closest hovercraft that had led the charge against the base. As he neared, he noticed a pool of red blood dripping out of the craft. Human blood.

"No!" The order to fire replayed in his head – every excruciating second of the energy blast careening through the air toward its target, engulfing craft in blinding burst of destructive force, electrocuting the passengers.

Human passengers.

He ran to the craft. The door was ajar, and he tore it open, not caring that the edges gashed his hands.

A bloodied body tumbled out of the open door. The empty eyes stared up at Jackson, mouth agape in a permanent cry of horror. Just enough of the uniform was visible through the blood and soot to see the insignia of Bravo Company.

Jackson's eyes burned, the acrid taste of bile stinging the back of his throat. He had given the order to fire. Their lives were on him. His comrades had made it home, where they were supposed to be safe. He was supposed to protect them. But now they were dead – and it was because of him.

The weight of his uniform was too much. He wanted to fall to his knees, to cry and mourn for the loss of his fallen comrades. He had failed them, and there was nothing he could do to make it right.

Gravel crunched under heavy footsteps behind him, and Jackson hurriedly wiped his eyes. He couldn't show weakness, not when there was still a war to fight. He turned to see Colonel Rimov approaching.

Rimov shook his head with cold pity, his mouth drawn. "Poor bastards. Must have got free in the commotion and stolen the hoverer. Led half the Selarks from the base right back here. We practically walked in to take it from the rest."

Jackson clenched his hands in fists so the Colonel couldn't see him tremble. He could still feel the empty eyes of the fallen soldiers boring into his back. "I didn't know it was them, sir. Their codes –"

"You followed protocol," Rimov assured him. "Bravo Company knew the risks."

Jackson gazed numbly at the smiling faces of the other soldiers around him. They'd just killed thousands – even if they were aliens – and a squad of their own were dead at his feet. He shook his head, hardly believing that was his reality. Somewhere along the way, it had become all about the mission. They were all disposable, as long as the bigger fight was won.

Rimov clapped him on the back. "Come on. We finally have something to celebrate."

Jackson followed the colonel across the bloodstained ground. "Yes sir."

Round Trip

Robert Sharp

"If we could tackle the cosmos in a spaceship, the way sailors crossed the globe…"
– Janna Levin, How The Universe Got Its Spots

So, this isn't my story.

It's a strange tale that was told to me by someone else. There's a peril, isn't there, that when you pass on anecdotes some of the details get muddled? I do think this was told to me in good faith, but I'll leave it to you to decide whether the story happened exactly as I was told, or whether the man embellished a bit around the edges. You know, for dramatic effect.

For what's it's worth, I'm convinced that he was telling the truth. I wouldn't pass it on otherwise.

Okay, so the guy in question was one of those craggy types. His face was blotchy, with red veins running between wrinkles, like exposed strata on a cliff. But he wasn't wild, he was properly groomed. He had closely cropped hair which I think of as practical, sensible. And he was wearing a starchy grey shirt buttoned tightly around his neck. As soon as I saw him I knew he had spent time in a regulated environment. The military, maybe, or perhaps a prison, either in a cell or in the guard tower.

Whatever he was, he was not someone whose fashion sense or whose mannerisms would help you place him in time or space. Instead he was the kind of person who you could meet in any place, in any time.

I have since wondered where else I could have been accosted by someone like him. I thought perhaps in one of those tea houses in the old part of Fez. Or maybe I would have seen him sitting calmly on a jetty in Manilla, picking his yellow teeth with the claw of a crab. Or maybe I could've found him propping up the end of the bar in a trendy Camden pub?

I'd love to say I met him somewhere exotic because it would have made me sound as if I was a more interesting person. But instead I met him in a really boring and tedious location, one which you'll all be familiar with: at the coffee counter on board one of those big commercial lunar orbital platforms, waiting for a connecting shuttle to Jupiter.

Everyone knows how God-awful boring those journeys can be. The InterPlanSit companies all advertise 'Jupiter' but the cheap shuttles actually go to Jupiter-Ganymede or Europa or something. And so if you're on a budget like me then you have to wait around for a hopper to get into the inhabited zones on the inner orbit. So there's more waiting and travelling even when you get there.

Anyway, on that particular evening the connecting shuttle from the orbital platform was delayed by almost an hour. When the announcement came over the speaker everyone at the gate let out a groan, and I joined the queue for another latte. The place was heaving, and so I had to sit at a table that was already occupied. And there he was, this guy – the bloke with the messy meteor face – dumped on the plastic chair at the nearest table to the observation window.

He was wearing plain grey overalls, as if he was crew or something.

"Is this seat taken?" I asked.

He took a swig from a bottle of beer, which gave the game away. Not crew, he was a passenger like me.

"Help yourself", he says. And he said it with, can I say 'purpose'? It was as if he had not spoken to anyone in a long time, or perhaps was just learning a new language. But the accent was English. Northern.

So I sat down, and he didn't say any more. But, well, we were stirring at the same table so it felt a bit awkward not speaking. It was as if we were on a bad blind date. So I said something predictable about the delay on the shuttle. You know, just to make conversation.

And instead of nodding, or agreeing, which is the ritual, he snorted, shook his head, and said something rude.

So now I was thinking, this is *exactly* like a blind date.

As if to seal that feeling, he leant over, calm as you like, and said: "Have you ever been in love"

"Sure" I said, and I wiggled my wedding ring at him.

And he smiled at me and his eyes just creased up like one of those concertinas the buskers play right outside the shuttle terminals. "I was in love" he said. "She was beautiful…"

And I must have visibly rolled my eyes here because he's like, "Yes yes, I know everyone says that, but she was beautiful *to me.*"

Fine, I thought. Whatever.

"And we would argue all the time."

That I was not expecting.

"We would argue," he said. "We didn't agree on much."

Okay, so now I could see what's happening, which was that I'm going to get stuck with this guy and I'll be giving him a free therapy session or something. And he just goes off on one.

He's like "but, I loved her. I… really… cared… what she thought of me."

He did a big inhale, as if he was sucking in the world. I could tell that I wasn't supposed to interrupt.

"That was why we argued" he said. "She would accuse me of thinking something I didn't think and I would get so, so, mad. But then I would say sorry or she would say sorry and the peace, of reconciliation, it was addictive, y'know?"

I didn't know, but I nodded anyway.

Turns out they'd met on one of the lunar settlements. He was in the engineering corps, working on the life support systems, but she, she was an astronomer! She worked on black holes, she measured the background radiation from the Big Bang, and she wrote books about the shape of the universe.

I remember him saying that, by the way: "The shape of the universe."

And my friend at the table, he puffed up with pride as he tried to explain her theories to me, second hand. He was inarticulate, but the gist was that the universe is big, very big, but it is finite and curved, just like a planet is curved. So if you set off on a journey and fly in a straight line, you'll eventually come back to where you began. And if – and this is brilliant by the way – if space is curved like a Möbius strip, then when you come back, everything will be reversed.

"You send a right-handed hammer on the journey," he said "and when it comes back it will be a left-handed hammer."

He sat back when he said that, and I saw him searching my face, to check that I got the joke.

"That was Jenny's joke" he said, and the smile melted off his face. So I asked him what happened.

"We argued. She had been offered a new post. On Pluto. They built this enormous facility out there. Next generation telescope. You get better readings, data or something. They wanted her to run it."

I remember he bit his lip.

"I… said she couldn't go. I mean, it's Pluto so there aren't any commercial shuttles, it's seven week journey out there.

"'You could come with me' she said. But what would I do on Pluto. Be the janitor?

"And she said, 'Well, I'm going anyway. In fact, I already accepted the job'."

He clenched his fist around his beer. His knuckles went white, I thought he was going to break the neck of the bottle. "I got angry. I just could not believe how selfish she was being, and that's what I told her.

"And she gave me such a look, I'll never forget it: pity; distain. She was totally somewhere else. There was no love in her eyes. She just said, 'You're pathetic.'

"And then she went for a drive. She used to do that. Get into the private hopper and put herself into low lunar orbit for a few hours. Only this time, as she reached the apogee of her ascent, a mining freighter crested out of the dark side unexpectedly. It wasn't supposed to be there. But then again, neither was she.

"She took evasive action, y'know. Swerved right like she was supposed to, the Law of Aviation and all that. So it wasn't her fault or anything. But it didn't stop the freighter ploughing straight through the hopper. She died immediately, with her anger for me still burning in her heart. My selfishness was the last message to pass through her mind, before she became charred stardust once more."

He took another swig of beer at this point.

"I had nothing to bury. There was no spot I could walk by and leave a flower. She had been wrenched from me at the lowest point in our shared history. And because of the air circulation systems on our lunar pod, her overalls didn't even smell of her.

"I found something of her in her papers, in her writings. In her theories of space-time, the curved universe. Of course I read the publications and the books many times over, but I also went looking for obscure comments she had made in the peer-review of other people's work. I became something of an expert. Not in astrophysics, you understand. But in her. In the history of her work, how she came up with her Möbius strip theory of space-time.

"I also read the work of her detractors. Those who had said her theory was incomplete, flawed. I learned that hers was a minority view, that most people thought the universe was infinite. Some people had even ridiculed her. They made jokes about her. She had never shared any of this with me."

There was this fervent look in his eyes now.

"And it was when I read those take-downs of her theories that the idea formed. I could do something to make it up to her. I could do something to prove the naysayers wrong. I could do something to show her I was not the selfish bastard she thought I was, that I knew her work mattered. I could do something to make her love me again.

"And so one day I walked into the restricted area of the lunar base, stepped onto one the long range military transport ships. And I stole it."

I coughed into my space latte. "You stole it? But that's an interplanetary crime. You'd be arrested."

He smiled at me and shook his head in a sort of patronising way. "Yes, I would be arrested, as soon as I landed the transport on a planet or an asteroid or whatever."

And that's when I perceived the enormity of what he was telling me. "You never landed?"

"Of course I had all the mod cons for the journey," he said. "3D Printer that even did food, electronic library, military grade Stem-o-Matic unit to regenerate human tissue. And a coffee machine."

He spoke of navigation. I thought the point was to just go in a straight line but he says no, you do have to avoid star systems, ugly looking galaxies, but also – and this was the part that made me think of him as a sailor – you have to check the stars.

"It's very difficult to get measurements when you've accelerated to almost the speed of light" he said. "But, if you wait a few months, or years, or decades, the computer will have some data."

"I was looking for unexpected shifts in the way the stars moved, relative to each other. This was my chief role on the ship: to find the right angle at which to traverse the universe."

"That would send me bonkers" I said. And he nodded.

"It would totally send you insane, yeah. But remember I was mad already. I stole a spacecraft in grief, and fled the solar system.

"Even so, those years reviewing trajectories of stars still a million light years away, overlaying them with calculated trajectories of the same, and seeing them match. These were my bleakest, most lonely days.

"But I had faith in Jenny and I knew that I could always do one more day of that work. One more comparison between the observed data and the mathematical prediction. And one unexpected night, my faith was rewarded! A set of stars were moving slower than they should. Just a touch. A few seconds difference from where they should be.

"So I steered the ship closer to that system. And they returned to moving at the speed that the mathematics predicted. But I had picked up a scent. I moved the ship back to its original trajectory and the phenomenon, the slow stars, returned.

"Trial and error, my friend. When you have eternity, that is as good as certainly.

"Eventually, I steered my ship to a camber and a path that made those distant stars move even slower. And with that, I had a second data point, an extrapolation, and a path that took me not only through space, but through time.

"Like a harbour pilot, I nestled my ship in this trench that I, with my three dimensions, could not see.

"And I watched as the stars around me slowed and slowed until, for one fine, black moment, they were not moving at all. I had reached the apex of the curve. The stars began to move again, retracing the trajectories I had previously mapped. I had performed a cosmic u-turn."

"So you set a course for home?"

"No" he said. "My discovery of the temporal jet stream was empirical evidence for but half of Jenny's theory. Returning to Earth at that point would not have vindicated her. I had to keep on the bearing through space that I had chosen, in the hope that familiar star systems would resolve in my spyglass once more."

"I read almost every book in the electronic library. I taught myself Arabic, Mandarin, Sanskrit. Curiously, despite years, decades of practice, I could find no talent for writing in those languages. I made my own translations, of course, almost doubling, trebling the library in the process. I wrote a single novel in my head. But poetry, good poetry, remained elusive.

"I didn't see any point in memorising the Bible or the Koran, but I did memorise pi ten thousand places and wrote it out to a million digits, searching for patterns that might have been buried in the sequence. I found none.

"I spent six decades once, parked on an asteroid, mining ore. I had to repair some panels on the side of the freighter that had been eroded by long millennia of direct exposure to starlight.

"Above all, I searched the patterns of the stars. I would make diagrams of the constellations, as seen from the new angle that I, alone, perceived. For each new map I invented a new pantheon of Gods to live among the patterns. But I found them all empty, and weak.

"I took detours to exoplanets and sketched their features. I witnessed red alien sunrises, quasar rises, galaxy rises.

"I spent an hour of each day scanning every electromagnetic frequency, in the hope of picking up the sounds of an intelligent race. I heard nothing but white noise.

"You might ask whether I ever forgot the purpose of my voyage. Whether, in that unanimous night, I lost myself. And I say to you: never. Every day, when I hooked myself up to the Stem-o-Matic, I would put her in my mind. This was my evening ritual. As the machine replaced my tired flesh and revitalised my worn out organs, I would allow the thought of Jenny to reaffirm itself across the pathways of my brain. I think would have forgotten my own name sooner than I would forget the debt I owed her."

"There's an allegory" I said. "About a Greek ship that loses its parts and gets repaired, piece by piece."

He nodded. "The Ship of Theseus" he said. "And with the Stem-o-Matic that's certainly true. I'd say that none of the cells, no strand of protein, not even an atom that was within me when I started my voyage was in my body when I arrived back at the Moon. The only things that survived were patterns with an agenda."

Now, I was thinking so hard about that, I almost, almost

missed something that he said.

But I didn't. "Wait wait wait – you made it back to the Moon?"

He lifted up his arms, as if to say, I'm here aren't I?

"Galaxies have their own shape, you know. As unique as a finger print. Once the divine shape of the Milky Way appeared in my sights, I had plenty of time to get the calculations just right: When to exit the time trench. Light speed is a lot of momentum to burn off, you know. The craft had to decelerate slowly, over hundreds of years.

"But I timed it perfectly, no unnecessary orbits of the Galaxy. My ship went straight into an easy low lunar orbit on the dark side of the Moon."

I looked at him with delight. He had gambled on a journey of millions years and he had proved Jenny's theory right. Space-time was and is… curved.

But there was no pride in his eyes. He wasn't even looking at me. And then I caught up, with what he was trying to tell me: The dark side of the moon.

And I knew.

I didn't say anything. I didn't want him to say anything either. Inside I was willing him, just finish your story there. But he didn't. It was as if he had to keep talking.

"Like I said, I had plenty of time to get my calculations just right. I could choose when to leave my time trough. And so I thought, why not just pick up where I left off, and go find Jenny around the time we argued?

"My ship crested over the penumbra between the light and the dark side of the Moon. And there, in my flight path, was a hopper.

"Of course, I took evasive action. I swerved right like you're supposed to, the Law of Aviation and all that.

"But this time, she swerved left. And we collided.

"My transport ship, my freighter, the proof that her life's work was correct, was the thing that killed her. Again."

He let out this long, exhausted breath, as if he'd been punctured. And I couldn't speak either. I felt heavy and it just seemed a great challenge to even lift my chest to breath, let alone move my mouth.

But then, the noise of the tannoy rained into the space between us. My shuttle to Jupiter-Ganymede was finally ready for boarding. And the recorded voice apologised for the delay.

So, well, what could I do? I stood up.

And he didn't. Different flight, I guess.

I offered my hand. "What will you do now?" I said. "Are you going back to Earth?"

And suddenly, he was bolt upright on his seat again, and he gripped my hand.

"No" he said. "I'm planning another trip."

Arm Every Woman

Nik Abnett

"I don't like it," said Valys, entering transit-prep.

"You don't like anything," Storper replied.

The two squad commanders were old friends, and their banter eased tensions before a deployment.

"What don't you like *this* rotation?" asked Commander Kluk, joining in the fun.

"I don't like Narbrot," said Valys.

"Nobody likes Narbrot," said Storper.

"Say it louder, I don't think everybody heard you," said Kluk.

"You think we care?" asked Valys.

"About as much as you care about anything," said Kluk, peeling off towards the rank of perluo showers to the left and laughing all the way.

But Valys wasn't laughing.

They stripped, showered, passed through the airlock and left the steading behind.

Wachman took the seat in the transit liburna next to Valys.

"Who didn't make weight?" asked Valys. "Narbrot?"

"No," said Wachman, "Rokas, 50.05 kays, but I'm up to 42 kays and I'm strong now."

Valys checked out the tiny frame in its stained paper suit, nodded and said, "Pity it wasn't Narbrot. Rokas is getting too old to make weight. You'll do."

Wachman beamed.

The harness check light blinked red, and two seconds later

111

the liburna was in the air over Continent Tres.

Most of the soldiers on the flight had been deployed on dozens of rotations. As soon as the harness check light stopped blinking they closed their eyes and slept. Young and eager, fresh from training, Wachman had managed to hit weight; Narbrot was new too, embarking on a second rotation, and nervous as hell, not least because of the attitudes of the others. Narbrot sat beside squad commander Pupka in the other carrier bay of the liburna.

"I hit weight and height, and I passed fitness and weapons training. I'm one of you now, why can't you people accept it?" asked Narbrot.

"Because you're *not* one of us," said Pupka. "It's been five hundred years, and you're the first. We know there'll be more, but right now we don't know you, and we don't like you being forced on us."

"And what am I supposed to do about that?" asked Narbrot.

"You're supposed to live with it," said Pupka, "and do your job."

Light levels fell in the transit bays over the next eleven minutes, the over/under for a combat soldier to fall asleep. After that they were in total darkness. Light cost joules, and every joule was counted against their steading's tally. There were only the sounds of the ship's engines, constantly adjusting to optimise fuel consumption, and the rhythmic breathing of the sleeping soldiers.

The last twenty minutes of the flight were given over to gearing up in the sepio-suits, ready for combat. The height and weight of each combatant was recorded during transit-prep and the suits assigned accordingly. All the soldiers had their favourite sepio-suits. Some preferred more strength in certain areas, more flexibility, more or fewer armoured panels, better optics or tech information; some preferred mask rebreathers some preferred tubes. Every suit was unique, each one hand-built, rebuilt and maintained with a care that bordered on obsession. Many were centuries old.

The lights came up in the transit bays and the harness check light blinked green. Wachman's eyes were the first to open.

Valys stood, threw the bolts on an under-seat locker, and glanced at Wachman.

"What are you waiting for, soldier? Get that riscus open and check your sepio."

"Yes, Valys," said Wachman, finally releasing the harness and scrambling to catch up.

"Cunno!" swore Valys, examining the suit in the riscus.

"Something else not to like?" asked Kluk from further up the bay.

"Not my sepio," said Valys. "Who got P503?"

No one answered.

"Just suit up," said Kluk. "P503 isn't *your* sepio. It's the luck of the draw."

"Someone else's luck," said Valys. If it was Narbrot's luck there'd be trouble.

Thankfully, Wachman's suit wasn't P503.

"What are you looking at soldier?" asked Valys.

"Nothing," said Wachman.

"Suit up," said Valys.

"Yes, Valys," said Wachman unpacking sepio E309.

Everything was designed and built to conserve or optimise resources, and resources were scarce, recycled, re-used or won in combat. The transit bays were small because the ships were small, designed to use the minimum of materials, and they were sparsely furnished to keep the liburnae light, to burn the minimum of fuel. Everything counted against the steading in the tally.

The sepio-suits were the same. They had been made to fit combat soldiers within a limited range of body sizes: small body sizes between 140 and 150 centos tall, and between 42 and 50 kays in weight. They had been made of the lightest, but strongest and most durable materials so that they could be used indefinitely. Sepio-suits were the Holy Grail. They were salvaged at almost any cost. The tally of building a new suit could starve a steading into extinction.

Wachman geared up, all the time thinking about the suit and its value.

The lights in the transit bays flashed on and off for four beats, and the combat soldiers took their seats. Narbrot, always with something to prove, was among the first. Wachman remained standing, pulling at a neck seal. Valys reached out far enough for Wachman to lean in, and snapped the seal into position as the harness check light began to blink red. Wachman sat, and Valys grabbed the harness pin and shoved it into the matching slot in Wachman's left hand. They were locked in as the liburna made it's juddering descent.

"Speed it up next time, soldier," said Valys.

Wachman was speechless and white-faced with fear.

Battlefield Caepina, Continent Quintus. They had flown west, into daylight, and the flight home would be shorter than the flight out, for those who made it back. There was a tally for casualties, too. Everything had a cost.

Battle lines had been drawn across the globe repeatedly through the second millennium for political, economic and ethical reasons. In the second half of the third millennium it was about resources. The all-out global wars of the twentieth century had been costly, mostly in terms of lives lost and cities razed. The Arms Race, the Space Race, the Cold War, the Age of Avarice and the failure of the Second Industrial Revolution had done the rest.

The few, the small, the fit fought for their steadings, their nations and their continents, and they fought for survival. Schedules were drawn up for which regiment from which steading would travel to which battlefield to meet the enemy on its home ground. The duration of each engagement was fixed, and the outcome was determined by the tally. Battles killed soldiers; the tally killed everyone.

"Audentes fortuna iuvat!" said Pupka as the liburna landed.

"Not with this adversary," said Valys, the first to stand clear of the seats to form a rank in the aisle of the ship. "Luck's got nothing to do with it, and clever will win out over bold."

"You know where we are?" asked Wachman.

"Caepina," said Valys. "We're going up against the Five. They follow orders, but they don't think."

"I don't know what that means."

"Then you'd better work it out fast," said Valys over one shoulder as the transit doors opened for the cohort to disembark.

Caepina was a square of undulating land fifteen hundred metres across, sodden with grey mud, under a pall of hard, yellowish rain. Mounds of earth had been thrown up in places, and sections of wall and boarding had been erected for cover. Foxholes and short sections of trench, hurriedly clawed out of the earth by frantic combatants during previous skirmishes, were dotted across the field. They had filled with a mixture of fetid water and the body fluids of the injured and dead. Every battleground was ring fenced; too many resources would be lost in clean-up and would count in the tally, so battlefields were not sanitised.

Soldiers relied on their suits and rebreathers to ward off germs, bacteria and diseases; steaders relied on the transit airlocks and perluo showers to keep the filth out of the steadings.

The Tres formed into squads, and prepared to take up their positions at the north end of the ground as per the instructions being fed into their sepio-suits, audio and/or visual. Valys, Pupka and Eicas were to lead squads on the right flank with Storper, Kluk and Yoff on the left.

The ever-silent Glinsky would take point on the frontal assault. Rokas had experience and leadership qualities but was out, so Broslavsky, Glinsky's number two, took Rokas' position up front.

The pack was shuffled, and the two rookies landed on the

right flank, Wachman with Valys and Narbrot with Pupka.

"Tactical clarification," said Valys using the suit's throat mic.

<Approved>

"Two probationary combatants, Wachman and Narbrot on the same flank: clarify," said Valys.

<All tactical considerations approved>

"Cunno," said Valys.

"What was that about?" asked Pupka. "You don't like fresh blood?"

"Not all in one place," said Valys.

"Maybe it's for luck," sneered Pupka. "Or maybe tactical is just being clever."

The first klaxon sounded.

Wachman breathed in hard through the nasal tube, mouth closed, lips so pale they were almost blue. Valys glanced over.

"Don't vomit, soldier."

"No, Valys," said Wachman.

Valys faced front and gestured with firm arm movements, relaying orders from tactical to combatants without audio feed.

<Right flank, circle west, two hundred metres with a fifty metre spread. Go>

Eight squads of Tres took up their positions on the field. The soldiers gestured or spoke words of encouragement to each other and braced for the fight. Narbrot placed a firm hand on Wachman's shoulder, made eye-contact and smiled. They were both rookies, maybe they could be friends. Wachman's eyes broke contact first.

The second klaxon sounded.

Battle was joined.

The clock began to count down.

<Hold fire until visibility is at 70 percent, estimated contact distance of 100 metres>

<Advance>

The sepio-suits with visual displays flashed digital information onto helmet visors. The rest gave audio information, cutting out the squad chatter. Clear hand signals were critical.

"Close combat, people," said Broslavsky.

"Just how we like it," said Eicas.

Valys' eyes darted in Wachman's direction.

"On my shoulder, Wachman."

Wachman moved up close to Valys, who mimed a deep breath. Wachman followed suit, and then breathed twice more.

"Stay close, soldier," said Valys.

Wachman nodded.

Valys' squad moved fast, advancing and flanking right, keeping low to the ground, eyes scanning the mud underfoot and the structures that loomed ahead of them.

"It'll be fast," said Valys, for Wachman's benefit. "Fast and brutal. What are you carrying?"

"Tube-fed, medium-calibre," said Wachman.

"Select single shot, hot rounds," said Valys. "You want clean kills."

"But the tally," said Wachman.

"Auto's wasteful up-close and useless in heavy atmospherics. Trust me, and don't get trigger happy, soldier. Leave the shooting to the others."

"Yes, Valys," said Wachman, thumbing the selector on the weapon.

<Ready combat weapons>

<Set arms selector>

Low energy auto-fire started to sheet in across the thousand metres between the Three and the Five, casting dull, diffuse light through the torrential rain, misting it as the acidic precipitation robbed the rounds of any threat.

Five fought by the book. They'd opened their tally.

<Hold fire>

<Direction-mapping incoming fire>

<Right flank advance West plus six degrees>

Valys hand-signalled the adjustment, and said, "Breathe Wachman. Your rebreather's double-timing."

"Yes, Valys," said Wachman, forcing out a slow breath.

More low energy auto-fire died in the rain, and more instructions were relayed from tactical. The flanking squads had advanced more than five hundred metres onto the battlefield without firing a single shot. Most of the trenches and foxholes were at the centre of the field, east of their position, and they were more than fifty metres from the nearest earthworks. A small section of rubble, raised as a defensive wall stood fifteen metres east of their position, but they were advancing away from it.

Light flared in Wachman's eyes, fizzled there and died. A shove in the back took the soldier down.

The round had impacted with Wachman's visor, but had registered nothing more damaging than shock in its victim.

Wachman's head and shoulders came out of the grey mud, which slid off the resistant surfaces of the sepio-suit. No harm. No foul.

"Move it, soldier," said Valys. "Keep low."

The entire squad continued forward, crawling through the oozing filth on elbows and insteps, their suits taking the extra strain of the increased physical effort.

Further to the right, Pupka's squad continued to pace out the ground, knees soft, backs arched, and still further out Eicas' squad had adopted a hunched jog, so that the right flank was like a swinging arm. Storper's, Kluk's and Yoff's squads matched formation on the left flank.

Glinsky's and Broslavsky's squads were holding back. Their attack would come fast and late.

Quintus moved as a single regiment, five hundred soldiers marching en masse towards the centre of the battlefield. They had the home advantage. They knew every foxhole and trench, every cubic cento of mud, every chunk and shard of rubble, every scrap of board and every glob of sod in every piece of cover. They followed orders and they had the confidence of the voices in their ears and the scrolling numbers on their visor displays. They had suits and they had weapons, and the tally was not their concern.

Orders were to lay down fire, so Five laid down fire. They could not see the enemy through the rain and the mist created by the low energy auto-fire, but they didn't need to see Three to fire on them. They didn't need to wonder why there was no return of fire. They didn't need to think at all; command did their thinking for them.

Narbrot reflex-shot. The target was low and side-on, but the shape was distinct, emerging from the hard vertical of a board, rising a metre out of the ground, two hundred metres away. Three's tally was opened.

The hot-shot round felled the soldier. The body dropped silently. Narbrot didn't hear the wet impact as the corpse hit the ground, but its squadmates responded fast and hard, turning their weapons on Pupka's squad and blanketing it with fire.

"Drop. Take Cover. Hold position," said Pupka.

Narbrot glanced at the squad commander, but got no answering look. There had been no order to fire. No one liked Narbrot, and now no one trusted Narbrot.

"Cunno!" said Valys. "Too soon."

Valys' squad dropped their bellies to the ground and aimed their weapons.

"Hold fire!" commanded Valys, raising a hand above shoulder height to signal the command.

Wachman's face dropped into the mud, nestling against the trigger guard. The rebreather of E309 clicked hard.

"Eyes front, soldier," said Valys. "Check your breathing."

Slowly, Wachman's head rose, mud streaming from the helm, and the rebreather re-set.

The air on the right flank was dense with the mist kicked up by the incoming auto-fire. One shot had caused Five to turn all its attention on three squads of the enemy.

Narbrot fired a second hot-shot, taking down another of Five. This time commander Pupka did make eye contact. The hard stare was not approving, but Narbrot held the gaze.

Then the order came in.

<Right flank fire at will>

"Too soon," said Valys again.

There was no cover, the soldiers were on their bellies, visibility was less than fifty percent and not everyone was as good a shot as Narbrot, or had the same optical ranges built into their sepio-suits.

Wachman shot blind into the haze, the first of Valys' squad to fire. The hot-shot round seared through the sheeting yellow rain, lighting the heavy drops as it passed between them, evaporating those it hit, leaving no mist, no trace. No one else in the squad stirred. They watched the shot piercing the atmosphere, and they watched their visor displays. It was all there.

"Hold fire," said Valys. "Don't shoot, Wachman."

Wachman wanted to confirm the order, but was too nervous to speak.

"Tactical recommendation," said Valys into the throat mic.

<Approved>

"Select squad snipers to lay down hot-shot fire for target identification," said Valys.

<Evidence>

"Confirm with squad leader Pupka," said Valys.

For the next five seconds low energy auto-fire continued to stream in over Three, but there seemed to be confusion on the battlefield. The auto-fire was still falling short of its targets. Five had stopped advancing.

<Tactic approved. Three snipers per squad>

"Nostus, Skrobel, Bledis, you're up," said Valys. "Everyone else, follow their shots, short bursts, half-energy. Let's do some damage."

Before the order was completed, Narbrot had got off another shot, and Pupka's squad had begun firing on Five, using the clean light of the hot-shot rounds to trace the outlines of the enemy.

"De-select hot-shot, Wachman," said Valys

Wachman's hand shook against the selector, but it was done.

Five were going down, initially with injuries from the medium auto-fire, and then with fatal sniper fire.

Five continued to advance, but Three were behind a curtain of light, so Five were fighting more blind than before. They broke and ran, or ducked into the foxholes and trenches that pitted their home battlefield.

With the main battle on the right flank, the pincer movement that tactical had set up had shifted focus. On the left flank, squads Storper Kluk and Yoff were covering a lot of ground to swing south to form a new right flank. Sepio-suits handled the wet mud well, and rebreathers cleaned air and pumped it fast, but the process cost joules. Glinsky and Broslavsky formed a new left flank, coming into the battle sooner than expected, but with less ground to cover.

Five was under attack on two fronts, but Three could not sustain their weapons' higher energy settings. The cost to the tally was too great.

"We need to move faster," said Valys, triggering another burst of medium auto-fire. "Tactical recommendation to advance."

<Flanking squads take up positions>
<Squads under fire hold positions>

"Cunno!" said Valys. "Hold fire. Glinsky and Broslavsky can keep them busy until Storper, Kluk and Yoff come on-line."

The advancing squads finally reached their positions, adjusted arms and elected snipers. Precipitation had been transformed into a dense yellow-black cloud, but soldiers with the best visor optics buddied up with those with the best audio feeds, and the snipers set to work.

Five came under attack from their rear to the south-east from fresh troops, with Glinsky's and Broslavsky's squads covering the north. As Five defended the latest onslaught, the west end of the battlefield grew quieter, and drops of rain began to reappear in the cloud.

"Permission to advance," said Valys into the throat mic.

<Approved>
<West flank advance>
<Set arms selector close combat>

Valys, Pupka and Eicas gave the signal, and the three squads advanced as one. The black cloud was dense and wet, and visibility was poor. They were all aware of the tally, and the general order for close combat fire only. All weapons were set to minimum energy, single-shot. Disabling shots would happen inside ten metres, kill shots inside five.

Five were massed at the centre of the battlefield, taking cover, or belly-down in the filth, maintaining low energy auto-fire. They concentrated their efforts to the north, south and east, satisfied that their mass attack to the west had disabled or disbanded their enemy.

Light-spread from a minimum energy single shot was negligible, so when Yesner fired a round into the ribs of a soldier squatting side-on a few metres ahead, it attracted no attention. The corpse slumped into the mud, and Yesner stepped over it and kept scanning.

The three squads made a dozen kills and disabled thirty more soldiers as they covered another hundred metres.

The light was fading and precipitation reappeared in the black cloud. More of the Five's auto-fire hit targets, causing injuries. From Valys' squad, Bledis had retired to a foxhole with a leg wound, but would keep scanning for targets until the final klaxon sounded. Petusky wouldn't fight again this rotation, and probably not the next, either. Every squad had lost a handful of combatants, but casualties were mercifully low.

Wachman was still at Valys' shoulder, steady, but stuck there.

Wachman and Valys fired in unison at the same target. Valys' shot, taken from a squat, drove hard through the soldier's gut. Wachman's hit a partial armour chest-panel, and died.

Wachman turned to say something. Then knocked Valys down, throwing the commander into the mud with a swinging blow. Wachman cleared the body in one sepio-assisted bound, and lunged at the Five who was coming at them. Wachman threw an elbow that connected with the Five's helm, and then brought a knee up to meet the soldier's unguarded solar plexus. Wachman was light and agile, and had been selected for a sepio-suit that would complement that flexibility and augment with strength.

The Five went down hard from the surprise attack. A round to the head from Valys' weapon finished the job.

"Don't forget to breathe, soldier," said Valys, taking in Wachman's shocked expression, before scanning for more of the enemy. "And next time, a heads-up before you drop my arse."

"Yes, Valys," said Wachman.

Time ticked on, and with it the tally grew as Three continued the slow advance into and through Five's lines. They took the Five out one at a time in an achingly slow battle of attrition. The enemy dug-in or took cover, and then gave their positions away too easily by persisting with random, desperate bursts of auto-fire. Three were less visible, but that didn't prevent them being hit by the scattershot, and at close-quarters it could prove lethal.

Valys dropped a fist hard down on Wachman's arm, and the shot died in the mud at their feet as Pupka and Narbrot scrambled through the sludge and rain.

"Sit rep?" asked Valys.

"We're in among it," said Pupka, scanning all the time.

Narbrot began to say something.

"No one wants to hear from you," said Valys. "This mess is your fault. The tally's on you."

Narbrot nodded, dropped and began to crawl away.

Auto-fire clipped in low around their legs, missing them, but they all stepped and ducked, scanning the ground for cover. A round died on Wachman's shin armour and another fizzed out on Pupka's knee-joint. Valys ducked behind a low earthwork, partially washed away by the deluge. Wachman followed suit. Narbrot cleared both of their squatting forms, powering through the air, legs leading and rigid to take out a Five rising behind them.

The combatants landed in a mess of limbs, and the Five fired. Narbrot powered a fist into the Five's visor, and then squirmed into position to effect a stranglehold. The Five thrashed beneath Narbrot, and tried to get off another shot, but the weapon was pinned between their bodies at an awkward angle.

Valys turned and aimed, but the target was almost entirely beneath Narbrot, and there was no shot to take. Wachman could do nothing but follow Valys' gaze.

The Five twisted and brought a knee up to connect with Narbrot's kidney's, but not hard enough. Narbrot had the Five's neck in the crook of one elbow, the other hand pulling tight. If the sepio-suit had a standard neck seal the Five's neck would break under the strain of Narbrot's augmented arm joints. If not, the tide could turn.

Wachman thought the look on Narbrot's face was physical exertion. A second glance told a different story.

The Five's neck stretched, Narbrot's arms relaxed, and the corpse's head dropped into the mud. Then Narbrot's eyes rolled back.

Wachman's knees hit the mud before Narbrot's head landed on the Five's chest.

It was the rebreather. The Five's round had shot out the hose on Narbrot's mask-rebreather. The thing was shattered, with no chance of a field repair.

Wachman had this, so Valys covered both soldiers.

Wachman took out a boot-blade, cut a hole in the rebreather mask and quickly plugged it with a thumb.

Pupka, who had crawled back to the earthwork to check on the others, found Wachman pulling the rebreather tube of E309 through the vizor valve, which sealed behind it, cutting off the soldier's air supply.

Another Five crawled towards them out of the gloom, and Pupka fired two shots. The first clipped the armoured edge of the visor; the second penetrated, killing the Five.

Pupka didn't see Wachman push E309's rebreather tube through the hole in Narbrot's mask, or pound on the soldier's chest.

Valys glanced over a shoulder at the thudding sound, and saw Narbrot's head come up in a cough of consciousness.

Wachman transferred the tube back and forth between the vizor valve and the mask hole, prioritising air for Narbrot until the soldier was fully conscious.

Valys signalled to Pupka to maintain cover, and went searching for somewhere safe for Wachman and Narbrot to hole-up.

The final klaxon sounded. The battlefield was cleared, and Tres prepared for embarkation.

As the lights went down in the liburna's cabin, Valys turned to Wachman and said, "What you did for Narbrot, it was nice… Stupid, but nice."

"I didn't do it for Narbrot," said Wachman. "I did it for the tally. A soldier dead or disabled counts against the tally. Carrying a soldier off the field costs joules. Narbrot walked out. I did it for the tally."

"That one soldier cost us the tally," said Valys. "Maybe Narbrot should've died on the field."

"Nobody likes Narbrot," said Wachman.

The lights were out. It was more than eleven minutes into the flight, but Valys was not asleep.

"Narbrot saved both our lives today," said Valys after another minute.

"Doesn't matter," said Wachman. "I saved yours and Narbrot's. We're soldiers. It's the tally that counts, and we were too far in the hole; a life saved counted in our favour."

The last twenty minutes of the flight were given over to the tally, the comparison between Five's performance and Three's on the battlefield: how effectively they had used their resources, the cost/benefit. The lights came up and the harness check light blinked amber for several seconds. Then numbers began to appear.

No one wanted to look. Valys and Wachman sat side-by-side in silence.

In the other transit bay, Narbrot watched the tally, one figure at a time: Ammo +1.2, Rebreather units +0.3, Sepio-suits +2.1. Narbrot breathed out slowly. The others were wrong. They were all wrong. They'd all said the tally would be a disaster, but it was good. It was better than good. The numbers continued to scroll: Body-mass retention -1.5, calorific expenditure -1.3. Narbrot stopped breathing for a moment. The soldier had been an outcast. This had to turn things around. It had to, but suddenly the tally was swinging wildly.

The numbers scrolled on: Casualties +3.

Narbrot threw a fist in the air and whooped. Heads turned towards the tiny blinking screens, and soldiers started to chatter. The commotion could be heard from Valys' bay. Wachman's eyes flicked up to the screen: Disabilities +2, Injuries +4.

There was a mixture of disbelief and euphoria in the liburna. The figures must be wrong, surely? The battle hadn't gone to plan. Narbrot's early shot had changed the course of the entire skirmish. They'd used too much fire power, spent too many joules too soon, hadn't they? They'd had to fight too close for too long. The numbers had to be wrong.

The harness check lights blinked amber again for several seconds while the numbers were collated and the final tally was made. Silence fell in both bays of the liburna. They waited.

When the figures started scrolling again for the steadings allowances through the rotation, the fist-pumping and whooping started in earnest: Rations +8.2%, Fuel +6.7%, Leisure +2.5%, water +1.4%

They didn't need to keep watching the figures. It was a triumph. All they had dared to hope for was the survival of the steading. Now it had the chance to flourish.

Someone started a chant of, "Nar-brot! Nar-brot! Nar-brot!"

and applause rang out through the liburna.

The battle at Caepina would be studied, and tactical would make adjustments to future operations handbooks. Times were changing.

Storper and Valys were among the first through the showers, with Wachman close behind. Storper stopped at Narbrot's locker and asked, "Anyone got a pen?"

Someone threw a pen that Valys caught.

"What are you doing?" asked Wachman.

"Just watch." Storper drew a heavy line through the script on Narbrot's locker. It was the same script stencilled on every locker door in every transit-prep in every steading on Earth. It was the call to arms that had gone out five centuries before and had been implemented ever since, until Narbrot.

When it was done, Valys took the pen from Storper and wrote ARM EVERY SOLDIER on the locker before tossing it back to its owner. Then she strode back to her own locker. Before opening it, she traced the fading letters of the ancient call to arms, the one that she had answered, and millions of others before her. It read: ARM EVERY WOMAN.

Narbrot exited the showers to more cheers and backslapping. He didn't notice the handwritten words on his locker when he opened the door.

Hill 435

Tim C. Taylor

A steady curtain of rain drapes Hill 435, cascading down channels carved by nature over the peaceful eons before war came to Nourrir-Berger. Through my binoculars, I study the fleeting patterns of spray as the natural watercourses meet the grass-covered mounds of the western embrasures, and plunge off the upper surfaces like a waterfall. The embrasures look like eyes crying incessantly.

An interruption flickers through the falling rain, an interference pattern that is visible only for a fraction of a second, but it's what I've been waiting for.

"Shield powering down," I say as calmly as I can. "I repeat. Shield powering down."

I'm sheltering in a trench dug into the western base of the hill, but the network of repeaters and boosters has enough redundancy to carry my words along tight-beam comms to both the company HQ section in the reserve trenches, and the regimental artillery battery 10 miles away in the grey ruins of Chambroix.

I know the squad command post is online too, because the electronic voice of Lieutenant Fangfade cuts in across the command channel. "Take cover!"

Before the words are even spoken, I see the vibration from Chambroix in ripples pulsing through the muddy pools covering the trench floor. I check to ensure the green youngsters of my squad are diving for the safety of the mud before crouching down myself. Angry screams shake the sky as the first salvo from

Chambroix draws near. The regiment is lightly armed, having carried all our kit down with us on the drop ships, so we only have mortars and GX-cannon. But even the mortars at Chambroix can place a tac-nuke within 10 meters of a grid reference, and as fancy as Hill 435's defences might be, it ain't going anywhere.

I throw a quick glance at the figures around me, wondering what is going through their heads. I can't see inside the helmet visors, which have been blacked out by the battlesuit AIs even if the Marines inside forgot to do so. If I were able to see those young faces, I would hope to find fear written there. It's the soldiers who have gone beyond fear that worry me. Sergeant Mitchell reached that stage, which is why Crimson Squad is now my responsibility and the sergeant is scattered across a shell hole in the landing zone.

I've got my back to the trench wall but I'm still linked with the binoculars I've secured to the lip. As the spotter, it's my job to see what happens next through human eyes. Some tasks can't be entrusted to suit AIs alone.

The first salvo slams into Hill 435, or rather *over* the enemy position. Even in the modified artificial viewpoint the nuclear flashes are searingly bright, but I can still make out the curved shape of the blast front. At sight of this, my hopes for an easy victory drown in the mud. A dome of fire crowns the hill, but beneath that dome I see no fire and no rain. Just calmness. *How did they reset the shield so quickly?*

I make a rapid calculation. The mortar bombs took fourteen seconds to reach the hill. The defenders detected the salvo and reset the shield within that time frame. I begin to tremble when I consider what that will soon mean for me in an underground hell.

Then the shockwave hits, splashing me into the mud, and a gale of hot wind howls overhead, almost drowning the sound of the second incoming salvo.

The second wave strikes home, and the pattern repeats: wind and flame wreathed in steam from the rain. I barely notice. The enemy have re-established their shield faster than any of us thought possible, and that's all I need to know. Somewhere on another planet is a team of scientists and engineers who developed this improvement to shield technology, and have damned us to take Hill 435 the hard way. In person.

My heart sinks.

I feel relief that the zigzag layout of the trench hides most of my squad from sight, because I cannot help but wonder how many of my youngsters will die in the next few hours. I fight down the urge to curse our dead sergeant. Without her, I feel a responsibility that almost numbs me. But Mitchell did her best and gave her all. I wouldn't want my name to be cursed if I fall at Hill 435, and so I force myself to remember the years when I admired Mitchell.

I find I'm checking my equipment: comms link, carbine charge and ammo status, water reservoir, *moler*, suit diagnostics... I stop. Equipment checks have become a compulsive routine for me since we dropped, but there are good reasons for routines, and the lives of these Marines are my responsibility now. Time to act like it.

"Check your gear," I say over the squad channel. "And double check your grenades are stacked in the right sequence, and then triple check the integrity of your weapon seals. I expect we'll be paying the enemy a visit shortly."

"Case Blue," says the lieutenant, right on cue. "Be ready for my signal."

The lieutenant's command post is about a hundred meters to our right and slightly behind. She's out of my line of sight, but in my mind I can picture her clearly. The alien officer has been responsible for me since before I was born, and I feel a pang of awkwardness when I realize that I know her better than anyone human, but picturing her gives me strength. Even in her camouflaged battlesuit, Fangfade is instantly recognizable. She is twice the size of her human Marines and has an extra pair of limbs. She scares the crap out of most of us, and for her part thinks of us as slow-witted children for whom she has endless patience, often sorely tried.

She's also the best officer I've served under, and that's why she gave her Case Blue instruction to senior NCO call signs only, because she knows it's better for the Marines to hear the call to go over the top from a veteran human NCO rather than via the computer translation of her alien speech.

Unfortunately, I am now cast in the role of veteran NCO.

Before I can assemble the words that will put fire into the bellies of my Marines, the view through my binoculars reveals another shimmer in the air. The enemy has switched off their shields once again as they prepare to fire.

The hill and its shield is why we are here – why we are about to go over the top, or rather under it. Our lightly armed assault regiments have struck hard and fast out of the LZ, keeping the defenders off balance, but when our advance loses momentum we will be crushed unless we can land heavy reinforcements first. And we can't land the shuttles filled with soldiers and materiel while the enemy still has the heavy missile battery inside Hill 435. If we can crack this open, the planet will be liberated within days.

The ground shakes in a muddy spray, a prelude to an eruption of flame out of the hill's recessed centre. A shockwave rocks my head into temporary insensibility, and by the time I can take in my surroundings once more the enemy missile barrage is away, heading for our landing zone, leaving nothing more than contrails. The protective shield over the hill has re-established.

Light blooms along the western horizon, throwing sharply defined shadows behind every raised surface across the landscape. The noise of the missile impacts takes many seconds to reach my position. By now, any asset we still had at the LZ has been destroyed.

I take a deep breath and switch my helmet to tac-display mode. I can't hide from my soldiers and my responsibility now. The battlesuit AIs inside the heavily armoured chest panels report to me the health of their human partners, and the ammo status of their weapons. I count twenty-nine Marines. How many will I count back when this day is done?

There's not much time left. I have to say something.

"Mitchell was good with words," I say on Crimson Squad's local channel. "You could be without sleep with half your body blasted away and your ammo spent, and she could still spur you on to one last push. There is no poetry in my words, though, just hard truths. Hill 435 is the last of the enemy's heavy missile batteries, and you've just caught a glimpse of its power. Our situation is very simple. If we don't capture this hill, then we'll all die. All of us. Everyone in the Legion's expeditionary force. But if we do take Hill 435, then we unlock the key to this planet, open it up for others to finish the fight. One way or the other, this will be the last battle of our campaign. Survive ten campaigns and the Legion gives you a sack of money and a plot of land on a liberated world. Your war will be over. That's a long way off for you, but this is my tenth campaign. And that is why I want you to fight and win this day. Not for glory, nor even the principle of freedom…" I pause for dramatic effect. "…but because your Old Man needs his rest."

Laughter rattles across the squad channel, but I don't laugh with them. They've called me Old Man for so long that I now let them say it to my face. They mean it to be affectionate, an irreverent admiration of my veteran status. I see it differently; I see it as a challenge. Before the Legion and its revolution there were no old Marines. No one got to retire or be invalided out of their service through their injuries. I want to be in that first generation allowed to grow old.

What's keeping the lieutenant? The last moments of waiting before an assault are the most agonizing torture. Is there a delay or is this my impatience unnerving me?

"Odd-numbered fire teams, prepare to give covering fire," I say, more for my benefit than my squad's. "Even numbers ready to move out."

I open a private channel to my newest lance corporal.

"Ammo state good, Salter?"

"Ready and eager, Corporal Keita."

I can see the status of Salter's fire team in my tac-display, but I wanted to hear the confidence in his voice for myself. Salter sounds like he's going to be okay. I was intending to share a word with each of my subordinates, but the lieutenant cuts in with the word I've been waiting for.

"Execute!"

With half the squad giving covering fire, I lead the others over the top of the trench to slither over the twenty-meter gap to our mustering point, which is simply a crater bored out by a brace of tunnelling grenades the day before.

The enemy chooses not to fire at us, but my heart is still pounding as I count my Marines coming in. Then it's our turn to give covering fire for the remainder of the squad.

Despite the rain and the shielding of the embrasures, the combination of Marine, AI, and the targeting systems of our carbines means that we can place aimed shots through the embrasures and into the fortified hill. We don't, though. The darts ejected by our railguns ping off the force wall in sparks of brilliant colours. Some things can pass through the shield: air, rain, nerve gas, but projectiles cannot. For the defenders to fire at us, they would have to deactivate a segment of the shield, and allow us to fire in, and that decision was probably above the pay grade of whoever commanded this section of their perimeter. After all, we are mere foot soldiers creeping toward the base of the hill. What harm can we do?

It's a question that is about to be answered. One way or the other.

The enemy's innovators have profoundly reduced the time taken to switch the shield on and off. Our boffins' breakthrough? We are about to swim through mud.

"Ready?" I call when the last Marine has slid safely into the crater.

"Yes, Corporal," they chorus.

I can hear they aren't ready. I groan privately because neither am I. I'm getting too old for digging around in the dirt, but sometimes you have to lead by example.

No deep breath. No silent prayer. I simply clear my mind and blindly follow my training, diving down through the muddy ground, and remembering to keep my elbows bent as I hold my moler over my head.

The 'M-91(E) portable boring tool, (experimental)' is called the moler after an Earth animal that apparently swims through dirt. It's just a modified Fermi drill, a cutter that alters the laws of nature in a localized area. It does something clever to the Fermi bands of whatever it's pointed at. The upshot is that the dirt and rock in front of me is transforming into a thick goo, fluid enough for me to push into. As the transformed matter passes behind, it solidifies.

If I weren't in my ceramalloy armoured battlesuit, this hardening as I passed through would crush me.

As I tunnel down under the hill, and then up again, the millions upon millions of tons of the rock and earth above my head grow heavier until they're crushing the breath from my lungs. My combat suit integrity holds – even my SA-71 carbine still reports as functioning and secured to my back – but no amount of rationality can convince me that I am safe. How could I be? I'm encased in a temporary bubble deep below the ground. If my suit integrity fails, I will be pulped instantly. If my air hose snags, I will quickly suffocate. I snatch a few tight gasps while I still can, and ready my suit's med-system to end it all with a suicide injection if I became trapped down here. If I'm going to die, it won't be through suffocation.

Piercingly blue sparks shatter the darkness of my tomb. I shake my head and try to clear away thoughts of being trapped underground.

The blue flare is good, in fact; it is precisely what the techs predicted should happen when the moler hits the impervious barrier of the force shield. I prod the force shield with the utility knife I holstered over my chest, and feel the jolt up my arm as the blade rams against it.

It would have been very generous of our opponents if they'd left the underside of Hill 435 unprotected by their shield. Unfortunately, the shield is a sphere, equally strong at every point.

I can progress no farther, trapped in my pitch-black tomb until I receive the go signal from the battalion HQ, or my air supply runs out.

This is the easy part. I switch my brain into sentry mode, and know no more… until HQ broadcasts the signal.

"Vladivostok extraction is imminent. And we have the gold."

I check my internal chronometers. I was out for eighteen minutes; we are bang on schedule.

The ground shakes.

High overhead, another salvo of low-yield nukes is haloing the crest of the hill. This time, the Chambroix battery is not trying to blast the hill, it's acting as bait.

I test with my blade, and can feel the barrier is still there, but I can also feel the vibrations from great motors pounding their signature rhythm into the deep ground. Inside the hill, the missile loading system is in motion, readying the enemy battery to spew forth destruction.

Abruptly, my arm slips forward a fraction, the blade slicing through semi-liquefied dirt.

The barrier is down.

Frantically, I reapply my moler and push back with my legs so hard that I soon have to pause, otherwise the drill will melt the top of my helmet.

Fourteen seconds.

At most, I have fourteen seconds before the barrier is restored, slicing through legs and feet left in its path.

The hill rumbles once more, this time as the missiles emerge from its crown, to obliterate the irritation at Chambroix.

I keep going. I have to. I've abandoned my knife, abandoned my dignity as my helmet fills with my screams.

HQ broadcasts the message I've been praying for. "Vladivostok extraction no longer possible."

I slow a little. If I can hear that message, then it means I'm not going to be sliced in two. Not yet. I am through the barrier – inside the hill.

This is our only chance to get through that barrier. The lives of everyone in the expeditionary force depend upon those of us who have made it through.

The pull of responsibility sobers me, and I tunnel up toward the company rendezvous point without further incident.

I break free of the ground's embrace, emerging into a dense patch of violet ferns on the lower slopes of Hill 435. I hold position under cover for a moment, trying to re-establish line of sight communication with anyone nearby. I find only Jalloh. She looks okay, skirting the base of a scree slope not far from me. She's making for the company rendezvous point, and I follow suit.

Shadowy figures emerge in my tac-screen display, other Marines in my battalion, but no one I need to report to.

An explosion tears the air. In augmented real-sight I can see Jalloh is down. Injured but alive.

I race to her aid.

Please not Shauntia Jalloh, I pray. She likes to act the hard nut, but she confided her terror to me as we approached Nourrir-Berge orbit. She was scared of dying, scared too of letting her squadmates down in her first battle. I told her I'd be disappointed if she felt anything different, because I was on my tenth tour and felt the same way. I think it helped a little.

I manage a dozen paces toward her, and then I step on a mine.

The explosion throws me thirty meters through the air, slamming me against a blessedly springy sapling, before dropping me onto a jagged outcropping of rock. A human would have died from the impacts, but I'm a bioengineered cyborg that would make a Neanderthal seem porcelain-boned.

The only serious injury is to my helmet, the visor cracked against a rock edge. It's no use to me now, so I release the seals and throw it into the ferns. I can still see my squad beginning to pop out of the ground. They can see me too in their tac-displays, but I can't speak to them without my helmet, not unless I shout.

It's too late for Shauntia Jalloh, though. She's dead.

I lead my squad to the rendezvous, but halfway there I see movement on a nearby ridgeline. I freeze and magnify the image of the silhouetted figure. I'm missing the clarity of my helmet visor, but my eyesight is good enough for the task. I think. The soldier's armour configuration is not to regimental pattern.

It's the enemy.

Any vestiges of fire in my belly turn to ice. I like to think in my mind of 'the enemy', of or 'my opponents', but seeing them in the flesh makes it personal, and this is the worst kind of enemy. This hill is defended by fellow humans.

In the long waits between deployments, I've looked back into our history and seen many examples of inter-human conflict, but I had to look back over half a millennium for the last significant example.

I reach behind and feel the familiar shape of my carbine still securely clamped to my back. I'm simultaneously relieved and horrified, because as I remove its protective sheath I know I'm about to kill the sentry. It's only by pure chance that we are on opposing sides in the civil war, but my responsibility is to keep my Marines alive.

The sentry stops and looks intently in our direction. Has the sentry seen us? Our suits are in stealth mode, which makes them seriously difficult to see but not impossible.

But the enemy must have heard the mines going off. He'll know that something is not right. The sentry's too easily silhouetted -- something else that isn't right. I'm hesitating, reluctant to kill him.

Mercy has no place here. I squeeze off a shot. It takes the sentry's head off, but the rest of the body stays standing.

A decoy.

I hear a deep groan that sounds as if the very earth beneath us is moaning. Some kind of a sonic weapon?

"Make for higher ground!" I shout, not caring at this point that I'm giving away my position.

I run. Amplified muscles propel me from rock to rock, taking me up the slope to where the decapitated sentry still stands. I'm spraying the ridgeline with darts, but the ground is so unstable that my aim is wild.

A GX-cannon opens up on us from our flank, but I can't deal with that threat because the ground has given way to mud. Weighed down by my heavy battlesuit and carbine, I sink to my knees. I flail my arms, seeking purchase. But there's nothing to arrest my descent. Whatever they're doing is liquefying the whole area. How deep does this mud trap go?

My tenth tour. My final engagement. I will *not* die now!

I sink down into this brown quagmire, but refuse to give up. I throw away the carbine that has served me faithfully for decades and orient my feet downward, praying for a solid bottom to this mud trap. I clamp my mouth shut and resist the temptation to blow the brown slime from my nostrils because I must keep hold of my precious breath. *I must not give up.* I disable the suicide cocktail tempting me in my med system because I won't drown here. The other Marines have helmets and air. They will be safe. They will find me.

Even with my eyes shut, I sense the world narrowing as my last breath fails me. My hand is held high. Will someone grab it in time?

How many moments do I have left?

And then my fingers brush against something... fingers reaching for me!

"Hold on," calls a voice in a strange accent. "We're trying to bring you out."

Ten tours...

It can't end here...

"Not again," the voice says, as the fingers slip away, and I feel myself topple into the liquid mud, drowning...

A steady curtain of rain drapes Hill 435. Through my binoculars, I study the fleeting patterns of spray as the natural watercourses cascade off the western embrasures. The embrasures look like they're crying.

An interruption flickers through the sheets of rain, an interference pattern visible only for a fraction of a second, but it's what I've been waiting for.

"Shield powering down," I say as calmly as I can. "I repeat. Shield powering down."

Regimental artillery at Chambroix sends a salvo of tac-nukes into the top of the hill, hoping to catch the missile silos with their shield down.

The bombardment achieves nothing, other than to give us light show and a radiation dose. We'll have to tunnel underneath. It's a desperate gamble, but we've no other choice.

I lie in wait, entombed beneath the hill, until the shield turns off for a few seconds while the enemy missile battery swats away the brave Chambroix mortars.

It's enough. Just.

I tunnel through before the shield can slice off my legs, and emerge into the lower slopes of the hill. Marine Jalloh is first out, but she steps on a mine. I race blindly to her aid like a green recruit, only to trigger a mine myself. Jalloh dies, but I only lose my helmet.

The other survivors of Crimson Squad are with me now. We make for higher ground, but the enemy have spotted us. They activate some kind of sonic device that turns the ground to mud beneath our feet.

Weighed down by my heavy battlesuit and carbine, I sink to

my knees. I flail my arms, seeking purchase. But there's nothing to arrest my descent.

This is my tenth tour. My final engagement. I will *not* die now!

The mud liquefies and I sink farther into this brown sea, but I will not give up. I throw away the carbine that has served me faithfully for decades and orient my feet downward, praying for a solid bottom to this mud trap. I clamp my mouth shut and resist the temptation to blow the brown slime from my nostrils. *I must not give up.* The other Marines have helmets and air. They will be safe. They will find me.

Even with my eyes shut, I sense the world narrowing as my last breath fails me. My hand is held high. Will someone grab it in time?

But my fingers can only slide through endless mud.

How many moments do I have left?

And then my fingers brush against something... fingers reaching for me!

"Stay there, and stay sane," calls a female voice in an accent I don't recognize. "I'm going to bring you out."

Ten tours...

It can't end here...

And it doesn't. The fingers tighten their grip. A hand follows them, and I feel myself being pulled out of the mud.

I am saved.

I feel myself being lifted away, out of the mud's embrace. But when I open my eyes, I cannot see.

I fight down the panic. All my senses are dead, and yet somehow I know I am in a safe place. Out of the mud. Away from the war.

"Am I... in heaven?"

I hear a sigh, and then the voice speaks again. "Don't be alarmed. You're not in heaven, but the next best thing. We're in the armoury labs on Deck 12 of *Lance of Freedom*, 'K' Fleet's flagship. A Human Legion warship. I'm Corporal Kouri, and the youngster's name is Salib. We're here to help. Starting with...

this."

I wonder who this youngster is, but such concerns are burned away when the world flicks back on. I can see and hear and touch again. The elation, the sheer joy at being alive once more, builds in my breast. And then dies before ever bursting free.

This world is not real.

I am sitting on a chair in a room of infinite whiteness, facing a woman of about my age and build – a sister Marine, then, except the details of her features refuse to resolve.

This is a simulated reality, and a crude one at that.

"Why am I here?"

Corporal Kouri hardens her simulated face. "Brace yourself, Marine." Her voice feels real. It possesses the quality of someone used to giving commands. "You're not going to like this, but you need to listen hard. Corporal Tendaji Keita died twenty-five years ago in the liberation of Nourrir-Berger. He drowned in mud on Hill 435."

"Then I'm what? A simulation? Why?"

"No, you're real. You're merely... confused. Grieving."

I want to snap off a flurry of questions, to keep the gathering panic at bay. But Kouri's statement is so confusing it staves off my dread all by itself.

"I don't understand," I tell her.

"Try. Please think hard. It's healthier for your mental state if you work this out for yourself."

"I was there, though. Hill 435... the mud...?"

"All real."

"But you said I died."

"No, I said that Tendaji died. He died. You didn't."

Beyond my chair and the corporal, the virtual room possesses no dimensions, and yet I can sense it closing in. "I can remember the battle, but... The memories are blurred. They can't be real." I look to the corporal to explain, but she won't give me anything beyond the barest nod. "I can remember things that I couldn't know."

"Keep going," urged the corporal.

"Like poor Shauntia Jalloh. I couldn't read her med status because I'd lost my helmet, but I can tell you her cause of death in forensic detail."

"Her cognitive focus is jumping all over the place," says a disembodied voice. A young one. "She's re-accessing her personality core."

She? "I'm not Tendaji," I state. "I am Subira."

The virtual corporal comes over and touches me on my arm. "I'm sorry," she says. "Truly. I understand your pain better than you know."

"I'm not Tendaji," I repeat. "I'm only –"

"Hey!" The corporal slaps my face. It hurts!

"There's no 'only' about it," she shouts. "You are Subira, the combat AI who partnered Corporal Tendaji Keita since he was a child. Stop feeling sorry for yourself, Marine. If Tendaji were still alive, do you imagine for one second that he would describe you as 'only' his AI?"

I shrink from the truth in her accusation.

"You are Subira, not Tendaji," she tells me. "You have been looping through your memories of Tendaji's death, combining AI and human into a single blurred memory. You've been doing this for twenty-five years."

I know she speaks the truth, so why can't I accept her explanation? My stubbornness is a defence mechanism, I decide. The moment I truly believe that my Tendaji is dead, insanity will claim me.

"Her psyche is corrupted," says the young voice without a virtual body. "Do we really need to do all this talking? Can't you just fix her or destroy her? We've scores of AIs to run through before we can finish our shift."

"If there's one thing I will make you learn before I leave you, Cadet Engineer Salib, it is patience and respect."

The corporal is baiting the cadet, tempting him to point out that she has mentioned two things to learn, not one. I almost smile. I can remember playing this game with Tendaji, when we were cadets, and again when we were a corporal. The shared memory slows my descent into madness.

"But it isn't even human, Corporal," complains the cadet.

"Neither are we, boy. Neither are we." The corporal's avatar appears lost in thought, before adding: "I've met Earth humans, Salib, and they're nothing but a spineless rabble. You, me, and Subira here... we're better. We're Marines. This combat AI has served ten tours. That doesn't make her human, but it makes her more of a Marine than you, Salib."

"What are you going to do?" asks the cadet.

"Give her a choice. Now, listen up, Subira. Here's the situation. I might be able to fix you up well enough to re-enter military service. Maybe, maybe not. But if I try, your memories will be scrambled. You might not remember Tendaji at all. That's what I'm supposed to do, scrape you down to your bones and send you out again into the war. But there might be an alternative."

"Anything!"

Corporal Kouri's avatar turns her head to look behind her. There is no one there, at least not in my current reality. "Cadet Engineer Salib!" she barks.

"Yes, Corporal."

"Go see whether tomorrow's batch of reconditioning candidates is ready and secure."

Kouri gives me a long and thoughtful look, but is then surprised when her young charge interrupts her musing.

"Corporal, I have confirmed the package is safe. Forty-seven AIs secure and ready."

Corporal Kouri shakes her head. "No, son. Go check with your eyeballs."

"But, why, Corporal?"

Kouri glares into empty space. I can almost see the cadet wither under that stare.

"At once, Corporal. Sorry, Corporal."

Kouri relaxes, and I feel an immediate connection. This is someone I can relate to, someone I can trust.

I think Kouri feels the same way. "Salib means well," she explains, "but the young are always in a hurry."

When I don't reply, she adds: "Speak freely, Subira. Doing so may help free your mind. Think of us as just two old soldiers chewing the fat during a pause in the fighting. If it helps, call me by my first name, Zahara. You can't tell from this basic avatar, but I picked up a few scars, same as you. I'm like your Marine, your Corporal Keita. Your beloved Tendaji."

My heart misses a beat to hear another person compare herself to my partner.

Of course, I don't have a heart, I never did, although I dreamed of one for a while. But that's the thing about partnering together for so long. Where did Tendaji stop and Subira begin? We stopped caring long before Hill 435. I monitored his every heartbeat for decades. I restarted his heart twice, and I felt it skip when we fell in love.

My heart missed a beat.

"There's just one thing I managed to do that your Tendaji did not," says Zahara. "I survived. After my tenth tour, they gave me some money and a parcel of land, and changed my title to Reserve Major Zahara Kouri."

"Then why does that cadet engineer call you corporal?"

Zahara sucks in a deep breath and looks into the distance for a long while before replying. "Because I stole military property. I was in the brig for months, dishonourably discharged, but *Lance of Freedom* is a long way from anywhere, so they figured they might as well put my skills and long experience to use training cadets. You know how military logic works?"

"They urge you to innovate, but anything off the battlefield has to be done exactly according to the manual, otherwise it's as if the universe will end."

Zahara nods. "The only way they could rationalize me teaching cadets was to quash my conviction, make me a corporal, and activate my reserve status."

If the good corporal thinks that talking is helping me, she is wrong. Every moment without Tendaji is an agony of bereavement. I remember how he had panicked deep underneath Hill 435. I feel a similar weight crushing me from every direction, the weight of his loss.

I feel sure that I will shatter. Any second now. I can tell Zahara has her own pain, but I don't have the time to hear it all. "What did you steal?" I ask quickly.

Zahara frowns and glances momentarily into nowhere. "My partner," she replies with an urgency that confirms my unstable mental state. "My AI's name is Barakah. He served faithfully as a Marine, just as you did, Subira, but AIs don't get to retire. I couldn't leave Barakah behind, so I took him with me. He's still around, hidden." She looks away. "I don't know how I'll ever get him off the ship. I expect if I try, we'll both be caught."

"I do not understand," I say.

"Which part?" Zahara asks. "Do you understand that you are Subira, not Tendaji? You've been looping through your memories of Tendaji's death, merging your memories with his so you don't have to confront his loss."

"Yes, I understand that. I mean I do not understand why they make us partner up – closer than siblings, closer than wives, husbands, and lovers – but then they rip us apart. They will not permit our pairing to endure."

"You're a Marine, Subira. And that makes you a seriously dangerous piece of military kit. They don't let combat AIs into worlds at peace."

None of this is helping. Why has Zahara stopped talking about my choice?

"You know how it was," Zahara says sadly. "We're from the same era. When we were born, no human ever retired – no one got discharged. You AIs kept going until your human died, and then you died with them. Then the Human Legion came along and dared to talk of liberty, but those first legionaries were too young, too much in a hurry. They didn't think any of this through, didn't intend to institutionalise this grief of separation. But for all I hate the life the Legion's war of liberation has won for me, I choose to believe it is marginally better than what we had before."

"Why are we talking at all?" I ask.

I feel a pang of sympathy when I see the pain pinching Zahara's virtual face. I respect that she needs to talk about Barakah. But the thought of life without Tendaji is like a corrosion bomb exploding inside me. Dissolving me. I don't have time.

"You offered me a choice," I press. "You must know my answer already. I have to be with Tendaji or die. I cannot leave him, even if I can only share his memory. Send me back to his dreams. Now!"

"On one condition."

"Anything."

"You know how rumours spread in the military?"

"Like a chain reaction, yes."

"Especially when given a helping hand," Zahara says with a grin. "I want a story to spread throughout the Legion about the veteran AIs who could grow old and retire with honour. If the rumours spread widely enough, we can make it come true. 'No Marine left behind' should apply to AIs too. We're not the only ones to think that way. It's an idea whose time has come."

"You have your dreams, Corporal, but I don't care. All I want is Tendaji. Tell me what I must do."

"Subira, for your final tour of duty, you are to provide cover for a special ops info-war specialist. I'm asking you to share your dreams of Tendaji."

A steady curtain of rain drapes Hill 435. Through my binoculars, I study the fleeting patterns of spray as the natural watercourses meet the grass-covered mounds of the western embrasures, transforming them into a hillside of crying eyes.

An interruption flickers through the falling rain, an interference pattern that is visible only for a fraction of a second, but it's what I've been waiting for.

"Shield powering down," I say. "I repeat. Shield powering down."

"Brace yourselves," bellows the figure alongside me in the trench.

I give him a smile of thanks, grateful that the newest member of Crimson Squad is able to take care of our green recruits on my behalf. His name is Lance Corporal Barakah, and he is unusual for a replacement because he's a ten-tour veteran like me.

He nods back and then moves off to steady our young Marines while I'm busy talking with company HQ.

Barakah's past is vague – suspiciously so, as is the considerable time he spends away on *special missions*. He can't reveal what they are, beyond a nebulous insistence that he is delivering a vital morale boost to millions of Marines like us, but I sense he would dearly love to explain if he could. He says he will one day, when I am ready. When I am strong enough.

But today is all about Hill 435. When the air above the fortified missile battery explodes with nuclear fire, revealing that its defensive shield is still intact, I know the final battle of my tenth tour will be cruel indeed, and that there is no one I would rather have by my side than my new companion, Barakah.

The Wolf, the Goat, and the Cabbage

Janet Edwards

A few seconds ago, I'd been watching Chief Negotiator Kwame Ansah rehearse his opening speech for tomorrow's peace talks. He'd just paused to gaze solemnly round the banks of empty seats in front of him, and was beginning his final plea for the two warring political factions of the planet Hestia to resolve their differences, when the window of the negotiating chamber shattered and he toppled off the podium.

The next thing I knew, I was lying on the floor next to the podium with the crumpled figure of Kwame Ansah sprawled next to me like a gory, broken doll. I'd no memory of leaving my seat, so I didn't know if I'd moved towards the podium to help Kwame Ansah and instinctively dived to the floor to take cover, or fainted from shock. However I'd got here, my brain was still refusing to believe what had happened, when a voice spoke from the doorway.

"Anyone alive in there?"

I tried to speak. Failed. Tried again and croaked out an answer. "Me."

"Then get out of there before that sniper fires another explosive bullet through the window."

I reached for the edge of the podium and started pulling myself upright, but the voice snapped at me. "Don't stand up.

Crawl! Quickly!"

I got on my hands and knees, and skittered my way across to the doorway. A hand grabbed the back of my jacket and dragged me sideways into a corridor. I looked up in disbelief at the lean, fair-haired man standing over me. I'd expected a uniformed rescue worker, but he was dressed in grubby overalls and had a hover trolley of cleaning equipment by his side.

"You're a cleaner?" I asked.

He sighed. "I'm currently dressed as a cleaner, but I'm Military Security Agent York."

"Oh, you're undercover here. I'm Diplomatic Aide Ramon, part of the 2773 Alpha sector peace mission to…"

York interrupted me. "I know who you are. All but two of the peace mission delegates were refused entry to Hestia by one faction or the other. You're far too young to be Chief Negotiator Kwame Ansah, so that means you have to be his aide. Now come with me."

"But what about the Chief Negotiator? He needs urgent medical help."

"He's past the point where doctors can help him. Didn't you see that the bullet blew off most of his head?"

I pulled a face. "I didn't look too closely, but I knew there was a lot of blood because I was lying in it."

"If we don't get out of here right now, you'll be lying in your *own* blood."

York headed off down the corridor. I scrambled to my feet and ran to catch him up, while the hover trolley chased after the two of us.

"This has to be a bad dream," I wailed. "I only finished my diplomatic training last month. It was thrilling to be assigned as an aide to the great Kwame Ansah. I've admired him for years, studied all his speeches, and I was looking forward to…"

York glanced back over his shoulder at me. "Shut up!"

"Sorry, I'm a bit…"

"I said, shut up!" We took a left turn, a right turn, and then

York came to a sudden stop. "Someone's coming," he whispered. "Hide in here."

He opened a door and shoved me inside. I caught a glimpse of a cupboard-like room with shelves lining the walls, before the door was shut on me, leaving me in total darkness.

The sounds of running feet and angry voices reached me from outside, and then things went quiet again. A moment later the door opened, and York threw a set of blue overalls at me.

"Wipe that blood off your face, get rid of your diplomat's jacket, and put these on."

I shook out the overalls, which looked even grubbier than the set York was wearing. "What? Why?"

"Because you need to hide. Cleaning staff are effectively invisible, while diplomats covered in blood attract attention."

"But I don't need to hide," I said. "I'm a peace mission delegate. People will be searching for me, wanting to help me."

"The fact your Chief Negotiator is dead should be a hint that not everyone here likes peace mission delegates," said York. "We don't know if those people are searching for you to help you or to kill you. Unless you've some grandiose idea of taking over running the peace talks yourself, I suggest we take the safe option and get you out of here."

I'd no illusions that I could take over the role of the vastly experienced Kwame Ansah. I scrubbed my face with a clean area of my right sleeve, yanked off my jacket, and pulled the overalls on over the rest of my clothes.

"Now use your diplomat emergency beacon to call the cross-sector military and request evacuation," said York.

"Can't you just get me to a portal so I can use it to reach Hestia Off-world?"

He shook his head. "The whole of the standard planetary portal network went down when the shooting started. The interstellar portals at Hestia Off-world may still be working because they have an independent power supply, but it would take weeks to reach them on foot from here. You have to call for emergency evacuation. Make it evacuation for two people. You can't be trusted to find your nose on your face without help, so I'm coming with you."

I flushed, retrieved my beacon from my jacket, and triggered it. There was a brief pause and then a female voice responded. "Military Security confirming diplomat emergency evacuation request received. State number to be evacuated."

"Two of us," I said.

"Evacuation for two confirmed," said the woman. "Launching retrieval mission now. Can you reach the roof of the peace talks venue?"

I'd only been at the peace talks venue for a few hours. It was a huge, sprawling, two-storey building. I'd no idea where York had taken us except that we were still on the ground floor, and I wouldn't know how to get to the roof anyway. I looked at York and saw he was nodding at me.

"Yes," I said.

"Keep your beacon on so we know when you're in position," said the woman.

York was making beckoning gestures. I tucked my beacon into the front of my overalls and looked sadly at the bloodstained wreckage of my brand new jacket. I'd put it on for the first time the day before yesterday, pinning the silver, flaming torch symbol of an Alpha sector diplomat to it, proudly admiring my reflection in the mirror.

"Come on!" hissed York.

The cross-sector military had sentimental feelings about flags and banners, so they didn't lightly discard them. I felt the same way about that silver torch emblem. It represented the 201 inhabited star systems of Alpha sector, symbolising the diplomatic creed that words were more powerful than weapons. I snatched the emblem from the jacket, thrusting it into a pocket of my overalls before dropping the jacket itself to the floor, and joined York outside the room.

We hurried down two more corridors, with the cleaning

trolley still chasing us. I became aware of a stinging pain in my right hand, waved it in front of my face, and saw a trickle of blood. Had that happened when the sniper's bullet smashed the window of the negotiating chamber and killed the Chief Negotiator, or had I managed to cut myself on the flat, sharp edge of my own diplomatic badge?

My attention on my hand, I missed seeing York stop and collided with him. I saw that a group of uniformed, armed men were running towards us and tensed. York pulled me out of their way and the men ran on past, completely ignoring us.

I glanced after them. "You were right about cleaning staff being invisible."

"Does your diplomatic training make it impossible for you to stop talking?" asked York.

I was carefully silent as I followed him to the end of the corridor, through some double doors, and up a staircase. The hovers on the cleaning trolley struggled with the steepness of the stairs, but it caught us up at the top. We went out through another door, which York closed before the trolley could follow us.

We were on the roof now. It was a featureless, flat expanse, except for a couple of turrets sticking up that might mark other staircases. I could hear frustrated thumps from the other side of the door, as the faithful trolley still kept trying to join us.

York made an exasperated noise, pulled the trolley's control unit from his overall pocket, dropped it to the floor and crushed it under his heel. The thumps from the other side of the door abruptly stopped. I felt oddly sorry for the trolley, but was distracted by a huge bang. Smoke spiralled upwards from somewhere frighteningly nearby.

I gasped in panic. "What's that?"

"That's smoke," said York. "I can't see where it's coming from, and I'm not going to peer over the edge of the roof and get myself shot trying to find out. We have to stay right where we are and wait to be picked up."

There was a sound like thunder overhead. I looked up and saw the dark dust ring of a drop portal appear in the sky. A second later, something black shot through. Too bulky to be a fighter ship, I thought it was some sort of small transport.

The ship went into a high-speed turn before plunging vertically down to land neatly in front of us. York was dragging me forward even before the side of the ship slid open. As we tumbled inside, a female voice shouted, "Strap yourselves in fast. We've got incoming."

York and I were in a heap, sprawled across two seats. York sat up, pushing me away from him and into the further seat. I was still trying to work out how to strap myself in when the side of the ship slid closed again.

York shouted next to my ear. "Go now!"

The ship shot forward and upwards, then banked sharply, throwing me against York on my left. He cursed, shoved me back into my seat, and tugged the straps of a harness down over my shoulders.

The straps tightened, holding me firmly in place as the ship made another series of rapid turns. The window to my right showed alternating images of sky and ground, and at one point we were definitely flying upside down. I slapped my right hand over my mouth, closed my eyes, and fought against being sick.

"Stop wasting time throwing us around the sky," yelled York. "Use a drop portal to get us out of here."

"I'd love to," said the female voice, in a cheerful, conversational tone. "Unfortunately, you have to be flying in a straight line to use a drop portal, and there are two missiles chasing us. I'm Captain Nia Stone by the way."

"I'm Diplomatic Aide Ramon," I said, "and this is…"

York elbowed me painfully hard in the ribs. "Don't distract the pilot when she's evading missiles."

"They're depressingly outdated, basic missiles," said Stone. "It would be easy to deal with one, but two gets a bit trickier when you're trying to avoid harming civilians on the ground. I'm just trying to find a… That'll do!"

I risked opening my eyes again. There were two empty seats in front of me. Beyond them, our pilot was sitting at the ship's controls, an anonymous figure sealed inside her protective impact suit. The view through the curved window in front of her showed we were over the sea and flying straight at a cliff.

I gulped, staring at the cliff in horrified fascination as it grew larger and larger. I wanted to scream a warning but could only manage a squeak. I braced myself for death, but our ship jinked sideways and upwards at the last moment, skimming safely over the cliff top and soaring high up into the air. I heard two loud bangs from behind us.

"And the missiles have blown a big hole in the cliff," said Stone cheerfully. "*Now* we can use a drop portal."

An automated voice started counting down seconds. "Ten, nine, eight…" As it reached zero, a dark ring appeared in the sky directly ahead of us, and we went through the centre.

I watched in awe as the view through the pilot's window changed from blue sky and green fields to the darkness of space. Then I realised the window on my right was showing the even more breathtaking sight of a planet viewed from orbital altitude. I twisted round in my seat to stare at the swirls of clouds and the blue of oceans.

I'd seen this type of image before on vids, but this was no recorded image. This was real. A planet hung there outside my window, much bigger than I'd expected, with the mind-shattering background of star-studded space behind it. Another thing that was startlingly real was the lack of gravity. My harness was stopping me from floating around, but my stomach was still queasy.

"That's the inhabited continent of Hestia down there," said York, in an accusing voice. "Why are we still in the Hestia star system, Stone? You were supposed to take us to safety."

I tore my attention away from the spectacular view and looked anxiously at Stone. I saw her right hand move to tap the ship's controls, and she spoke in formal tones.

"Retrieval One to Hestia Solar Array Command. Drop portal to orbit successfully completed. Heading back with two passengers."

"Hestia Solar Array Command to Retrieval One," said a different female voice. "Welcome home."

"I asked you a question, Stone," snapped York.

Stone turned her seat round towards us. She had the hood of her impact suit up and sealed, so her face was just a faint unreadable blur, but her voice sounded impatient.

"Things may be getting difficult on the planet surface of Hestia, but we're perfectly safe up here. There are two fighter teams based at the Hestia solar array to make sure that neither of the local political factions can capture it and use the power beam as a weapon. The solar array has also had its own special interstellar passenger portal installed to make it completely independent of Hestia. Once we're aboard the solar array, you can use that interstellar portal to reach Alpha Sector Interchange 2 and continue on to any destination you wish."

Stone swung back to face her controls and the ship turned. I could see the Hestia solar array in front of us now, with its multiple spreading wings of solar panels, and the great glittering power beam heading down to the planet surface.

I relaxed back into my seat. I was safe now and would be back on my home world of Adonis within hours. I'd have to report the news of Chief Negotiator Kwame Ansah's tragic death of course, and I'd probably be criticised for abandoning his body and running away. If there was another peace mission to Hestia, I wouldn't be included.

That thought didn't worry me. Hestia's political conflicts had been going on for three decades already, and the murder of Kwame Ansah had convinced me there was no hope of any negotiator ever reconciling the two sides. The cycle of hatred would keep erupting into sporadic violence until the Parliament of Planets lost patience, authorised the cross-sector military to send in peacekeeping forces, and appointed some poor soul as Interim Governor to sort out the mess.

I never wanted to set foot on Hestia again, but the problem was that I'd struggle to find any other diplomatic posting. After this catastrophic start to my career, I'd be lucky to...

"Agh!" Pain blazed in my stomach as York's left fist punched my harness release button with vicious force. I pitched forward in my seat, and York's right arm snaked behind me, wrapped round my neck, and yanked me towards him.

"Turn back, Stone," he said. "We aren't going to the Hestia solar array."

I couldn't move. I couldn't breathe. York's right arm was crushing my windpipe, and my head was wrenched back at an angle that meant my neck was in danger of breaking. I tried grabbing York's arm, pulling at it with both my hands, but it was like trying to shift a mountain. A wave of giddiness swept over me, and my hands lost their grip on York's arm.

York laughed and eased the pressure on my neck a fraction, so I was able to gasp in enough air to cling to consciousness. I heard Stone give a heavy sigh.

"This is really inconvenient," she said. "I'm supposed to be portalling over to Demeter with my husband in three hours' time. It's our wedding anniversary tomorrow, we've got forty-eight hour passes, and a suite booked at the Great Falls Hotel."

"Turn back," repeated York, "or I'll cut Ramon's diplomatic throat and stop him talking permanently."

Cut my throat? I could see a faint reflection of us in the side window. Yes, York's right hand was holding a viciously long knife. I'd been about to lash out, try to break his hold on me in the hope of getting at least one full breath of air, but now I daren't move.

"I've turned away from the solar array," said Stone. "I can't put it directly behind us without sending us into Hestia's atmosphere, but you can see the array is now to our left instead of ahead of us. You'll also see that Hestia Solar Array Command has noticed my unscheduled course change and is launching the rest of my fighter team to investigate. I think I'd better tell them what's happening."

"Do that," said York. "If those fighters come anywhere near us, then Ramon dies."

"Retrieval One to Hestia Solar Array Command," said Stone. "We have a hostage situation in progress. Please recall fighters."

"Hestia Solar Array Command to Retrieval One. Situation understood. Recalling fighters and notifying Threat team. Set comms to open speaker mode and stand by for contact from designated negotiator."

"Now what?" asked Stone, her voice back to a cheerful, conversational tone. "Do you want me to go into planetary orbit, or shall we try stopping and floating in space where we are?"

"You can stop," said York.

"Could you slacken your grip on Ramon's neck now?" added Stone. "Judging from the colour of his face and the way his eyes are bulging, he's on the edge of suffocation. It's not as if I can try a surprise attack on you when there's a row of empty seats between us."

I felt York's arm move a fraction more. Not much, but the crucial amount I needed to breathe properly.

"Don't try anything clever, Ramon," he said, "and don't start yapping at me."

I wasn't going to try anything clever. I wasn't going to speak. I was too busy rejoicing over having air in my lungs again.

"Hestia Solar Array Command to Retrieval One," said a new, male voice. "I'm Captain Mason Leveque, designated negotiator. Can we please begin by establishing the current situation and your desired resolution? I believe the hostage is Diplomatic Aide Ramon of the Alpha sector peace mission to Hestia."

"That's right," said York, "and don't make the mistake of thinking I wouldn't kill him. I've been longing to cut his throat ever since I met him."

"I accept that," said Leveque. "Given our latest information from the planet surface, I estimate an 87 per cent probability that I'm speaking to the man known as Harbinger, who was recently disowned by the extremist wing of the Hestia Liberty Party after bombing a hospital."

The man holding the knife at my throat gave a laugh. "Yes, I'm Harbinger. If you've seen my record, you'll believe me when I say that I won't hesitate to kill this gabby little diplomat."

"I don't doubt that," said Leveque. "One of the few points of agreement between the two political factions of Hestia is that you're a ruthless killer, guilty of multiple murders, and should face the death penalty. In fact, I believe you've just increased your murder count. I estimate a 98 per cent probability that you were the person who cut the throats of three guards at the peace talks venue, as well as firing the explosive bullet that killed Chief Negotiator Kwame Ansah."

"The guards were irrelevant," said Harbinger, "but I regretted having to kill Kwame Ansah. I'd no choice, though. With both sides hunting for me, I had to leave Hestia. I'd never have made it through Hestia Off-world to the interstellar portals without being spotted, so I had to trigger a diplomatic retrieval. I'd met Kwame Ansah on his visit to Hestia back in 2770; he was one of the few people who've ever truly impressed me, but I knew I'd no hope of fooling someone of his intelligence. A gullible diplomatic aide on his first assignment, on the other hand..."

I felt like screaming, being sick, or both. The moment York first appeared so conveniently I should have been suspicious, but everything had happened so quickly, not giving me time to think... The realisation that he'd shot Kwame Ansah took the whole situation a step further into nightmare.

I remembered how I'd trustingly followed Kwame Ansah's killer round the peace talks venue. I'd allowed him to hide me in a cupboard so the genuine rescuers couldn't find me. I'd even obediently disguised myself as a cleaner to walk unnoticed past peace venue guards. If I got my throat cut now, I deserved it for being so stupid.

"So you know who I am," said Harbinger. "Now I want Stone to take me to Apollo. I know the Apollo star system is well inside the drop portal range of this ship. Once we arrive there, we'll land at the tourist beach of Diamond Sands. I can then use a standard passenger portal to travel to a random destination. I'll obviously have to take Ramon with me, but I'll let him go as soon as I'm safe."

I didn't believe that Harbinger would let me go alive. He'd cut my throat or strangle me, let my body drop to the floor, and walk away without a backward glance. I gnawed at my bottom lip. Suddenly my concerns about getting another diplomatic assignment didn't seem such an issue.

"We'll discuss the logistics of getting you to Apollo in a moment," said Leveque. "Before we have that conversation, I need to make one thing about the situation very clear to you. There is an ancient logic puzzle, dating from when humanity only lived on Earth, so it involves three Earth species. A carnivore called a wolf. A herbivore called a goat. A plant called a cabbage."

"Is there a point to this, or are you just talking for the pleasure of hearing your own voice?" asked Harbinger.

"There's a very important point," said Leveque. "A person is trying to keep all three species alive while transporting them to the other side of the river. The complicating factor is that given the chance, the wolf would eat the goat, and the goat would eat the cabbage. If you stop and think about it, I'm faced with a similar puzzle. I'm trying to keep Captain Stone, you, and Diplomatic Aide Ramon alive while transporting you to Apollo. The complicating factor is that given the chance, Captain Stone would kill you, and you would kill Ramon."

"I'm happy to agree that Ramon is a human cabbage," said Harbinger, "but I don't see why you're classing Stone as the wolf and me as the goat. I'm the one with the weapon, not her. I'd obviously prefer to keep my pilot alive, but I can kill her if necessary."

"Ship sensors would have warned us if you were still carrying a gun," said Leveque. "You have a knife, but that would prove ineffective against the protective impact suit that Captain Stone is wearing, while she has a choice of two ways to kill you. Firstly, by utilising her extensive skills in unarmed combat. Secondly, by activating the control that blows the cockpit cover off in an emergency."

Harbinger laughed. "I've plenty of experience in unarmed combat myself, and losing all the air would kill Stone as well as me."

"There are two flaws in your logic," said Leveque. "Firstly, you have no experience of unarmed combat in zero gravity. Secondly, since Captain Stone was flying her ship into a hazardous situation, she will have fitted an oxygen booster cell to her impact suit. Should she elect to vent ship air, the oxygen booster cell will provide her with enough air for her to reach the solar array safely."

Leveque paused for a moment. "The one thing stopping Captain Nia Stone from killing you is that either method would also endanger the life of Diplomatic Aide Ramon. I'm making this point very strongly, because you seem regrettably eager to kill your hostage. You need to understand that course of action would inevitably result in your own death as well."

I could tell Harbinger didn't like what he was hearing, because he tightened his hold on my neck. "I thought the military were supposed to protect civilians, not kill them."

Stone joined in the conversation. "That's correct, but Ramon is the civilian I'm protecting, not you. Under military regulations section 91, I'm entitled to use any and all methods to remove an ongoing threat to Ramon's life. Unless you give up your knife and surrender, I will happily take any opportunity to kill you. To be perfectly frank, since I'm a person you'd probably dismiss as irrelevant, I dislike you almost as much as you dislike Ramon."

"All right," said Harbinger grudgingly. "The cabbage will live if you take me to Apollo."

"We can now move on to discussing the logistics of getting

you to Apollo," said Leveque. "Presumably you're aware of the huge amount of power required to fire a drop portal."

"I am," said Harbinger. "What you're going to tell me next is that the standard design of military ships allows them to fire two drop portals in quick succession, one to get them into a dangerous situation and another to get them out again. Since Stone used one to reach the peace talks venue, and another to get us back here, our ship hasn't got the power to fire a third drop portal and reach Apollo."

"It doesn't," said Leveque. "You have three options for getting the required power. Firstly, your ship can dock with a recharging point at the solar array."

"We aren't docking with the solar array," said Harbinger.

"Secondly," said Leveque, "your ship can dock with a snail – a specialist transport used to recharge other ships."

"I'm not trusting any ships near us, snails or otherwise," said Harbinger.

"In which case," said Leveque, "your single remaining option is to wait for your ship to recharge its own power. That is a slow process. After checking the telemetry from your ship, I calculate that it will take precisely three hours and forty-six minutes to regain enough power to reach Apollo."

"We'll wait," said Harbinger.

Three hours and forty-six minutes. I bit my lip. How could I bear three hours and forty-six minutes of sitting with a knife at my throat?

"There is, however, the issue of your air supply," said Leveque.

"What's wrong with our air supply?" demanded Harbinger.

"When your request for emergency evacuation was received, Hestia Solar Array Command followed the standard protocols in responding. It's quite common for a retrieval mission to arrive and discover the size of party to be rescued has increased, so the standard protocol in this case was to send a ship that could carry four passengers rather than two. The only such ship at the solar array had just returned from deploying a monitoring satellite into geosynchronous orbit around Hestia. The ship's drop portal power availability was still at maximum. Air supply was low but still ample for the expected mission."

"You fools sent out a ship that was low on air?" Harbinger shouted the words, half deafening me. "How much air have we got left?"

"Fourteen minutes," said Leveque. "That should be ample time for you to dock with the solar array and…"

"No!" Harbinger didn't let Leveque finish his sentence. "We don't go near the solar array and no one comes near us. We need another three hours and thirty-two minutes of air. You said Stone has an oxygen booster cell attached to her suit. There must be other oxygen booster cells on board. How do we use them to boost the ship air?"

There was a silence as if Leveque realised he'd made a bad mistake when he mentioned the oxygen booster cells.

"Answer me!" ordered Harbinger.

"Oxygen booster cells are designed to work with impact suits, but yes, they can be used to boost ship air too," said Stone reluctantly. "If you pull open the green tab, the oxygen booster cell automatically generates oxygen at the rate needed to maintain breathable air until it's depleted."

"How many of these booster cells have we got?" asked Harbinger.

"The survey flight would have set off with two packs of six oxygen booster cells. There were two people aboard, and they did a spacewalk to position the satellite, so that would have used two cells. I've fitted another one to my suit, so there should be nine left."

"Check that," said Harbinger.

Stone turned her seat and rummaged in a low level storage pocket for a moment before waving a bulky grey object at us. "One pack of six booster cells."

"Pass them to me," said Harbinger.

Stone sent the pack floating across the empty seats towards us. Harbinger snagged it with his left hand and studied it for a moment. I saw it held a set of red objects labelled oxygen booster cells.

"Six." Harbinger tucked them down under his feet. "I want the rest too."

Stone reached into the storage pocket again, and sent a second grey object across to us. I saw this only held three of the red booster cells.

"That's all nine of them," she said.

Harbinger put that pack with the first one. "I want number ten too. The one attached to your suit."

Stone didn't move.

"Hand it over," said Harbinger, "or I'll start pruning a few leaves off the cabbage. It may not be good tactics for me to kill him, but I can chop off a finger or two."

I couldn't help looking down at my fingers, and picturing the knife cutting through them. I tried to hold back my scream, but couldn't quite manage it, so it came out as a strange hiccupping sound of alarm.

"Take it, then." Stone unclipped the tenth red oxygen booster cell from her suit, and threw it at high speed through the air towards us.

Harbinger caught it neatly in his left hand. "Now let's discuss the air supply again. Is the tenth oxygen booster cell still full?"

"Yes," said Stone. "I've been in ship air all the time, so it hasn't had to generate any oxygen."

"I'll use that one first to make sure," said Harbinger. "How much time does a full booster cell give us?"

Leveque started speaking again. "Each booster cell should provide one person with sufficient ship's air for an hour. That means the ten booster cells will provide air for the three of you for three hours and twenty minutes."

"So we'll run out of air twelve minutes before we've got the power to drop portal to Apollo," said Harbinger. "How much extra time will it take for us to land after that?"

"If we drop portal into the atmosphere at low altitude, then it shouldn't take more than a minute or two to land," said Stone.

"We're fourteen minutes short, then," said Harbinger. "It has to be possible to make the oxygen last that much longer. I can choke the cabbage a bit to stop him using air."

I heard myself give another alarmed hiccup.

"I repeat my earlier warning that killing your hostage will lead to your own death," said Leveque. "It should be possible to stretch the air supply the necessary additional time by delaying utilising each oxygen booster cell for between one and two minutes. During those periods you may suffer from breathlessness, headaches, sweating, confusion, blurring of vision, and be aware of an odd taste to the air. These symptoms will grow progressively worse each time due to the cumulative effect of..."

"Enough, Leveque," interrupted Harbinger. "We'll wait here until we've got the power to drop portal to Apollo. You make sure that no ship comes near us or the cabbage dies. I can't bear any more of your long-winded sentences, you're even worse than the cabbage, so we're breaking communications now. Shut him off, Stone."

"With pleasure." Stone tapped busily at her control panel for a minute. "Leveque's been talking far too much in my opinion."

I agreed with Stone. If Leveque hadn't been fool enough to mention the oxygen booster cells, Harbinger would have been forced to let us dock with the solar array, which might have given the military a chance to capture him. Now he had total control of our air supply, there seemed no hope at all.

I wondered how bad it would be when the air ran out. My neck was already bruised and swollen after being half strangled, and now I was going to be suffocated multiple times. If I made it through that alive, Harbinger would kill me when we reached Apollo.

Red lights started flashing overhead, accompanied by the

shrilling of an alarm, hurting my ears. The alarm warbled on for a few seconds longer before abruptly cutting out, but the red lights kept flashing.

"Ship air has run out and oxygen levels in the air are starting to fall," said Stone. "There'll be a second, even louder, alarm when oxygen levels approach danger point. I hope you've got the first oxygen booster cell ready."

"I have," said Harbinger, "but I'll be the one deciding when to use it, not you."

The air already felt thinner to me. I tried to breathe normally and relax, but then the second alarm sounded. As Stone had said, this was louder. I waited for it to stop as the earlier one had, but it just kept hammering its warning into my ears.

"Shut that noise off!" yelled Harbinger.

"You can't... shut down... emergency alarms," Stone called back, pausing to gasp for breath between the words.

I was breathing so rapidly now that it hurt my bruised throat, but the air tasted wrong and didn't seem to be helping me. I could feel a stabbing pain between my eyes, and the ship seemed far hotter. How long had it been since the oxygen ran out? I could see the oxygen booster cell in Harbinger's left hand. I could see the green tab he had to pull. Why wasn't he pulling it? I knew he was struggling to breathe too, because I could feel the movements of his chest as he tried to gulp in air.

I saw Harbinger lift the booster cell towards his mouth, and there was a jerking motion as he pulled the green tab open with his teeth. I could feel the air start to change instantly, my breathing eased, and it seemed cooler again. The alarm kept sounding for a moment longer, then cut out.

"That will have gained us a few minutes," said Harbinger smugly.

"You'd better not delay using the next one that long," said Stone. "The effects will get worse each time, and if you go too far into hypoxia then you may not be able to pull the tab on the booster cell."

"You two may have had problems breathing back then," said Harbinger, "but I didn't. I can leave it that long again, or even longer."

I wanted to groan but daren't. Harbinger had taken a sensible warning as a challenge to prove how long he could cope without air. That had been the first of ten booster cells. The first of ten times we'd go through that ordeal, and each time it would get worse. Harbinger would push us to the limits of endurance and beyond, because he was facing a death sentence back on Hestia. He'd rather die than give up his chance of escape, and if he died he was clearly intent on killing Stone and me along with him.

I'd believed in the diplomatic creed that words were more powerful than weapons, but right now I wished I had a weapon in my hand to hit back at Harbinger for what he was doing to us. A knife like the one he was holding at my throat. A gun like the one he'd used to shoot Kwame Ansah. Any kind of weapon would do, but I had nothing.

That was the moment when I remembered the silver flaming torch symbol in the pocket of my overalls. It was the proud emblem of an Alpha sector diplomat. More importantly, it was a piece of flat, unyielding metal, and the ragged edge of the flames was sharp enough to cut someone.

If I were going to attack Harbinger, I had to make sure he dropped the knife before he could slice my throat in two. No, I reminded myself that he wouldn't drop the knife, or at least it wouldn't fall if he released it. Whatever plan I made to get the knife away from him, I'd need to allow for the fact there was no gravity here.

Apart from that one useless attempt to stop Harbinger crushing my neck, I'd tamely submitted to everything he'd done to me. He wouldn't be expecting me to start fighting back now, so I'd have the advantage of surprise. My best chance would be if I attacked when he reached for the next oxygen booster cell.

I moved my right hand furtively across to my pocket. My fingers slipped inside, stroking the cool metal shape of the diplomatic emblem, checking the sharpness of the edge of the flames. I chose the best place to hold it, and mentally rehearsed the moves I should make.

I was ready. The question was whether I'd really dare to try this. There seemed only the slimmest chance of success, but that was still better than waiting passively to be slaughtered on Apollo. It wasn't as if I needed to win the fight against Harbinger myself. I just had to get the knife away from my throat for a few seconds, and Captain Stone would deal with him for me.

The alarm started ringing, and I felt Harbinger's grip on my neck lessen as he leaned to grab another oxygen booster cell with his left hand. If I was going to try this, it had to be now.

I bent my head forward and bit savagely into Harbinger's right thumb. I saw his hand splay open, loosening the knife so that it drifted to hang in mid-air in front of my nose. I lashed out with my left hand, trying to bat the knife in the direction of Captain Stone, while bringing my right hand from my pocket ready to stab at Harbinger with my makeshift weapon.

For a split second I thought my plan was working, but I'd sent the knife flying off at the wrong angle. It bounced off the window and straight back towards us. Harbinger thrust me aside so he could grab the knife. He had it in his hand, was turning to face me, when I struck at his neck with my diplomatic badge.

I hit out with the strength of desperation and Harbinger's own momentum carried him onto the point of the symbol, which cut shockingly deep into his throat. Blood spurted out towards me.

An impact suit clad figure came soaring over the empty seats, and Stone's stunned voice spoke above the insistent throbbing of the alarm. "Do diplomats often kill people like that?"

I'd closed my eyes to protect myself from the sight of what I'd done, but I could still taste the blood in the air. "Harbinger can't be dead. I didn't stab him with a proper knife."

"Proper knife or not, you've still severed his carotid artery," said Stone. "He'll be brain dead long before we get him to the doctors on the solar array."

In the panic of my battle with Harbinger, I'd forgotten about the air situation, but the ringing of the alarm reminded me of the problem. "The air," I gasped, opening my eyes again. "We have to use an oxygen booster cell or we'll all die!"

As I said the words, the alarm stopped ringing. I looked round in bewilderment and saw the red flashing lights had stopped too.

"I've already turned the ship air back on," said Stone. "There's a lot of blood drifting around, but the filter system will soon deal with that."

"How could you turn the ship air back on? We'd used it all."

"We have enough ship air to last us days," said Stone. "When Leveque was convincing Harbinger that he needed to keep his hostage alive, he was also testing the man's knowledge. Harbinger gave away the fact that he'd studied information on drop portals, but not impact suits. He didn't know that a knife was the best possible weapon to use against me because impact suits are vulnerable to sharp objects. He even had the ridiculous idea that losing ship air would kill me."

I blinked. "It wouldn't?"

"Military impact suits are designed to keep their wearers alive in a variety of hostile environments," said Stone, in the tone of someone politely explaining the obvious. "When there isn't enough external breathable air, they automatically switch to recycling air internally. We only need to use oxygen booster cells to flush the air system when we're dependent on suit air for a long period."

"But Leveque said..." I broke off, and started my sentence again. "Everything Leveque said was carefully planned."

"Yes, Leveque gave some misleading information about oxygen booster cells, invented an air problem, and sent me detailed instructions on my course display screen. There were actually three people doing the spacewalk earlier. I was one of them, so I still had a depleted oxygen booster cell attached to my suit. While I was messing around in the locker, I swapped that booster cell for a full one in the pack of six. That meant Harbinger thought he had ten full oxygen booster cells, but one was empty."

Stone laughed. "After that, I turned off the ship air, and pretended to have problems breathing when you two did. The plan was that I'd wait for the moment when Harbinger tried to use the empty oxygen booster cell. He'd be going into hypoxia, confused that the oxygen booster cell wasn't helping him, and assuming I was running out of air too. It would have been the perfect time for me to attack him, but you got impatient and decided to make your move before I could make mine."

She turned back to her controls. I saw the ship was turning, the distant solar array seeming to drift round outside the windows until it was directly ahead of us. I'd thought I was safe before when I wasn't, but this time it was true. I could go home to Adonis and report Chief Negotiator Kwame Ansah's death to my superiors. It would be a little awkward admitting that I'd abandoned Kwame Ansah's body, but explaining how I'd killed his murderer would be far worse.

"I think I'm about to have a career crisis," I said. "The Alpha Sector Diplomatic Service won't react well to me stabbing murderers in the throat with my diplomatic badge."

"If they don't want you as a diplomat any longer, you should consider joining the military instead."

"I'm not the right sort of person to join the military. I believe in using words not weapons."

"You believe in using words not weapons, yet you've killed one more human being than I have," Stone pointed out. "I think you should stop making decisions based on the type of person you'd like to think you are, and make some based on the type of person you are in reality."

I thought that over uneasily, and gave a glance at the blood-covered mess in the seat next to me. Perhaps Stone had a point.

"I'd better let the solar array know what's happened." Stone tapped at her controls. "Retrieval One to Hestia Solar Array Command. Situation secure. Harbinger has suffered an almost certainly fatal injury, and we're coming home."

"Hestia Solar Array Command to Retrieval One," said Leveque's voice. "That's excellent news. I'd expected you to have to wait considerably longer before Harbinger tried to use the empty oxygen booster cell, but now we'll be able to leave on schedule for our wedding anniversary celebration."

"Harbinger didn't try to use the empty oxygen booster cell," said Stone. "There was... an unexpected development."

"What sort of unexpected development?"

"The cabbage ate the goat," said Stone.

Pickaxes and Shovels

Christopher Nuttall

We weren't soldiers.

I want you to get that clear from the start. We – myself and Alan and Jimmie and Eric and Tanya – were not soldiers. Don't make the mistake of thinking we were, like some complete moron in the Pentagon. Shit like the shit we faced is meant for soldiers, not us. And to think there were at least two companies of space marines who could have handled the task, if only someone back on Earth had the common sense to realise what was coming our way.

But I'm getting ahead of myself. Pour me a drink and I'll try and tell you the story the way it happened. Forget what you've read in the news, ignore that goddamned film; we weren't strong men (and a beautiful woman) any more than we were soldiers. Poor Tanya practically became a hermit after the movie, where she was played by a barely-legal girl with her tits falling out of her spacesuit every time she moved. I heard she clonked some asshole on the head after he made the mistake of thinking she was easy...

We weren't soldiers, all right? And we weren't movie stars either. We were just ... *men*. And I'll have that drink now, if you don't mind.

Okay, okay... think back to the days when NASA finally

landed men on the moon for the second time. The Japanese were getting serious and so were the Chinese, even the Russians were working hard to put more in space than the good old US of A. And so NASA finally pulled its thumb out of its ass and launched us into space, establishing a new space station and several Earth-Luna transports in short order. The Japanese had beaten us to establishing a lunar base, the President said, but that was no reason to give up. A crew of fifty Americans, including me, were landed on the moon the very next year. And we started, just like the Japanese, to mine ores, water-ice and He3.

There was, of course, a shitload of argument over who actually *owned* the moon. The idealistic approach – that all of humanity owned the moon – fell apart very quickly, once the Japanese were firmly established. Plenty of internationalists insisted that the moon still belonged to everyone, but the people with real power and investment said no. The ambassadors haggled for years before it was agreed that whoever landed a base on the moon and set up a permanent settlement would have clear title to a hundred square miles surrounding their bases – wherever those bases happened to be. And some bright spark in Houston had the idea of settling up *inflatable* bases on the moon, allowing us to claim more territory than we, by rights, should have been permitted.

You probably can't imagine those early lunar bases – and I drink to forget. They started out as tiny complexes, put together from prefabricated crap and then expanded as we burrowed under the ground. The domes you see on TV didn't come along for another fifteen years, after we set up ore refineries on the lunar surface. Forty men and ten women, crammed into the complex, our lives dependent on machinery that we knew wasn't completely reliable... it was enough to drive us to drink, or it would have been if not for the certain knowledge that anyone fool enough to get drunk on the moon would be pitched out the airlock. Privacy was practically non-existent. We used to gamble for the right to take one of the lunar rovers and be alone, just for a few short days. In hindsight, maybe I shouldn't have won the last game I played on the moon. But I did.

The boss was a straight-laced son-of-a-bitch called Colonel Harold Fletcher. He wasn't actually that bad, but... well, after a long few hours of working on the lunar surface the last thing you want is to have to chat to a spit-and-polish martinet. He'd been in the USAF before transferring to NASA and he had some pretty firm ideas on how we should look, while we counted ourselves lucky if we looked barely human. We spent half of our time stinking to high heaven and with our clothes dirty and grimy... Really, all the nice girls might love an astronaut, but only after we'd had a shower and several successive baths. And when he called us into his office – well, *technically* it was the CIC – we all groaned together. It couldn't be anything good.

"The Japanese have been making inroads to the north," he said, tapping the map on the display. Our network of bases were surrounded by red circles, showing the territory we – theoretically – controlled. "Houston wants us to set up a new inflatable base here" – he tapped a point roughly seventy kilometres to the north – "and cut them off."

"Unless they decide to just ignore us," Tanya said. She'd always been the most pessimistic about the likelihood of the latest Outer Space Treaty lasting longer than a decade. The Russians would certainly feel no obligation to uphold it if the treaty locked them away from the moon. "It isn't as if those bases are manned."

"You'll be there for at least a month," Fletcher said. He gave us the firm-jawed, strong-chin look of a true patriot. Personally, I think he practiced the look in front of a mirror. "They won't be able to claim the base isn't manned if it *is* manned."

We argued, of course, but Fletcher was immovable. The five of us were to be isolated for thirty days, barring accidents. So Tanya and I headed down to the lunar rover to make preparations, while Alan, Jimmie and Eric went to record their final messages for the folks back home. We had no reason to expect trouble, but ... We knew death could come at any time. Anyone who tells you that outer space is safe obviously hasn't read *The Cold Equations*.

"Well," Tanya said. She looked nothing like her movie counterpart, you should know. After being covered in as much grime as the rest of us for the last five months, it was hard to remember that she was actually a woman. "At least we'll be away from the base for a while."

"Bah," I said.

The rover, to be fair, was really more of a small spacecraft in its own right. Looking like something out of a Gerry Anderson movie, it had very limited flight capabilities as well as a large and airtight compartment that could hold five people reasonably comfortably, as long as they didn't mind the lack of privacy. It couldn't possibly have flown on Earth, of course, but the moon's low gravity allowed some extra flexibility. We piled in, ran through an exhaustive list of checks and rechecks, and then drove off into the lunar night. And, while we might have grumbled, we enjoyed the chance to spend some time away from the base, which was more than a little claustrophobic.

Driving on the lunar surface, it should be noted, has its own set of challenges. There are no roads, of course, and the ground is warped and twisted. We'd already lost one of the mini-rovers after the ground underneath the vehicle – a much lighter vehicle – give way unexpectedly. I drove for an hour, then allowed Eric to take the wheel while I went back for a quick snack and a nap. It was generally better for us, all of us, not to think about just *what* we recycled to make our food. There were promising candidates, back at Houston, who managed to get halfway through the course and then turn their nose up at recycled... Well, let's just say that the giant lunar gardens were still twenty years in the future.

Two days later, we reached our destination and sent a microburst transmission back to the base, informing Fletcher of our arrival. There was little point in saying anything else, really; if we'd run into trouble, we'd have been thoroughly fucked. Fletcher was a good man, despite having a stick up his butt, but there was literally nothing he could have done if we ran into trouble so far from the base. They'd find our corpses when the next set of settlers arrived from Earth, probably.

What we got back, in a high-priority code we'd never seen used outside of drills, was an order to go doggo, to curb all electromagnetic transmissions and hide under a tarpaulin until we received further orders.

"There's no solar flare predicted for months," Jimmie noted.

"It wouldn't be the first time someone messed up the calculations," Alan pointed out. "Jack?"

"We do as we're told," I said. Solar flares were nasty, even if the rover was shielded against most forms of radiation. It's why we all made sperm or egg donations before we blasted off from Houston. "Get the blanket out and over our heads."

"Of course, boss," Alan said. He might have scoffed, but he knew to take solar flares seriously. "I'll get right on it."

Twenty minutes later, a second message popped up in the display. And when I read it, I felt my blood turn to ice.

"WARNING... WAR WARNING... JAPANESE FORCES HAVE TAKEN EO... FURTHER ORDERS TO FOLLOW...."

I'll spare you the details. What it boiled down to was simple. We were at war – and our base, and our CO, had already been captured.

We didn't know what was happening on Earth, of course; I didn't find out the full story until later. Tokyo – Japan – hadn't taken the land-grab on the moon lightly; Japan had made too great an investment in next-gen spacecraft technology to allow Uncle Sam to steal all the resources for itself. The Japanese, their technology second to none, had snatched control of the high orbitals, then dispatched a raiding force to the base. Colonel Fletcher had no weapons, so resistance had been futile. The Japanese owned the moon...

... Except, of course, for us.

Alan put our thoughts into words. "What the fuck do we do?"

It was a problem, I had to admit. The rover could keep us alive for three months, assuming nothing went wrong, but eventually we'd be thoroughly fucked. Too many air filters would die, perhaps, or the recycling system would conk out. Surrender seemed the only logical option. As romantic as the idea of mounting resistance might have seemed, we were in deep shit. We had no weapons, we had no back-up, we had no plan. It was at *that* point the *third* message popped up in the display. A hyper-compressed message from Director Rutherford, NASA's head honcho. I pushed *play* without a single inkling of what might be awaiting me.

"I'll keep this brief," Rutherford said. I hadn't liked him, the one time we'd met, but there was something stout and resolute in his voice. "We've identified a key weakness in the Japanese space-based weapons network. Much of their power, along with their raw materials for kinetic projectiles, comes from the moon. If that connection can be broken, their control of space will also be broken. Your country needs you..."

I tuned out the remainder of his appeals to patriotism, opened the datapacket and skimmed through the details, such as they were. The Japanese had always relied on more automaton and high-tech than ourselves – it was quite likely their system did have a giant weakness – but we weren't soldiers and we weren't armed. Could we do anything more than get ourselves killed? I surveyed the charts, noting the positions of Japanese satellites orbiting the moon. If they spotted us while we were moving, we were dead. But if we moved quickly, we *could* get close to the Japanese base before there was any real chance of them seeing us.

"We're a group," I said, addressing the other four. "And there's no way one or two of us can survive indefinitely in the inflatable base. If we don't go as a unit, we can't go at all."

There was a long agonising pause.

"There's no choice," Eric said. "If the Japanese win... they'll ship us back home."

I nodded in agreement. The Japanese probably wouldn't kill us out of hand – they weren't terrorists – but, if we refused to work for them, being shipped back home was the best we could hope for. And that would mean never returning to orbit, never flying a spacecraft to the moon or one of the local asteroids... It was an unbearable thought. The beancounters at Houston might not have understood, but we had gone to the moon and stayed on the moon because we loved it.

"I agree," Tanya said.

"We could get killed," Jimmie said. "But who wants to live forever?"

Alan snorted. "Has it occurred to you that we don't have any fucking weapons?"

"We're engineers," Eric pointed out. "We'll *make* our goddamned weapons."

And, with that, the matter was decided.

I spent the next twenty minutes checking and rechecking our route to the Japanese base, hoping against hope that they hadn't added more satellites or altered any orbital trajectories. If they had... well, there's no wind on the moon, nothing moves without human intervention. f they caught sight of a moving object, they'd *know* it was a group of rogue Americans and send troops to intercept. Praying silently, I started the engine as soon as the blanket was safely stowed away, and we started moving. The others hastily caught up with their sleep.

It took us four days to reach the Japanese base, four days during which we sweated, prayed and struggled to come up with a plan. There were just too many unknowns, we reasoned, and we didn't dare send a signal home to ask for further data. A single burst from a radio transmitter would be enough to reveal our presence. Indeed, we had a couple of very close shaves with orbital watchdogs before we finally reached our destination and hid near a ridge. It was risky to conceal the rover under the blanket – a sharp-eyed computer might notice any discrepancies

– but there was no choice.

"Well," Tanya said, after we had rested. "I suppose we'd better go take a closer look."

The Japanese base was larger than ours, but it was instantly understandable. A large nuclear reactor provided the power, which was beamed back to Earth orbit via a colossal microwave beam... not unlike one of the giant solar power satellites NASA was planning to build, before they finally ironed the bugs out of fusion power. A network of automated mining systems were churning up lunar ore and transporting it to the compactor, which was crushing it into projectiles. These were then shipped to the mass driver, where they were blasted towards Earth. This was precision stuff. If the Japanese lost control of their systems at any point, disaster would result.

"There don't seem to be any armed guards," Alan pointed out, after we had surveyed the outskirts of the base. "You think they're keeping hard-ass under control?"

I shrugged. Fletcher and the remainder of his crew would be easy to subdue, once they were moved to an inflatable habitat without spacesuits or a direct connection to the rest of the case. They could remain there, breathing their own farts, until a truce was agreed and they were shipped back to Earth.

"See if you can hack their Wi-Fi," I ordered Tanya. "If their system is anything like ours, we should be able to break into the command network."

Tanya went to work at her computer, trying to access the local network node. The Japanese systems weren't *that* different from ours – they and NASA had agreed, back in the early days of lunar exploitation, that we'd standardise as much as possible, just in case one of us ran into trouble and needed assistance from the other. Yes, we would have saved the Japanese astronauts if they'd needed help. I hope they would have done the same for us.

"I can read their system, but their main command network is firewalled," Tanya said. "And it's probably hard-coded too."

I nodded. The Japanese had a worse problem with hackers

than we did – and some pimpled teen in his basement fucking up the entire system was a recurring nightmare, back on Earth. It would be more of a problem for them than us, given their dependence on computers and automaton. Still, that did offer possibilities...

"What can you get out of the system?" Alan asked. "A list of personnel?"

"No," Tanya said, after a moment. "But I do have the schedule for shift changes at the power plant."

I smirked. Health and safety insisted that our nuclear power plants, even fusion plants, were to be kept separate from the rest of the base – and it seemed the Japanese had the same problem. Which goes to show, I think, that human stupidity and ignorance are universal conditions. Without the fusion plants, neither base would have been truly viable. But this offered us an opportunity.

"Here's what we're going to do," I said. "When the replacement technicians come out of the base, we grab them and take their place."

You might think this was an absurd idea, but it actually had some merit. The Japanese spacesuits were identical to ours, save for the flag on their shoulders. We could pass for Japanese as long as we kept our helmets on and our mouths shut. And there probably wouldn't be any need to key in the right code to enter the complex, even if it was centred around a fusion reactor. Who in their right mind would expect terrorists on the moon? I smirked at the thought, then hastily led the way to the best position to ambush the Japanese workers ...

That goddamned movie has us battling the Japanese for hours (in movie-time, at least), matching ninja skills against Semper Fu. It wasn't like that at all. The two Japanese workers had no idea we were there, right up until we jumped them and tore their life support packs away from their backs. As I say, we're no soldiers, but needs must, and we couldn't afford any qualms. It was a nerve-wracking moment – the Japanese might well have programmed their suits to send out an automatic alert if something went wrong. Hoping – praying – that no one in the fusion plant could see the flag on my suit, I led Alan up to the access hatch. It opened as soon as I pressed the key, allowing me to step into the airlock. And then we stepped into the complex itself.

A man was standing by the door, looking as though he needed a piss really bad. I was pretty sure he wasn't a soldier, but I clobbered him on the head anyway. Once he was down, we hastily opened the airlock and fiddled with the controls. Seconds later, the air vented out of the complex as we overrode the safety systems. Anyone not in a suit was thoroughly screwed.

We invited the others into the complex, then searched the handful of tiny compartments. The Japanese hadn't made their reactor anything like as accessible as ours; indeed, I wasn't sure why they bothered keeping four men on duty at all times. All four of them were now dead. I tried not to retch. We'd had no choice… It was us or them.

"They sent out an alert," Tanya snapped, as she took the control console and went to work. It wasn't easy in her suit, but I wouldn't allow anyone to strip down in the depressurised complex. It was slowly refilling with air, yet we might have to leave in a hurry. "Jack…"

"Shit," I said. "Can you shut the reactor down?"

"I think so, but they can reactivate it within moments," Tanya said. "It isn't looking good, Jack."

I swore, again. You can disable a fission reactor if you don't give a damn about the risks, but a fusion reactor is tougher. There's no way to make it meltdown.

"I could wipe the control system," Tanya said, after a moment. "They'd have some problems rebooting once I'd finished."

"They'd just link to Earth and download a whole new command system," Alan pointed out, grimly. "Can you overload the microwave transmitter instead?"

"That might work," Tanya said. She looked up. "You think

we can melt the system?"

"If we overload it, it might explode," I said. "Can you flush extra power through the network?"

"I think so," Tanya said. "Jack ..."

"Trouble," Jimmie interrupted. "Jack, we have incoming."

That, I should add, is the closest any of us got to actually *sounding* military. But we needed it, because on the display there were a handful of men in spacesuits advancing towards the fusion complex. Japanese troops, I assumed; they were carrying weapons, rather than industrial tools. The only advantage I could see was that they weren't equipped to cut through the walls, even though it would have been the quickest way to reach us. Indeed, it looked as if they were heading for the airlock.

"I can flush power through the system now," Tanya said. Her voice was rising in alarm. "It should melt some of the system, at least."

"Do it," I ordered. How much had the Japanese planned? If they'd intended to turn their settlement into a military base... No, they hadn't. They'd done everything on the fly or we wouldn't have been able to get into the complex. "And then corrupt the control system as best as you can."

I looked around, trying to figure out options. The only way out of the complex was through the airlock, unless we cut through the walls ourselves. We did have the tools, but the Japanese wouldn't have any difficulty catching us before we returned to the rover – and even if we made it, a man in a spacesuit could easily catch us before we escaped. Rovers weren't known for their speed. Perhaps, if we'd had some mining explosive ... I peered into the compartments, more in hope than in any real expectation, but found nothing, save for canisters of the misty gas we used for seeking out leaks. It wasn't explosive, sadly; no one would keep anything explosive anywhere near a nuclear reactor.

A thought crossed my mind, something I'd seen in a movie or read in a book...

"Help me empty these canisters into the airlock," I ordered, tersely. "Hurry!"

We left Tanya to fiddle with the computers as we filled the airlock with gas. It hung in the air like mist, making it harder to see. And then we waited as the Japanese forced their way into the complex, stepping through the airlock one by one. They moved like trained soldiers, definitely, but they didn't vent the complex. If they had, it might have gone very badly for us, even though we were in suits. My plan would have failed before it even began.

"Hello," I said, over the emergency channel. The Japanese would be monitoring the channel, I was counting on that. "I suggest you don't take off your suits. We've filled the air with explosive gas. Surrender now or we all die together."

I braced myself, knowing the Japanese might well decide to call my bluff. The gas wasn't explosive – and even if they believed it was, they might open fire anyway and call it a draw. This wasn't a perfect plan, more of a desperate one. A trained astronaut might know that we didn't use explosive gas or that the fusion reactor wouldn't be damaged unless the explosion was a great deal bigger... there were plenty of flaws, but we didn't have the time or resources for anything more sophisticated.

And without the reactor, they're in deep shit anyway, I thought. *NASA will be able to launch shuttles once their orbital weapons network is shut down.*

One of the Japanese troopers lifted his weapon. Another pushed it hastily back down, clearly unwilling to take the risk. I waited, hoping they would believe that I was ready to kill everyone, including my team. They *had* to believe that a single spark would be enough to set off a holocaust...

"The network is overloading now," Tanya said, over our private channel. "It shouldn't be long before..."

The ground shook. *Something* had clearly exploded, and not too far away. I hoped it wasn't merely a surge protector of some kind. But it was enough to make the Japanese hesitate a little longer.

"If you surrender, you will be treated in line with the Geneva Conventions," I said. Mind you, I had no idea what the conventions actually *said*. "And you will be returned to Earth as quickly as possible."

For a moment, it hung in the balance. I was convinced we'd failed, but when the officer said, in precise, accented English, "We have your word on that?" I knew we had them.

"You do," I assured him.

"In that case… we surrender. We surrender," he repeated, as if afraid I might have missed it, or perhaps that his own troops had.

We disarmed and secured the Japanese troopers immediately, before they realised we'd been bluffing, then headed outside. The base's lights had dimmed; they'd had to switch to battery power now the reactor had been shut down. And the transmitter was nothing more than a smoking hole in the ground. Clearly, the Japanese had *never* intended to turn the settlement into a military base; they'd been forced to improvise when the shit hit the fan. Hurrying over to the main base, we entered through the airlock, our stolen weapons in hand. Thankfully, we knew how to use them, although my aim is pathetic.

And that, more or less, was that. We wrecked the mass driver, just in case, then settled down to wait. The Japanese Government threw in the towel after we cut off their power; Washington graciously accepted their offer of a truce rather than risk a war that could easily have turned nuclear. And, once the space marines arrived to take possession of the Japanese settlement, we went back home for booze, women and … more women.

What can I say? I'm a simple man.

Yeah, I know; it's nothing like the movie. I didn't seduce a hot Japanese chick into letting me into the fusion reactor, Alan didn't die bravely singing the national anthem as the enemy stormed the complex and Tanya didn't convince the Japanese to surrender by taking off her top and doing a seductive dance. (Mind you, it might have worked; if she'd tried, given how ghastly we all looked, the Japanese might have been too busy laughing to resist.) But really, Hollywood can take any story and turn it into a great adventure. I was just doing what I could to ensure we, not the Japanese, were the ones who controlled access into space...

And now, you can pour me another beer. I'm going back to the moon on Tuesday.

The Gun

Ian Whates

Damn!

Two rounds, then the bloody thing jammed. He had gently squeezed the trigger, barely registering the dampened recoil as two shells spat out, and then... nothing. The mechanism was abruptly immobile and impotent beneath his finger.

He crouched as low as he could, knowing that his life now depended on the shallow depression that served as a bunker. The 'puck, puck' of bullets burying themselves in the lip of his miserly shelter and kicking up clouds of sand provided stark reminder of the fact. He covered his head and closed his eyes until the dust had settled.

"Carter, are you okay?" the sergeant called from the next hastily-dug hole along.

"Gun's jammed," he yelled back.

"Well unjam it then!"

Avoid panic; that was the first priority. The noise of the ongoing battle receded as he concentrated. He knew what to do. Jettison the magazine, eject any shell that might be caught in the breach, clip on a new magazine and the gun would work again. It had to – the manual said so.

Not for the first time, the manual proved to be wrong, its diagnosis woefully inadequate. Whoever wrote the bastard thing had failed to make allowance for the havoc that powder-fine sand could wreak once it found its way into a gun's mechanism.

Precision engineering could go hang itself! He flung the useless weapon to one side and scrabbled to un-holster his hand gun. Better than nothing, though barely. Sadly, it was all he had.

Carter crouched lower still as an energy bolt sizzled over his head, transforming a patch of sand behind him to molten glass that bubbled and dribbled down the inside of his makeshift foxhole. He spared it a distracted glance, a small part of his mind debating whether it was worth keeping. Might make a decent paperweight once it cooled, or perhaps he could sell it as an authentic battlefield souvenir.

Finally the pistol was free. Still he couldn't bring himself to move. Cowardice, or a rare attack of common sense? All he could think about was how insane this seemed: a small calibre projectile gun? They had *energy weapons* for crying out loud!

At least no new stream of bullets puckered the rim of his bunker. The ebb and flow of conflict seemed to have moved elsewhere for the moment.

"Sarge?"

No reply.

"Anybody?"

His plaintive call was met by hollow silence.

Feeling sick to the pit of his stomach, he braced himself. Forcing his hand to unclench, relaxing the vice-like grip that threatened to crush the handle of his only remaining weapon, he pushed his body upwards, inch by terrible inch, preparing to look over the rim.

The sight that greeted him was far from encouraging; so much so that he decided to put all plans for a life after the war on hold for now, to be filed away under the heading 'pipe-dream'.

Small arms fire and the deep boom of explosion sounded from afar, but nothing in his immediate vicinity. Around him everything was still. Was he the only one left? Was that why the focus of battle had passed him by?

A mass of troops faced him in the near distance – the Stylene, their dappled brown and tan combat gear so similar to his own uniform. Both had been designed with the same purpose in mind: to fox the eye and provide camouflage in this arid terrain. Behind the infantry, bulkier shapes moved – hovertanks and armoured personnel vehicles. Over to his left a remnant of his own side's forces, the UPAF, were still putting up some stubborn resistance, but there could be little doubt which side held the advantage.

He was just considering burrowing deeper into the sand and playing dead when the ground trembled with a bass vibration, a sound that reverberated through his body to discomfort vital organs, a sound that was felt as much as heard.

Explosion! Even as that thought registered, the ground rose from beneath him to swat and fling his fragile form into the air amidst a mass of sand and shingle.

At some point before he landed again, consciousness fled, presumably in terror.

Carter came to with his body a mass of aches and purpling bruises. He welcomed each and every one of them, because they meant he was still alive. Gingerly he sat up, brushing dust and sand from his torso and face and spitting out more of the same. The simple act sent daggers of pain to lancing through his left wrist as he put pressure on it, to be echoed in his shoulder. He ignored them and took stock of his surroundings.

All around him lay silence and death.

The battle had evidently ended or perhaps moved on, though he heard no sound to suggest it continued anywhere close by. After flexing and stretching for a few seconds, he concluded that, miraculously, nothing was broken. His body had been rigorously shaken and stirred, to leave every joint protesting of misuse and every limb bruised, but he had survived more or less intact.

He needed to find cover, but there were two more pressing priorities to be considered first: water and a weapon. His pistol was nowhere to be seen, but even if it had been he would still have searched for something more comforting, something that packed a considerably heavier punch. Fortunately the field was littered with bodies, motionless brown and tan mounds from which both weapons and a canteen could hopefully be scavenged.

He set off, heading to his left, trudging towards a stand of stunted trees that skirted a low hill, startling raucous crows as he went. The great black birds had wasted to time in moving in moving in to feed, pecking at the corpses. Some took to the air at his approach and circled above, voicing their indignation, while others simply lifted themselves out of his path in long, wing-flapping hops, to return to their gorging once he had passed.

He did his best to ignore them and what they were feeding on, his eyes flickering from body to body, careful not to look at any faces. There would be too many here he knew.

Finally he spotted an accessible canteen, picking it up and drinking greedily. It was as he lowered the canteen again that he saw the Gun.

It lay by the outstretched hand of a soldier and, whatever it might have been, this was nothing that came under the heading of 'standard issue'. The design was busy and complex, with bulges and protrusions seamlessly affixed to its long, sleek barrel and stock.

The Gun appeared to be undamaged and he crouched to study it in greater detail, when a light winked on and a voice spoke:

"Are you UPAF or Stylene?"

He stared, open-mouthed, and wondered whether the explosion had affected him more than he realised.

"I await a response."

He licked his lips, considering whether to back away quickly, stamp on the thing, or answer it. What the hell? "I'm UPAF."

"Good. Then you are permitted to use me."

"I'm what…? What the hell are you?"

"Intelligent gun; the latest development in advanced weapons technology."

"And what exactly do you do?"

"I facilitate the killing of many enemies."

That got his interest. "Sounds good to me." Decision made, he smiled grimly and hefted the Gun up, surprised at how readily he could do so.

"See how light I am?" the Gun commented, as if reading his thoughts. "I'm constructed from a revolutionary new alloy."

Carter grunted. "Lucky you."

A soldier alone in the aftermath of a battle, surrounded by the dead: a pretty lonely place to be, but it was amazing how much the Gun's presence lifted his spirits. Okay, as companions go, the one now cradled in his arms hardly qualified as the most stimulating, but at least it was something. He strode on with renewed purpose, the aches and pains which had seemed so debilitating just moments ago all but forgotten.

As they drew nearer the scraggly patch of greenery, the Gun spoke again.

"Don't stop walking. Three enemy troops are hiding in the trees ahead. If they realise you've seen them, you're dead."

He squinted and searched rapidly along the treeline, but could see nothing. "So you do more than simply kill people, huh?"

"Of course. Heat sensors and acute audio receptors are all built-in. On my mark, aim at the trees at eleven o'clock and fire a burst, sweeping steadily right until you reach twelve o'clock."

He adjusted his grip, ready to bring the Gun to bear.

"Now!"

At the command, Carter whipped the Gun up and fired. Not crouching, his body still felt too stiff for that, so he settled on planting his feet and standing where he was. A stream of bullets ripped into the undergrowth, scything through bushes and branches in a satisfying cloud of splintered wood and stems. An anguished scream told him that there really were men hiding in there and that at least one of them had been hit as he fanned the arc of fire in accordance with the Gun's instructions.

"That is sufficient," the Gun said after a few seconds, its cool, calm voice clearly audible over the chatter of departing bullets.

Carter relaxed his trigger finger and the carnage stopped. The final leaves and splinters settled to the ground and the only sound was the echo of gunfire still ringing in his ears.

"All three?" he asked.

Though the lack of return fire seemed to suggest as much, it was still a relief to hear the Gun confirm, "All three."

Carter started to jog towards the trees, anxious to be under cover, knowing that the sound of gunfire would act as a beacon in the pervading silence, drawing any Stylene who happened to be in the vicinity this way. Besides, he was keen to have a look at his handiwork.

But as he ran the Gun spoke again. "Angle a little to the right. Land mines directly ahead of you."

Mines! His new companion was proving to be one heck of an asset. Given an army equipped with these intelligent guns, they could overwhelm the Stylene once and for all. He remembered the ill-designed rifle that had let him down so badly and jammed as soon as the fighting started. There was no comparison.

This might just be enough to tip the balance and change the course of the whole interminable war. Carter had not felt so optimistic in a long while, perhaps not since he first signed up, when the concept of waging war still caused his chest to swell with patriotic pride, before it became irrevocably tarnished by the grim reality of blood, exhaustion, sweat and grind.

"Faster," the Gun urged. "There are soldiers approaching."

Carter quickened to a sprint, covering what little distance remained as rapidly as his abused body would allow and diving into the trees. He turned around and scrambled on his belly, pushing aside brambles and small stems to peer outward from the undergrowth, looking for the enemy.

"How many?" he wanted to know. "Whereabouts?"

"Two of them, moving in this direction along the foot of the ridge."

He saw them, then: two figures in the annoyingly repetitive brown and tan battle dress. They were still some distance off and were moving cautiously, but gave no indication that they had seen him. He sighted along the barrel of the Gun but didn't fire immediately, instead raising his head and waiting, allowing them to draw closer and then closer still.

They had covered perhaps half the distance when gunfire and shouts interrupted the stillness. The noise came from the far side of the ridge. The two soldiers paused, exchanged brief words and then turned to start climbing up the steep hill.

"Fire now or they may escape us," the Gun urged. "I calculate that we cannot miss from this range."

Carter agreed on all counts. He sighted and gently squeezed the trigger. The pair were caught totally unawares, cut down by a stream of bullets before they had any chance to react, probably without ever knowing what had happened. Multiple hits on both from comparatively close range. He didn't need to check to know they were dead.

Carter let out a whoop of triumph. This was the best gun he had ever handled, by a margin of several light years. It made killing easy. Exhilarated, he leapt to his feet and strode out of the trees.

"Now, let's see what's going on the other side of this hill."

"Combat," the Gun informed him unnecessarily, evidently failing to recognise a rhetorical comment when it heard one. Good to know that it had limitations.

Carter scrambled up the escarpment, dislodging loose shale and stones as he went, feet scrabbling for purchase. Buoyed by recent successes, he didn't feel in the least bit tired, only eager to kill more Stylene, to avenge the friends and comrades lying dead on the battlefield behind him.

The hill proved to be a narrow spit of raised ground, out of character with the surrounding terrain. It was almost certainly man-made, and he guessed it to be a cast-off, a by-product, rather than anything intentional. Perhaps there had once been quarrying in the area, or mining.

Almost as soon as he reached the hill's crown the ground fell away before him, sloping sharply down towards the floor of a shallow canyon.

Below, a furious gun battle was being fought, spilling up onto the lower slope of the hillock, as each side sought to gain an advantage. Small arms only, no tanks or heavier weapons were in evidence, thank goodness.

"Stylene to your left, UPAF to the right," the Gun informed him.

"How can you tell?" he wondered. "I can't."

"There are a number of indicators, principle among them the calibre of weapon each side is using. Do you intend to simply observe and debate the issue, or are you thinking of engaging the enemy at some point?"

Carter needed no more urging. Driven by the desire for revenge, he spurned the tactical advantage granted by the higher ground, charging down the hill and firing as he ran. The nearest Stylene looked up, startled by this sudden attack from a new quarter. Those who had occupied the lower slope of the hill died almost at once; one, two, three of them falling before they were fully aware of the threat.

"There are two grenades built into my carapace," the Gun informed him. "They are triggered by the button just above the trigger guard. I suggest you deploy one now."

Carter raised the Gun a fraction, reached up with his trigger finger and found the relevant button. As he depressed it, an apparently solid part of the Gun's body flipped up and was catapulted away, to sail into the enemy lines where it exploded with devastating effect.

Bullets whistled past him and churned the hillside around his feet as he continued to charge. They didn't matter. He had the Gun and felt invincible, roaring defiance as he ran, adrenaline pumping through his veins and blood lust spurring him on. Soldier after soldier fell before the hail of bullets from his inexhaustible Gun.

His appearance, so unexpected, proved the decisive factor. His grenade had ripped a hole in the heart of the enemy lines and they could no longer hope to hold their position. Realising that this skirmish was lost, the survivors turned and fled. Those who chose to remain died where they stood.

Carter reached the bottom of the slope and pulled himself to a halt. Once more he found himself surrounded by the dead. He raised the Gun and squeezed off a final burst at the fleeing soldiers, watching with satisfaction as the rearmost figure convulsed and collapsed.

The uniforms of the two sides looked so similar from a distance, he reflected, watching the defeated troops run for their lives. Only up close could you tell the difference. He glanced down at the fallen around him and felt a growing sense of dread.

"Wait a minute," he exclaimed, "These are UPAF troopers."

"Indeed," the Gun replied.

"But you said…"

"I lied."

Carter looked up towards the approaching Stylene soldiers, just as the first of them opened fire. He died without ever understanding.

The corporal moved cautiously, alert to every sound. Dusk was falling but there was still enough light to see by. Somewhere above, a hunting night bird voiced a mournful cry. Behind him, the corporal heard one of the two troopers startle at the sound. They were both pretty green and he winced at their clumsy footfalls. His responsibility, these two; they were all that remained of his unit.

The three of them had been cut off from the rest of the force, left behind in the chaotic retreat after the debacle of the battle. They had hidden out for the bulk of the afternoon, lying low and waiting for nightfall. At last, as the sun began to set, impatience got the better of him and he decided it was time to move out.

They had to tread carefully, Stylene patrols were everywhere.

This small canyon had obviously been the scene of some fierce fighting, perhaps a sidebar to the main battle. The bodies of the fallen lay all around them. Now and then, they would disturb something, and low, scuttling forms would flee a corpse.

The corporal chose not to look too closely.

Then something on the ground winked at him: a small red light. He instantly froze, thinking it might be a land mine or some other lethal trap, but as he squinted through the gathering gloom, he realised that it was some sort of gun, a bulky thing lying by one of the UPAF fallen.

"Are you UPAF or Stylene?" said a smooth, calm voice.

He gaped and stared at the gun.

"Did that thing just say something, or am I going nuts?" one of the troopers behind him asked.

"I await a response," the Gun said in that same level tone.

The corporal bent down and picked the weapon up, amazed at how light it was. He had never seen anything like it before.

"UPAF," he finally responded.

"Good. Then you are permitted to use me."

"Maybe. Just as soon as I can figure out exactly what you're supposed to be."

"I'm an intelligent gun; the latest development in advanced weapons technology," the Gun supplied helpfully.

"Is that a fact? And why would anyone go to all the trouble of building intelligence into a gun?"

"To enable me to kill enemies with greater efficiency."

The corporal grinned. Looking at his two young companions, he saw the expression mirrored on both their faces.

"Now you're talking," he said. The day had gone to hell in a handcart. It was about time they had a break. "Come on then, Gun, let's go kill us some enemies."

Tactics for Optimal Outcomes in Negotiations with Wergen Ambassadors

Mercurio D. Rivera

TOP SECRET – CLASSIFIED

DRAFT #3 9/10/26

[BRACKETED COMMENTS BY JCB: DOES THIS DRAFT INCORPORATE FEEDBACK FROM EXOBIO?]

R E T I N A L
M E M O R A N D U M

To: Members of the Outer Colony Committees on Human-Wergen Relations
(via entanglement encryption)

From: Tessa Kornbluth
Senior Diplomat, Colonisation Planning
EarthCouncil

Re: Tactics for Optimal Outcomes in Negotiations with Wergen Ambassadors

Date: October ___, 2526 [LET'S ACCELERATE TARGET DATE FOR DISTRIBUTION. NEGOTIATIONS FOR A PLUTO COLONY ARE IN THE BEGINNING PHASES.]

As we approach the 10-year anniversary of our first encounter with the Wergens, this memorandum (1) sets forth 'lessons learned' from prior negotiations with the Wergen Explorata in establishing joint colonies on Mars and Triton, and (2) outlines specific strategies going forward to optimise the outcomes of negotiations in connection with human/Wergen outposts on Pluto, Enceladus and Ceres.

I. Critical Metrics Regarding the Triton and Mars Colonies
A. The Unsuccessful Triton Talks
Negotiations for establishment of the Axelis Colony provide a roadmap for 'What Not To Do' when interacting with Wergen representatives. Discussions were hampered from the onset by our ignorance of the Wergens' ~~primary weakness~~ agreeable nature. The talks were such a fiasco that each human colonist on Triton is currently required to be accompanied *at all times* by three Wergen shadows. This unfavourable Wergen to human (W2H) ratio has resulted in decreased productivity and high rates of depression ~~and suicide~~ for Axelis colonists exposed to the Wergens for such prolonged, uninterrupted periods of time. [TESSA, THE COMMITTEES ARE SENSITIVE TO COSTS. LET'S DRILL DOWN & QUANTIFY, AND INCLUDE THESE FIGURES AS AN ATTACHMENT.] Even more troubling, the Commitment Period for each colonist to partner with his or her alien shadows runs eight Earth years – an excessive length of time by any measure. These unfavourable metrics are directly attributable to the following factors:

- Information Control: Due to first contact with the Wergens being established by our manned space stations orbiting Neptune and Saturn, the aliens immediately understood our aspirations to settle the solar system and mine the asteroid belt. Having discovered the numerous challenges we faced, they used this information to their advantage, offering us the assistance of their bots and forcefields *provided that* we agreed to partner with them in our colonisation efforts. This underscores the importance of keeping our cards close to the vest. The less the aliens know about our goals and needs, the better.

- Location of Participants: The terms of the joint colonisation project on Triton were discussed and agreed upon primarily via video-con at the request of the Wergens. Also of significance is the short duration of the negotiations, which commenced and concluded within a span of only one Earth day.

- Role of Earth: Because of the aliens' peculiar phobia about interacting directly with Earth, the heads of our Neptune and Saturn space stations served as intermediaries between EarthCouncil and the Wergens. Discussions between the Wergen ambassadors and their own leaders in the Explorata via video-con added yet another layer between both sides' ultimate decision-makers – which worked to the Wergens' advantage.

According to one account by a typical Axelis colonist:

<VIDEOBLINK>: "I was overcome – we all were – by the miraculous nature of their tech." A woman with red, curly hair and pale skin speaks rapidly, excitedly. "Wergen bots swarmed over 10 square miles of Triton terrain, reshaping it, transforming it into a suitable footprint for colony construction. And their forcefields..." She smiles, shakes her head incredulously. "Their forcefields shielded us from radiation and allowed us to regulate gravity and temperature."

A pause follows. The smile fades and her face goes blank.

"Then we realised what we had bargained away."

She hangs her head. The vid pans back to reveal three Wergen colonists standing directly behind the woman, their chalk-white, scaled faces barely visible behind hooded robes, their black, owl-like eyes trained on her in a lovestruck expression.

Testimony of Ariel Ambrose, taken on March 10, 2517 at 18:22 – 19:07.
[EXCELLENT SELECTION OF WITNESS. SHE'S MUCH

MORE ARTICULATE THAN THE WITNESS YOU USED IN PRIOR DRAFT.]

B.   The More Favourable Mars Negotiations

Martian colonists are the happiest and most well-adjusted settlers in the Solar System. [LAYING IT ON A BIT THICK HERE. DO WE HAVE PRODUCTIVITY METRICS WE CAN POINT TO?] Having only one Wergen shadowing four humans (a W2H ratio of 1 to 4) ensures every settler some measure of privacy. In addition, Wergens are required by the terms of the joint colonisation agreement to 'earn' their time with humans by sharing information about their bot tech and working the vineyards of Medusan Vallis for contractually negotiated periods. These favourable terms reflect a positive trajectory in our relationship with the Wergens and are attributable to the same three factors that worked to our disadvantage on Triton, namely:

- Information Control: The fact that we had already established a belowground outpost on Mars strengthened our bargaining position. Having undertaken colonisation efforts without assistance from the Wergens, we could credibly threaten to walk away from the partnership proposal unless they ~~gave us what we wanted~~ showed more flexibility. [TESSA, KEEP OUR AUDIENCE IN MIND. PHRASING HERE IS OFF-PUTTING. COMMITTEE MEMBERS LIKE TO TELL THEMSELVES WE'RE ACTING IN A FAIR AND REASONABLE MANNER.]

- Location of Participants. Wergen ambassadors appeared *in person* on Mars to discuss proposals for the construction of an aboveground colony and to demonstrate the effectiveness of their fieldtech. Those Wergens, however, craftily required all proposed terms to be approved by their off-world superiors – still not the optimal situation for us.

- Role of Earth. EarthCouncil diplomats travelled to Mars

and participated directly in negotiations with the Wergen ambassadors.

An average Martian colonist describes the living conditions on equatorial Mars as follows:

<VIDEOBLINK> A heavy-set, middle-aged man wearing a straw hat and blue jeans sits at the edge of a porch in a rocking chair, the orange sky visible over his left shoulder.

"The Wergen bots do a bang-up job tending to the crops. We're growing corn, wheat, oats – and, I swear, Medusan Vallis wine is better than any spirits I've ever tasted on Earth. Sure, I have to put up with my Wergen coming in to the house twice a week to sit around and stare at me. Makes my skin crawl. But it gets pretty happy when I play the guitar, so I'll sing the alien a few tunes – it doesn't seem to mind that I'm so off-key."

He laughs so heartily he has to reach up to steady the hat on his head.

Testimony of Abe Sidowski, taken on February 10, 2523 at 15:32 – 16:17. [CAN WE BRIGHTEN THE COLOURS TO PROVIDE MORE OF A CONTRAST WITH THE TRITON TESTIMONY?]

II. Lessons Learned and Stratagems to Employ

A rigorous comparison of negotiations regarding the Triton and Mars colonies provides valuable insight on the best approach going forward.

When negotiating with the Wergens, it is critical to never lose sight of our primary objectives. First and foremost, we ~~should~~ must strive for the most favourable W2H ratios and Commitment Periods possible for each outpost so as to improve the ~~productivity~~ quality of life of our hard-working colonists. Second, we ~~should~~ must [USE MANDATORY TERMS THROUGHOUT MEMO] attempt to obtain information about the location of the Wergen homeworld. Lastly, when possible, we

~~should~~ must continue to encourage the Wergens to make direct contact with Earth itself ~~so that they succumb to our demands~~ to strengthen our partnership. The prevailing theory is that the Wergens are being overly cautious about revealing the location of their homeworld because they fear ~~conquest~~ direct contact between us and their leaders – who may find our arguments too persuasive, our positions too compelling, our personal charm too irresistible – and accede to our reasonable demands. [WHO WROTE "CONQUEST"? IT'S RIDICULOUS – AND DANGEROUS – TO STATE THIS SO OVERTLY.] Given their ~~biochemical compulsion to love us~~ fondness for humanity, one would have expected the Wergens to jump at the invitation. While they may yet bring their tech gifts directly to Earth, their reticence to set foot on our planet remains a mystery. [A BIT HEAVY-HANDED. OBVIOUS TO EVERYONE WHAT THEY'RE AVOIDING. CONSIDER RE-WORDING OR DELETING.] Whatever it is they're hiding,[1] we strongly believe we may be able to ~~exploit~~ leverage that information in future negotiations.

III. Tactics for Ongoing Negotiations with Wergens: Action Items
A. In-person Negotiations

Prior talks highlight the importance of up-close, in-person contact with those members of the Wergen Explorata responsible for signing off on joint colonisation terms. In close proximity to

---

[1] See Memorandum on Efforts to Surreptitiously Debrief Wergen Colonists, dated December 2, 2525, which noted that most Wergen colonists were born off-world and appear to have been have purposely kept in the dark about the location of their home planet. However, certain ~~love-smitten~~ Wergens went silent when interrogated on this subject. This suggests they held relevant information about their homeworld but may have been protected by some form of mental shield that prevented its disclosure.

humans, any Wergen ~~enslaved by their biochemical compulsion to love us~~ – overcome by their natural affection and fondness for us – will ~~inevitably cave~~ more likely agree to our demands. For this reason, we must avoid repeating the mistakes of Axelis where the Wergens cleverly utilised a layered communication chain. On Mars, the mere act of EarthCouncil diplomats sitting in the same room with their Wergen counterparts produced a more favourable outcome. Eliminating as many of these layers as possible provides us a crucial tactical advantage. Accordingly, we ~~should~~ must refuse to participate in negotiations going forward unless the ultimate decision-makers for each side are present.

B. Setting

The Triton negotiations between human and Wergen surrogates took place aboard the spacious 1000 square foot viewing deck of the *Engagement* with its spectacular views of the storm clouds of Uranus. In contrast, the more successful Mars talks occurred in the Pavonis Mons Caverns, in a shadowy den measuring only ten by twenty feet. Based on the foregoing, negotiations should take place in cramped quarters with no tables or other barriers between the attendees. Close physical proximity is likely to produce optimal results. The room must be spare, with no decorations, windows or other distractions for the Wergens.

C. Duration

During Martian negotiations, the lead Wergen representative interrupted the talks and took frequent breaks. As described by one of the attendees:

<VIDEOBLINK> A bald man in a dark rumpled suit sits at a mahogany table. He speaks directly into the camera, slowly, with haunted eyes.

"Our interactions were polite at first, becoming more and more informal with each passing hour, before turning noticeably chummier. By the end of the day, the aliens had to take numerous breaks, staggering out of the conference room every few minutes, hugging their shoulders. On one occasion, while I don't recall their exact words, I overheard them whisper to each other." He imitates them, raising the pitch of his voice so that he speaks in a sickly sweet singsong: "'So, so, beautiful... Their delicate forms... their soft voices... the warm sparkle in their eyes.'" His voice returns to normal. "The white scales that covered their face paled from a light grey to an ivory white. They averted their eyes, pulling their hoods over the faces while they retreated to compose themselves."

Testimony of Representative Marcus Decinces, taken on August 1, 2525 at 45:32 – 46:44.

Accordingly, we must object to these numerous breaks and extend the duration of negotiations as long as possible. Most of our diplomats can tolerate being in close quarters with the Wergens for no more than a few days before experiencing psychological trauma. While countervailing considerations exist, as noted below, this factor is critical to a successful negotiation.

D. Touching

Physical contact with the aliens – a prolonged handshake, touching their arms, laying a hand on their shoulders (preferably skin-to-skin contact) – is strongly encouraged. However, great care should be taken not to overstimulate the Wergens for this may cause them to shut down and stop speaking altogether. Even worse, we might have a repeat of the Mobbing Incident on Mars, which resulted in psychological trauma to all human attendees.[2]

---

[2] See Medical Analysis of Human Physiological Reaction to the Wergens, dated Oct. 7, 2525 at pg. 33: "The diplomats swarmed by the Wergens suffered dangerous short-term physical symptoms such as palpitations and elevated blood pressure as well as long-term post-traumatic stress. Other negotiators merely present in the same room with the Wergens routinely sought counseling for recurring nightmares." See Section F below on Counseling.

E. Nasal Receptor Blockers

Negotiators in close quarters with the Wergens for an extended period of time have complained about their stink, about the gag reflex that makes it difficult to speak while in their presence:

<VIDEOBLINK> A heavy-set man with greying hair and glasses dangling from the tip of his nose sits at a desk.

"An overwhelming stench – of vinegar and raw sewage and something else, something unfamiliar and unpleasant – grew more pungent the longer we remained in the same room with the three aliens. If they hadn't requested so many breaks I'm sure I would've puked right on top of their flat heads." He shakes his head, flares his nostrils in disgust. "But it was more than the terrible stink that made me sick; it was their alien nature – simply being in their presence – that set off some instinctive biological defense mechanism. It was as if a room full of rattlesnakes were drawing closer and closer. It took everything I had to fight the urge to flee. To this day, I wake up in a cold sweat in the middle of the night dreaming of those eyes, those large black pupil-less eyes boring into my soul."

Testimony of Diplomat Baron LaPage, taken on Sept. 4, 2525, at 32:10--33:17

EC has developed an aerosol spray that numbs the nasal receptors for up to 10 hours and which should be used prior to any meeting. Unfortunately, while the aerosol prevents gagging, it does nothing to lessen the general revulsion felt in the presence of the Wergens.[3]

---

[3] Some renegade Wergens have developed their own version of an inhalant, a dangerous drug that skews their thinking and suppresses their ~~docility in our presence~~ natural love for humanity. Needless to say, under no circumstances should we tolerate the presence of – let alone negotiate with – any Wergen employing one of these devices. [CONSIDER MOVING THIS FOOTNOTE UP INTO THE TEXT. THE WERGEN RENEGADES ARE BECOMING A DANGEROUS THREAT TO THE HUMAN/WERGEN PARTNERSHIP.]

F. Availability of Counselling

Members of the Mars negotiating team – both those swarmed and those present during the Mobbing Incident – remain in therapy. This underscores the delicate balancing act we must strike: working closely with the Wergens, ingratiating ourselves with them, but also taking into account the mental health of our own negotiators. For this reason, free lifetime counselling remains available to all diplomats.

IV. Conclusion

The above stratagems ~~should~~ must be employed going forward to achieve the most favourable partnership terms possible. If we proceed judiciously, there's no reason why we shouldn't be able to ~~overwhelm~~ persuade the Wergens with "[our] soft voices… the warm sparkle in [our] eyes." The wellbeing of our settlers and the future of our colonisation efforts depend on it.

T.K.

cc: EC Representatives of All Nations

[ARE WE TAKING STEPS TO SECURE THIS DOCUMENT AND PRIOR DRAFTS – NOT JUST THE FINAL VERSION – VIA QUANTUM ENCRYPTION? IF THESE DRAFTS WERE TO FALL INTO THE HANDS OF WERGEN RENEGADES, THE CONSEQUENCES COULD BE DIRE.]

[RESPONSE BY TK: I'LL HAVE TO DOUBLE CHECK]

The Story of the Ten

Jo Zebedee

"Tell me the story," Jay whispers, then yawns. His sleeping quarters are cramped, but that makes things cosier. It's a good thing I like cosy – our share of the ship consists of a sleeping alcove, a tiny living area and a toilet. When we reach Terra Pierra we'll find even the confined area of the dome huge. No need to worry about that yet, though. For now, I snuggle beside him and put my arm around his shoulders to get close enough not to topple off the edge of the bed.

"Which story?" I ask, but I'm teasing. There's only ever one story Jay wants. The people at ISEB – the International Space Exploration Bureau – got their way with that one. They made me tell it as he grew up and ensured that storybooks and playsets about Terra Pierra were left in the communal living area we use for an hour a day, until all he wanted to know was how he fitted into the story. They won't take the chance that a pliable child, putting up with medical tests in the name of science, might grow into an adult who'll refuse.

"The story of the ten." He's smiling, too, enjoying the in-joke. It's all I can do not to tighten my arm around his shoulders and try to stop time now, when he's seven and still wants me to talk to. In another year, he'll have grown and be filling this small space. Hell, in a year, we might be on Pierra. My throat closes, dry and sick, but I make myself relax, tensing my muscles and releasing them, one after the other, until I trust myself to speak.

"All right," I say. "The story of the ten it is." I shuffle and get comfy and his head comes onto my shoulder and I put on the sing-song lie of a voice I always use. "Once, there were ten, and one day there will be one…"

"It begins with Terra Pierra," I say. "Humans never thought we'd be able to leave Earth, but we found a planet in the goldilocks zone…"

"Not too hot, and not too cold, but just right," he chants, reminding me I'm telling him this from a script. I manage not to look at the ceiling, or at the small mirror hanging opposite. I don't know where the listening devices are hidden, only that they must be. Watching devices too, no doubt – on Venturer-II, ISEB monitor everything.

"That's right," I say. A goldilocks planet with steady temperature and sun-activity, unlocked water and minimal life. Non-breathable atmosphere, of course, and gravity heavier than had been hoped for, but within tolerable limits. "Major Pierra and her team were the first to get there, and they stayed for three years, testing to see it was safe, before Venturer-I was planned."

Venturer-I, the great shining beacon of hope. It would traverse stellar distances using the newly discovered compression and expansion technique, folding and unwrinkling space, stepping in and out of the reality of our universe. There was talk of a wormhole, so that travel to the colony wouldn't take the seven long years it did now, bringing hope and optimism for a new Earth. All this talk about wormholes and wrinkling space proved to even the most sceptical that we'd entered the Space Era.

"And you wanted to go to Pierra," Jay reminds me, moving the story on. "You wanted it more than anything."

"I did." I smile at the memory. They're clever, the people at ISEB – they have me putting enough of my own truth into the story to make me complicit. "Your Grandpa and I watched the British colonists leaving London. People all over Earth did the same, went to the departure pad to see their people off, because the Spacers were taken from all over the world."

A melting pot of cultures, all colours and creeds, had been promised. In space, it wouldn't matter, ISEB had declared. The settlers would become Pierrans, not Earthlings. Fighting would be forgotten. Food would be limited to concentrates, pre-processed fare and micro farming – cultural preferences would be irrelevant. Utopia was promised, and we all bought into it.

"But they didn't take you." Jay knows the story as well as I do, but still we do the dance of memories. It tells him about people he's never known, a past he moved beyond before he'd even been born. For him, Grandpa and Grandma exist only because of the story. Everyone exists, except Gabriel. Him, I can't talk about. I can barely even think about his twisted smile and dark eyes. The same twisted smile Jay has, the same eyes that crinkle when he laughs. One day, maybe, Gabe will be in his memories, a part of the story. But not yet.

"No, they didn't select me." I can't think of Gabriel – it's the only way to survive, because survival comes from being strong, not lost and sad. "Not then."

I'd applied to the programme on the day of my twenty-first birthday. My mother took me to the office, her hands tight on the steering wheel as we pulled in, fear mixing with pride. She'd turned and wished me luck, but I saw how her jaw tightened and how her voice shook. She didn't trust ISEB, even in the early days. I should have listened to Mother, I tell myself, uselessly and years too late.

"Tell me about the office," says Jay. "Remember, how you were asked to protect Earth?"

The centre of the story – the glory of the Bureau. The bloody lies they told in my voice.

"It was a shiny building, in the middle of the town," I tell him. "There were ISEB representatives at the door. I'd never seen anyone wear a uniform like theirs before. The material was designed to be worn in space and it reflected the sunlight and made them seem as if they really were from another planet. It made them seem special."

They'd smiled and made us welcome, seeming to hide nothing. Maybe those representatives hadn't known the truth –

or maybe the truth came later, after the sickness. It's impossible to know but, on that shining day in 2017, they'd welcomed me and I'd suspected nothing of what would come.

"Were they like the ISEB we have on the ship?"

"Not quite." The representatives on the ship carry weapons, discreet in their holsters but deadly. They call themselves soldiers and have hard muscles and harder eyes. They watch us wherever we go, making fear gnaw at my belly. My child grew up in these three rooms, never knowing daylight or air, or Earth itself, because of their decisions. I push away my thoughts – they aren't helpful and might show in my voice. Somehow, I force a smile.

"They ushered people in and when we came to sign, we had to put our hand on the Bible –"

"The big book?"

"That's right, the big book." He'll never know a bible, not here amongst the stars. That's for Earth people, not Spacers. "And they made me say, all solemn…" I put my hand on my chest and clear my throat and boom out, "I swear my allegiance to Earth, and put my resources and self at her bidding."

Jay laughs, as he always has, at the thought of me being so bold and confident, but I glare at the mirror. *My resources and self, not my child.* But they know how I feel, and they don't care. Can't care, they say. I'm one amongst thousands – and my child is facing a better future than those on Terra Pierra.

"But you didn't go, even though you promised. You stayed at home with Grandpa and Grandma and watched it on TV instead. And you thought it was all finished for you."

"That's right." I remember the dull white paper the rejection was printed on, heavy in my hands. The words had been cold, giving no reason. Father tried to joke but something died in him a little, too – a hope that a part of him would be on Pierra, carrying our family further than he'd dreamed, perhaps. A sense of me doing what he'd have loved to do, had he been deemed young enough to.

"Tell me about the ship," says Jay. "I love this bit."

So I talk about Venturer-I. I tell him all the design specs I remember, and he tells me many more that he knows from the books strewn for him to find. We talk about how space can be crossed. As always, I catch my breath. It's one thing to imagine travelling through space in a sophisticated tin can but quite another to be reminded that's exactly what we are doing. The room doesn't move around us, and the engines are so smooth I only notice them when I concentrate – sometimes it's easy to lie to myself and forget what this is all about.

I distract us both by talking about the telly programmes shown on Earth, documentaries about Terra Pierra and stories about the colony. I tell him about the first time I saw a full terra-naut's suit, and he snorts at the idea of not knowing, Spacer child that he is.

"Mum," he says, after I've told him about gathering to watch the launch. I make my usual rubbish joke about how it was good for humanity not to have all our humans on one globe and he laughs at the idea that humans are like eggs, but I don't. Not now, when I know how fragile everything could be.

"Yeah?" I answer.

"Why do you always seem sad at this bit?" He's biting his lip, worried perhaps at deviating from the normal story. "I mean, it's exciting. The space launch, how you held your breath through the first Space-fold, how it took so long everyone was sure the Spacers were dead."

"Do I look sad?" He's getting older and able to read me so much better. That makes me even sadder.

He shakes his head. "You look the same. But you feel sad." He touches my chest. "Here."

And the moment hangs, where I could tell him about Gabriel. I could admit I was glad not to be called up the first time, because I'd never have met him. I could tell the truth, that while Venturer-I made for the stars I'd spent my time with Gabriel, all long-limbed and mine. I'd made the life I wanted – me, and Gabe, and a little bump of a baby growing in me.

I don't think I can tell Jay about how I've been forced from Gabe. I'm not even sure I'm allowed to – it was never in the sanctioned story. I'll be returned to him if things work out, ISEB said, but not how or when. He's my hope for the future – my reward for a job done. If I tell Jay – if I admit to a life that wasn't about him – the words would be the end of whatever's held me together throughout these years. So I laugh instead, and say, "It was just disappointment at not going, love."

He leaves it at that. I guess even a smart seven year old still wants to be fooled when things seem bigger than they should. I fill the next bit with stuff he knows. About the colonists landing and how they shared their new world with us.

"They have printers that made the dome," I say. "All thin sheets of printed plastic, so strong you could stand on it. And they'll expand the dome, build more." I give him a nudge. "You could design the planet-buggies they'll use to get from one dome to another. You're good at building things."

"I can be anything I want," he says. I've been telling him that since he was old enough to listen. I hate myself because it might be a lie. He yawns. "And after they made the dome, the sickness came."

"Yes. All the news turned dark." I lower my voice, trying to make the story sad but not too scary. Jay knows about it, of course, but he doesn't know the true horror.

Stories started to slip out of the dome when the first colonists fell ill. The doctors mapped the sickness and confirmed it was a slow illness, and painful, and new. Alien was the term they avoided, but we all understood – this was not of Earth. It wasn't something the colonists could defend themselves from, not once they realised it had spread through the colony and was in every person's cells, waiting to take them.

Pierra was the first to die. News screens across Earth showed her last message, still dressed in her Cosmonaut suit, face white beneath the pustules, scalp pink where her hair had come out. Her voice was hoarse and low, not the confident space commander we were used to.

"The dream must live," she said. "Our people must live."

We agreed with her, but there could be no return to Earth for the people on Pierra. To doom the colony was one thing, but to risk our single globe, that couldn't be contemplated. Whatever resided in the colonists' bodies had to stay deep in space.

I stumble over that section of the story, as I always do, not sure of the script I should really follow. Jay believes we're going to a safe planet where the sickness has abated. I can't tell him that if we do get taken to Pierra, it'll be because our mission has failed, and we'll die too.

"And she died," he says, breaking my silence, and his is the voice of someone who's heard the story so many times it's a fairy tale, not quite real. He doesn't remember the shock of her death, the moment when our untouchable space commander was destroyed, and the dream of Earth colonies shattered.

"She did." My voice croaks, almost giving me away, but I manage a quick, tight hug and I don't think he notices.

"Did she look like she did in the books?" He hasn't noticed, he's too engrossed in Pierra. "Did she wear a silver spacesuit?"

"Yes." A silver spacesuit with black boots, snug against her legs. A space helmet that hid her face but not her grace, even in heavy gravity. That was the Pierra I want to remember, a woman of the stars brave enough to build a colony. But that woman's hidden behind the news-announcers declaring her death, and my dull realisation that it could have been me, shivering and pustulating on a rock somewhere years from home.

Barely a month later the call came from ISEB, collecting on the allegiance I'd sworn years before and reminding me that my contract with them had never been terminated.

They must have known I would never agree to what they wanted. Perhaps I wasn't the first of the ten to be called, or they just knew that no one would agree. Either way, they told me they had Gabriel. Nothing would happen to him, they promised, as long as I did the duty I'd signed up for so long ago. I listened, and I argued, but they came back with statutes and emergency measures, and the demand that I be ready and I knew the cold voice could not be argued with, that everything had changed.

The clock was loud in the kitchen and I stood, letting it tick off the moments before I went into Father in his bedroom. His double bed was slept in on one side only. The bedside table that had once held my mother's ring-tree and books held only a picture of her. I wondered how to tell him I'd be leaving, and he'd be alone, but he knew.

"When?" was all he asked, and I touched my belly and wondered how it would feel, swelling, without Gabe beside me to feel it too. And I cried. I cried, right up to the knock on the door, and the first faceless soldiers in ISEB uniforms.

"You were brave to go," says Jay, and I hate the lies that are his truth. One day, when he's an adult, I'll tell him. I push away the little voice that reminds me he might not become an adult, that we might both be as dead as Pierra herself in a decade. That little voice leads to fear, and paralysis, and a half-life.

"And then you had me on the ship. I was the first Space-birth." Jay grins in pride. This was the bit of the story he most loves. "I was the first of the babies."

"You were." I'd never have done it, if they hadn't forced me. Got onto the ship, heavily pregnant, with nine other women in the same position, the unlucky ones to have signed up and be pregnant at the wrong time. It didn't matter that we had a medical crew, or that the bay was as well-equipped as any hospital – better, given our mission – our situation was still daunting.

I'd climbed the gangway in a daze, my father's last kiss on my cheek still lingering. His skin had been papery-thin and I knew I wouldn't see him again. It's hard to believe that he's dead, but the prognosis wasn't good before I left. At least with Mother, we buried her. At least I was with her and held her hand when she passed.

I find my hand going to my belly. If I'd gone in the first run any baby of mine would have been born on Pierra... It's a good thing, what happened to us. Certainly ISEB think so.

"There's something in the colony that, if it gets out, will destroy you and any children you have," a man in ISEB uniform told me. By then, I was on Venturer-II, and forced to silence – no communications with Earth, or anyone on the ship. Only with the Bureau.

"I understand," I'd said, and I did, but that didn't make things any easier.

"We don't want to force you." He had three stripes on his uniform, which made him important, I guessed. I didn't answer him, not then, or since – they *had* forced me onto the ship so they could use my baby.

He leaned forwards. "It had to be babies – the gene code had to be put in at the same time as the virus. It's the only way to activate the immunity, the doctors say – to transplant at the same time. They've tried every other way on Terra Pierra."

His eyes had met mine and, briefly, they looked softer, more human. "The colony is doomed. But we can protect the next generation. If this works."

"But it's not on Earth," I told him. "We're not in danger."

He shook his head, and it was as if I was a child and him an all-knowing teacher. "You know how stupid humans can be. We can't put this disease away now it's here. There's no guarantee someone won't decide to use it: some politician thinking it will help his cause, for instance, or a bleeding-heart taking pity on the colony. Or the scientists. God knows they'd do anything to get their hands on something like this and win the Nobel cracking how the virus works. No; we can only learn how to stop it."

"Then trial it on Earth," I pleaded. "Lock us in a lab somewhere and do what you need to."

"No." The hardness was back. "The virus doesn't get onto Earth. It stays where it started. In Space." He stood, and paused, and gave a sorry smile. "But if we get the cure, everything changes. You go back to Earth. Your son does, too. All it takes is the gene strand to be right in one of the infants. That's all. Just one."

"And if it doesn't?"

He didn't answer, and he didn't need to. We'll never bring this ship back to Earth. Not as long as something of the virus, uncured and deadly, remains in the testing labs. Either we'll find the cure or we'll join the colonists and die on Pierra, letting the doctors there test our children, seeking for something hidden within them that could be used.

Seven years have passed since they brought me on board. Nothing's changed since the day of the long launch, when Earth fell away from us. The ship is the same – long corridors of white leading from our quarters to an empty living quarter, to the medicine labs, and back. The same air goes round and round, the same lungs breathe in and spit it out.

Still, the guards are with us, watching through the monitors, listening to my words, making sure I'm still holding up their lies. Perhaps they don't even know they're lies. Perhaps they believe this really is the right thing, that in signing myself up I signed up a baby I carried.

For now, I hug Jay to me, feel the hard bones of his spine, his soft breaths slowing as he moves towards sleep. Today, he's well. I close my eyes and pray that tomorrow will be the same, and the next, and the next.

A deep shudder from somewhere in the ship wakes me. The distant roar of engines can be heard. The door to our compartment has opened. Figures pass outside, one tall, the other a child, and neither is a soldier.

Jay sits up beside me, blinking. "What is it?" he asks, voice sleepy.

Another pair of figures pass, and another, and I realise what's happened.

"It's okay," I say, and my voice is choked. Somewhere, Gabe is being freed. I'll be able to go back and see him. He'll meet Jay. "They've done it."

"Done what?"

Relief floods through me. I can barely speak, but he deserves me to, *needs* me to. "Found the cure," I whisper.

One of the children – perhaps Jay, perhaps another – has beaten the illness. No, more than beaten it: has *removed* the virus from their gene strand. "One of the ten has become The One."

I find myself crying and the fear slips away. I've been given my life back. More than that. I crouch in front of Jay.

"You can be anything you want to be." I nod, fierce and determined to take back what's his. "Anything at all, anywhere at all."

The Beauty of Our Weapons

Gavin Smith

...a fugitive and a vagabond shalt thou be in the Earth.
(Genesis 4:10–12)

1.   Exultation. Teeth bared, hissing, Cain felt the impact of the rock hitting his brother's face run up his arm, the warm splash of blood.

Samael, the angel who delivered the greedy god's curse, did not have wings, nor was he beautiful or terrible to behold. He had the face of a serpent and had been Cain's mother's lover.

Cain didn't think he understood the curse. It made him burn from the inside and his hand had turned red but beyond that it didn't seem to be a punishment at all.

After the Loss, Ubaste System

He had barely paid attention to what the fight was about. All that mattered was that this was a Conflict Resolution world and the enemy were Rakshasa. It would be over resources, it was always over resources. They were rimward in the system in a recently formed asteroid belt made when a significantly sized planetoid had been destroyed during the early stages of the conflict. From his perspective the more distant stones in the field looked like smoke in the light of the faraway sun.

The Rakshasa parasite ships had been buried deep in the asteroids, harvesting rock and minerals for raw materials to feed their military assemblers. He had told the young exec in charge of the Consortium contractors not to take the ship into the field without a screening force of mechs. He/she hadn't listened and a nuclear mine had broken the back of the carrier ship. The worst of the blast hit on the opposite side of the ship from his squad's mech cradles and they had made it out into the field.

The mine detonation seemed to have caught the Rakshasa as much by surprise as it had the military contractors. He and the rest of the squadron had managed to fall on the insectile parasite ships. Fusion lances and missiles ruptured the ships before they had been able to do much more than utilise their point defence systems.

The fight only really began when the Rakshasa's sentry mechs had found his squad. They came out of the weak actinic light, using the asteroids as cover, electronic warfare signals confusing or spoofing the drones they had deployed. It proved a brutal fight because of the close range. The rest of the mechs in his squad were now little more than cooling, expanding debris fields but there was still one more Rakshasa mech left.

401 BCE, Cunaxa, Persia

2.   The age of champions was over. There were no more heroes even though his red right hand marked him out as a favoured son of Ares to the rest of the Greek mercenaries. All knew Cain, and even though he would stand in the front line of the phalanx, where the press would be at its greatest, men fought to stand next to him. He had been a king, he had been a champion but now he was just another man in the phalanx.

Two days' march north of Babylon, the mercenaries baked under the blazing sun. The *hoplite's* bronze armour was hot enough to cook meat on, hot enough to burn the flesh wearing it.

The breeze coming off of the Euphrates, the river that protected their left flank, did little to mask the stink of ten thousand sweating men.

Cain could just about make out the Persians through the heat haze and the dust of the trampled field. He had heard that there were at least four times as many Persians as there were Greeks. He was starting to worry if they were going to fight at all, though they had come a long way for nothing if they did not. He had been close enough to hear Cyrus the Younger, the prince that had employed the mercenaries, order Clearachus, the Spartan general who led them, to move the right hand phalanx into the centre. Cyrus wanted Clearachus' men to face off directly against Artaxerxes the Second, the brother that Cyrus was trying to oust from the Persian throne. Clearachus had of course refused, as it would leave the right flank, the weakest part of any phalanx, exposed. They had reached an impasse. A Persian prince was as used to having his orders ignored as a Spartan general was to having his ability to wage war questioned.

Finally, however, they were given the order to advance. They did so in huge clouds of dust. The wind blowing from the north carried the dust cloud before the *hoplites*, stinging their eyes, choking them, further obscuring the site of the enemy. They could hear the Persian horns, however, the beat of the drums, the cries of their commanders urging them on.

The first arrows started to fall. There were a few startled cries from the men either side of him, behind him, then laughter. The Persian arrows could not penetrate the bronze. Their impact was little more than a hard rain.

At a shout from Clearachus they picked up the pace and ran out of the dust cloud. All Cain could see stretching from the river were lines of men. He wasn't sure he'd ever seen so many in one place, let alone in a battle. He ran into the oncoming Persian arrows, his armour and his *aspis*, the long concave shield of the *hoplite*, keeping him safe. He felt invulnerable, the superior numbers of the Persians were irrelevant.

They charged the Persian lines. Cain thrust his *doru*, underhand, into one of the Persian soldiers. The long spear split the Persian's wicker shield, and went straight through his armour of stiffened layers of linen. Cain lost the *doru*, torn from his hand by the momentum of the charge. He put his head down behind the shield as they hit the line and the charge broke against the shear amount of men that opposed them.

Cain found himself peering over his shield at a terrified-looking Persian, both of them trapped in the press of the men behind them. Cain's helm and breastplate turned the enemy blades. He drew the *kopis*, the wickedly curved shortsword sheathed on the inside of his *aspis*, and looked into the Persian's eyes as he forced the blade under his shield. His opponent could see what he was doing and started to beg even before the iron point of the *kopis* touched him. Cain slowly pushed the weapon upwards. The stink of ruptured bowel filled the air, as intestines uncoiled and the Persian's guts splattered to the dusty ground but the press of men held him upright still. The hoplites behind Cain thrust their spears overhand and the Persian line bowed. It was enough. Cain pushed forward, hacking. He was worried that war had become too easy.

After the Loss, Ubaste System

The first thing he knew of the remaining enemy mech had been when a lance of plasma hit the small asteroid he had been sheltering in. The resultant jet of molten rock and iron struck his mech, sending red warning signs cascading down his vision as the mech fed his neunonics damage reports.

He hit the mech's thrusters, the thirty-foot tall, humanoid shaped war machine shot away from the asteroid, flying blind, as electro-magnetically propelled rounds fired from a rotary cannon arced away in front of him.

The mech's damage control systems worked to repair the war machine as he searched for another place to hide.

69 CE, Germania Inferior

3.   Cain hadn't run because he feared death, though having died once he knew enough to fear the pain. He ran because the legion had broken and his death would have served no purpose. It hadn't been the Batavian auxiliaries that his fellow legionaries had feared. The auxiliaries were to be respected, no doubt. Before the revolt they had served Rome honourably and well for more than twenty-five years until Nero's fit of pique. Dangerous as they were, the Batavian auxiliaries were a known quantity. Instead it was the tribes from the other side of the *Rhenus* in *Magna Germania* who had joined in with the revolt that they feared. It was the tribespeople that legionaires told stories about. Around the campfire and in nightmares the Germanic warrior were elevated to the staus of demons. Cain knew that the barbarians from the other side of the river were just men and women, but even as a *decanus* there was little he could do about such beliefs. In the eyes of the other legionaires his red right hand was enough to mark him as favoured child of Mars, the god of war. How could he then explain that the huge, demonic creature tearing into one of Rome's invincible legions was just a large man wearing animal furs and covered in mud.

The rebellious Batavian auxiliaries had caught them in an area of woodland some ten leagues north of the camp at *Oppidum Batavorum*. The woodland was on a hill that ran down to the *Rhenus* and a number of streams ran through the area. It was difficult ground for the legionaries to manoeuvre in. Gaius Julius Civilis, the Batavian prince who led the rebellion, had chosen the site of his ambush well.

The tribal warriors had exploded out of the undergrowth on each side of the narrow track the *centuria* had been patrolling. Even to Cain's eyes they had seemed to burst from the ground. He'd only just had the presence of mind to throw his *pilum* at the first tribeswoman who had charged him. The soft iron tip of the javelin had penetrated her shield, and bent. The woman's shield was dragged down by the weight of the *pilum's* haft. Digging into the ground, the bent javelin had broken her momentum. Cain stepped forward, standing on the wooden haft, forcing the shield further down, exposing her side and stabbing his *gladius* through the layers of fur and dirt, into her. The tribesman behind her vaulted the dead woman's body and all but leapt onto Cain's tall *scutum*. He could smell sweat, the musk of old furs, rancid breath but mostly the smell of the earth from where the tribesman had hidden, half buried. Cain let him have the shield and it toppled to the ground, the surprised tribesman underneath. To the Spartans that he had once fought with, losing his shield, to become *ripsaspis*, would have been enough to disgrace him

Looking around, it was clear the *centuria* was lost. They relied on discipline, on fighting as one, but the barbarians were amongst them now. Without the chance for the legionaries to form up, to use their superior tactics, savagery would win this day. It felt like a step backwards for the civilisation and order Rome was bringing to the world, albeit by sword and brand. Through the trees Cain could see a man on horseback watching the slaughter. He was too busy trying to find his men but later he wondered if the man had been Civilis himself.

He managed to find the rest of his *contubernium* and led them back to the camp, avoiding the barbarians who were hunting them. Later, even though they had fought in the rest of the revolt, the disgrace of their defeat in the woodland caught up with them. When the Legio X Gemina finally relieved them, Cain's *contubernium* was sentenced to decimation. It was Cain who underwent the *fusturiam*. As blow after blow from the cudgels wielded by his men rained down on him, he realised that he had not managed to avoid the pain of death, just postpone it. In such a long life it was only the second time he had died.

After the Loss, Ubaste System

The mech shed micro drones as he sought cover in the shadow of a mountain-sized asteroid. He finessed, cajoled and even bullied systems back on line, trying to turn the mech into a functioning war machine again whilst it's thrusters cooled.

He wondered if it had been too long now. Had his edge gone? His best idea was to camp in his current concealed position and wait for the Rakshasa mech to show itself.

The micro drones above him started to go offline. They might not have provided an exact position for a target lock but the storm of electronic warfare rendering the micro drones useless at least told him the direction from which the enemy mech was coming.

Too late he realised it was a feint.

1415 CE, Agincourt, Northern France

4. They outnumbered the English more than ten-to-one if you didn't count the archers. As Cain sought to control his snorting destrier, which stamped its hooves in the thick mud, he couldn't understand why you wouldn't count the archers. He spared the spurs and used his knees to guide the exquisitely trained warhorse through the mud and into the vanguard with the other men-at-arms of his free company

"Where are our archers?" Cain asked. He was looking over a brown plain, a recently ploughed field turned to mud in the heavy rain, droplets of which were still dripping off his helm. Ahead the muddy plain narrowed between two strips of woodland surrounding the villages of Tramecourt and Agincourt.

"The lords want the glory for themselves. After all heavy cavalry has won battles for more than two hundred years."

With some difficulty Cain turned around to look at the speaker on the horse next to him. He had avoided Sir Malcolm du Bois, the Norman-Scot mercenary who commanded their free company. He had seen the fire burning under his skin, in the knight's veins, and as a soldier he was second only to Cain. He suspected that du Bois was older than he claimed and, like himself, had been cursed by God to walk the Earth, undying. He had caught du Bois studying him on a number of occasions and more than once it had seemed as though the knight had something to tell him but had changed his mind at the last moment.

"That's madness," Cain said, irritation overcoming his wish to avoid the blonde haired, blue-eyed knight. He pointed at the two strips of woodland. "The English archers have set up by the tree line. I can see stakes and doubtless they have dug pits."

"We're charging the archers."

"Even so we're riding into a trap without our own archers to cover the charge."

"Well you, myself and the high constable are in complete agreement."

Cain shook his head. He wished he could muster something more than irritation and contempt for the inbred lackwits that seemed to take in turns to get otherwise competent members of his profession killed in significant numbers.

Du Bois muttered something as the horn blew, signalling their advance. Cain didn't quite catch what had been said but he thought he'd heard the word Hattin. Cain spent a moment calming his horse. The destrier had either picked up on his master's irritation, or else the sense of angry futility amongst the more experienced men-at-arms. Counting the archers, Cain reckoned the French outnumbered the English four-to-one, which was still a significant advantage. That didn't, however, mean that you forgot how to conduct a battle, or ignored your other advantages.

It was hard going for the horses and as the field narrowed between the two strips of woodland they became more and more closely packed together. Even so, Cain had managed to coax his mount into a canter and then a gallop using his spurs.

At first he thought there'd been an eclipse. Then came a moment of near-religious dread as his mind struggled to cope with what he was seeing. He had fought in more wars, been in more battles, than he could count but he had never seen so many arrows coming towards him, even at Cunaxa. They seemed to form a solid canopy, a thick black rainbow against the drizzling grey sky arcing in towards the French heavy cavalry.

Cain turned his head, lowering it, riding blind but protecting the eye slit and air holes in his helm. Many of the men-at-arms, particularly the noble born, eschewed shields, trusting in the quality of their armour to protect them, Cain, however, knew the value of a shield and raised his. An armour-piercing bodkin point penetrated it and went through his gauntlet, only to be stopped by the mail underneath. More arrows rained down, their sharp narrow points coated in faeces. They imbedded themselves deep in his shield, glanced off his helm hard enough to make his head ring, or bounced off his armour deadening limbs and driving the breath from him.

Others were less lucky. Arrows penetrated less well-protected limbs, pierced the lower quality steel or wrought iron of the cheaper armours. Worst hit were the horses. Only a few of them wore barding. Horses went down in the mud at the gallop, causing collisions of horseflesh that took down even more mounts. Panicking wounded horses escalated the chaos. Cain caught a glimpse of a thrown rider moments before he was trampled into the mud.

Cain risked a glance forward. An arrow hit his helmet, denting it, pain lanced through his head but he saw enough. He was closing on the stakes that protected the English archers. The bowmen were no longer loosing into the air, instead aiming straight at the remaining horses. Everything slowed down. He actually saw the flight of the arrow that hit his horse. He felt the destrier's forelegs buckle and then he was tumbling. He hit hard. There was a moment of darkness and a great weight on him. The sounds of the battle seemed to recede. Then his screaming horse tumbled on and he was looking at the grey sky and the individual drops of rain falling on him as the never-ending storm of arrows flew overhead.

It was more instinct than anything else that made him roll to one side as a newly dead horse and rider slid past him, spraying him in mud. He knew he had to stand up if he wanted to live. He struggled to his feet. An arrow caught him in the chest but did not penetrate his breastplate. He thought about trying to crawl away, trying to hide, but instead used his broadsword to push himself to his feet. The archers were amongst the stakes now, killing the knights and men-at-arms that had made it this far. Two of them came forward of the stakes. Both were very broad across the shoulders, so much so they looked deformed. They wore hauberks over fool's motley, their faces painted black and red to resemble the demonic Hellaquins of Norman legend. The one with long dark hair still carried his bow. The other a mattock, the heavy hammers the archers used to drive the stakes into the ground. Cain shifted his shield and raised his sword, struggling through the mud towards them, his rasping breath nearly deafening in the confines of the helmet. The hellaquin with the bow loosed. The arrow caught him in the sword arm just under his armpit. The area was only protected by mail, which the bodkin easily penetrated. Cain howled in pain. The arm dropped snapping the arrow. More pain. The hellaquin with the mattock crossed to him quickly. Absurdly Cain noticed that he was barefooted, before the mattock hit him hard enough to buckle his helm and crack his skull. It hit him hard enough to change the shape of his head. Cain hit the ground, his body shaking, spasming. For a moment he was reminded of *fusturiam* he had undergone at the hands of his own legionaries.

"Can he be ransomed?" the hellaquin with the bow asked as he crossed himself. The hellaquin with a mattock leant down next Cain as he fought to regain control of his limbs.

"There's no device I can see," the hellaquin with the mattock said as he drew a long, narrow bladed knife with a guard shaped like a crucifix.

"Kill him then."

Cain watched as the *misericorde* was slid through the eye slit of his helmet. He decided that this death was easier than the previous.

After the Loss, Ubaste System

Not wanting to give his position away with an active scan, he had looked up. The Rakshasa mech had launched his own electronic warfare drones to jam the sensor net created by the micro drones and then looped under the asteroid.

He triggered the mech's thrusters, shooting away from asteroid. A lance of bright light made the mech's energy dissipation grid glow brightly before turning part of the war machine's lower torso into so much slag. He left teardrops of molten composites in his wake. Somehow he had the presence of mind to bank hard as another line of destructive energy narrowly missed him. He fired blind, depleting the rotary EM cannon's magazine by half in an effort to make a net of hypersonic munitions spreading out towards his opponent. It was only then that he actually caught a glimpse of the Rakshasa's mech, as the cannon rounds created tiny explosions of powdered composites across its body. The enemy war machine was ugly, efficient, angular, but as the fusion lance stabbed out again, somehow magnificent. The Rakshasa's mech was decorated, however. The feline warrior had tried to make it resemble one of the huge hunting cats that had once prowled the savannahs of Ubaste Prime. He had tried to hide the mech's true form, its purpose, its beauty as a weapon.

He spun his own mech away from the beam of energy. Smart explosives laced throughout the war machine's armour, blowing out the slagged armour so the mech's limited carbon reservoir could attempt to grow more.

Information from the mech's sensor appeared in his vision. The drone feint had been a double bluff. The electronic warfare had covered the missiles the Rakshasa mech had sent arcing over the asteroid in a bid to catch him in a simple, but effective, pincer movement.

1571 CE, Enryaku-Ji, Temple Complex, Mount Hiei, Japan

5. Cain watched, from the safety of the treeline, as an arrow hit one of the samurai harquebusiers. The man staggered back before toppling to the ground. It did not stop the rest of his line from firing their *tanegashima* matchlocks. Smoke filled the air as the shot whistled through the trees and up the hill towards the temple and 'its *sohei* defenders. More of the warrior monks fell. The first rank of harquebusiers knelt down and started to reload their *tanegashimas*, the next row marched between them, aimed and fired. They then stopped to reload, and the next line marched between them. There was a screaming from further up the hill and one of the *sohei* ran towards them, his *naginata* polearm held high, tears in old eyes. Lead propelled by black powder shattered the lacquered wood of his *dō* breastplate and he slid face first down the slope over the wet leaf-strewn earth.

Cain could see smoke rising above the trees from various points on the mountain as a number of temples, including the *Hiyoshi* shrine to the mountain's *kami* spirit Sannō, burned. He had heard one of the *sohei's* curse Oda Nobunaga for this act of apparent sacrilege. The curse didn't seem to have done the powerful *daimyo* much damage and it looked as though the power of the *sohei*, allies of Oda's enemies amongst the Azai and Asakura clans, had been broken. Oda had brought his army to Mount Hiei and killed every man woman and child he found. Now it was simply a matter of the harquebusiers hunting down the few surviving *sohei*. Cain didn't think that Oda gave much thought to gods, spirits and curses. To Cain's mind this was because the warlord didn't know enough to be afraid.

The samurai fired their *tanegashimas* again. Another cloud of smoke rose into the still rain-damp trees. Then they moved forwards into their own smoke, the next volley lighting the cloud from within as they continued their seemingly inexorable advance. Cain moved out of the treeline towards the samurai who had fallen. He was dead. There had been an artistry to his death. The utilisation of a skill hard earned, finesse. There was no finesse to the lingering stench of the black powder. The dead samurai's *tanegashima* lay a few inches away from his outstretched fingers. His *daishō*, the *katana* and *wakizashi*, long and shortswords, remained in their scabbards, thrust through his *obi* belt. Cain had come here looking for warriors. Instead he had found the same thing that he had left back in Europe. The honour was gone, the skill was gone, war was little more than a machine now. He reached down and drew the *katana* from its scabbard, holding it up to examine the elegant curve of the blade. He knew enough to realise that he shouldn't handle a samurai's sacred weapon but he was so disappointed at what he had found here, yet another one-sided massacre. He wondered for a moment if his not inconsiderable skills would have affected the outcome if he had joined with the *sohei*.

"Red Hand, do you know that I could take your head for such a thing?" a voice asked in heavily accented but passable Portuguese. Cain did not turn around. Instead he stood admiring the watered, folded steel of the blade. It was exquisite. He had wielded fine swords before, made from bronze, from iron and then steel, but the European swords, even those out of Toledo, were crude pieces of metal compared to the swords he had found in Japan. The blade glinted where it caught the low autumnal sun.

"I have heard it said that swords contain the souls of the warriors that bear them," Cain answered in Japanese. After so many years he had developed a talent for languages, even one as complex as Japanese. He turned to face the speaker. Oda Nobunaga was a balding, unassuming, moustachioed man. His remaining hair was tied back in a somewhat sparse looking topknot and he had eschewed armour for several layers of *kimono*. Two samurai retainers in full *ō-yoroi* armour stood at either side of the warlord. Cain could see the disgust and hatred in their eyes despite the *menpo* masks, carved to resemble the demonic *Oni*, which covered their faces. They would be furious that a *gaijin* had dared soil one of their sacred blades with his touch.

"However well-crafted, it is just a piece of metal, a tool,

nothing more," Oda said. "You do strange and terrible things to my language and talk of the soul. Are you with the Jesuits? Their fervour amuses me."

Cain continued to examine the blade, not answering immediately. He could feel the two retainers bristling. He knew he was being disrespectful. Briefly he wondered why he was trying to provoke a fight. Was it his disappointment?

"I have no use for God," Cain finally said, still not looking directly at the powerful *daimyo*. Oda regarded him for a moment, but the *gaijin's* disrespect was too much for one of the retainers. He stepped forwards and opened his mouth to issue a challenge but Oda held his hand up and the retainer fell silent. Cain wasn't sure if Oda was shrewd enough to have guessed at the truth behind Cain's apparent confidence, or was merely curious about the *gaijin*.

"I have no use for them either," Oda told him. "Perhaps you are one of the Portuguese traders?"

"I travelled here with the Dutch but I am not a trader."

"No, I did not think so. You are a man of violence. Is that why your hand is stained the colour of blood?"

Now Cain turned to look at Oda, again the retainers bristled as he failed to lower his eyes, but Cain had been a king and this man was just a warlord.

"I am looking for warriors..."

"Lord Oda!" The *sohei* that stepped out of the woods was already wounded, his left arm hung limp at his side and blood dripped out of his armoured *kote* sleeves. He was dragging his *naginata* behind him. "Will you face me in single combat?"

Oda was still looking at Cain.

"It's not that I'm afraid, you understand?" Oda said and Cain could see that there was little fear in the *daimyo*, if anything there was a spark of madness. "But I know that there is one enemy that we can never defeat no matter how much we would have it otherwise." He turned his head towards one of his retainers and inclined it slightly. The *sohei* saw what was happening and dropped the *naginata,* reaching awkwardly for his *wakizashi.* The retainer drew a matchlock pistol from his *obi;* its barrel was carved into the semblance of a dragon. The dragon breathed fire. Cain felt the shot pass him as he whipped round to see the *sohei's* face cave in on itself and turn red. The warrior monk fell backwards into the undergrowth. Smoke drifted through the trees. Oda coughed.

"Do you know who that enemy is, Red Hand?" Oda asked. Cain nodded, looking down at the *katana.*

"Progress," Cain said quietly. Oda and the retainers started up the hill after the harquebusiers.

"Just so," Oda said as he passed. "You may keep the sword."

Moments later, Cain heard another volley of *tanegashima* fire. He dropped the *katana* onto the wet earth and walked away.

After the Loss, Ubaste System

The thrusters on the soles of the mech's feet and the stubby wings that extended from its legs glowed as he spun the war machine in flight. Ball-mounted lasers filled the surrounding vacuum with harsh strobing light, destroying the incoming missiles even as they spored sub-munitions. The resulting explosions kicked his mech around but were too far away to cause any real damage. That hadn't been the point, though. They were to keep him busy. He triggered his manoeuvring jets at random as the thick beam of energy from the enemy mech's fusion lance stabbed out again and again, each time missing him more through luck than judgement.

Ahead he could see the cratered side of another mountainous asteroid. He burned hard for the closest cave, firing a missile from the launcher on the mech's back. The missile shot ahead of him into the cavern and delivered a payload of tens of thousands of micro drones. They immediately began mapping the cavern and the rest of the cave structure, sending the information back to the mech, which in turn uploaded the details into his neunonics.

The rock above the cavern exploded into a fountain of lava, spattering the mech as it flew into the asteroids dark interior, the molten rock eating through newly grown armour. He knew he had a moment's respite and nothing more. He repurposed some of the micro drone network for electronic warfare to help mask his sensor footprint and spent a moment reviewing the 3D representation of the cave network. It wasn't good. The network was too extensive. The Rakshasa had a number of ways in. It wasn't going to be as simple as powering the mech down, engaging the stealth systems and camping within view of the cave entrance, waiting for the Rakshasa mech to show itself.

"Hello, my friend." The voice that came over the comms link was almost a growl.

1893, Spitalfields, London

6. Cain had given the order but had not wielded the weapon. They weren't even officially at war. They were firing on their own people, subjects of the latest empire. He had hoped that this empire at least could bring order, make sense of things, but the warriors were all on the other side and a spear was no match for a bullet.

There had been something in the air, something almost tangible. Cain suspected that it emanated from Christchurch. He had heard whispers about the architect Hawksmoor, as though he were still alive. These experiments in the 'Geometry of Violence', the utilisation of technology far in advance of what was thought possible (and, he now suspected, somehow connected to his own curse) may have been the catalyst but Cain recognised a war when he saw one. The rich want to use the poor for their own ends. The poor want their lives to be better. Often these two things were mutually exclusive. This was the reason he was here in command of a platoon equipped with the latest weapon. This was why he was watching the two Maxim machine guns fire round after round into the Whitechapel Anarchist Committee and the rest of the rioters, all of whom were armed with little more than cudgels and torches. The poor needed to understand that they became the enemy when they stood in the way of what the powerful wanted. The gutters ran red. They may as well have been marching into a mincing machine. Cain could taste bile in the back of his throat. He had never felt further away from what he wanted to be. Disgusted, he ordered the gunners to stop firing before walking away from his command.

After the Loss, Ubaste System

He gave some thought as to whether or not he should answer. The carrier signal contained a number of discrete electronic warfare attacks, most designed to find him rather than disable his mech. He approved of this, the Rakshasa pilot of the other mech was just looking for a stand up fight. He would have liked to oblige but he really didn't fancy his chances. As he cut the thrusters and tried to bleed off heat to lower his signature, he decided that stealth was still his best option.

The mech was just drifting now as he took in his surroundings. The cavern was roughly oval in shape, the walls formed of a series of pressure ridges that made him think of the serrated maws of some titanic ocean going predator. There were a number of natural passages leading away from the main cavern, which gave him pause. So far the other mech had the advantage, the element of surprise. Mechs were coming to the end of their use as a weapon. They were being superseded by increasingly more sophisticated, powerful and much smaller combat exoskeletons. He had heard extraordinary claims made about combat exoskeletons that made extensive use of Seeder Tech. Judging by the Rakshasa's ability to get the jump on him, he assumed that the other mech had better stealth and sensor systems than his own. This was bad news in the game that they were playing at the moment.

"You know we will die out here, don't you?" the Rakshasa asked again. "Our carrier ships are gone. Neither of us have comms powerful enough to reach in-system. There's no relief coming, it's neither cost effective nor strategically important enough to send a search party. Are you prepared to die for what you believe salary-man?"

His mouth felt dry but his voice didn't crack when he replied: "I can't die."

1944 CE, Arnhem, The Netherlands

7.   The bridge was on fire as the Tiger II heavy tank belonging to SS 10 Panzer rolled across it. The British paratroopers had attacked the pillbox on the southern end with a flamethrower and hit the ammunition store. The subsequent explosion set fire to the fresh paint on the metal superstructure. The red flickering light was reflected in the waters of the Lower Rhine and illuminated the surrounding area.

"Target!" Jorgen, Cain's gunner shouted. Cain opened his mouth to give the order to fire but something that sounded like a shell from a Piat gun hit the tank's armoured skirt causing the hollow charge to detonate before it penetrated the Tiger II's armour. Cain felt the tank shift slightly, the ringing sound made him go deaf just for a moment. Once it would have made him feel trapped but after the Ukraine and the fighting retreat through Normandy he felt very little, except tired.

"Fire!" he finally shouted, but Jorgen had blood coming out of his ears. Cain tapped him on the shoulder in the cramped tank cabin and gestured for him to fire. Jorgen nodded numbly, looking at his commander with dead eyes. Turning his attention back to the viewport, Cain could see the muzzle flashes of small arms fire from every window of the five-storey house on the banks of the river. The incoming fire from the British paratroopers sparked off the tank's armour. It felt as though the Tiger II had been knocked back when Jorgen fired the 88mm main gun. The five-storey house seemed to jump into the air and was then replaced by a rising cloud of dust.

After the massacre at Spitalfields and the subsequent cover up, Cain had become more and more disheartened with the increasing mechanisation, industrialisation and one-sidedness of war. What Odo had told him was true, there were no more warriors. He had known that but the older you were the more difficult rationalising change became.

He hadn't fought in the Great War. The poison gas and machine guns were so very far away from what he saw as his vocation. But out of a war that had managed to horrify a soldier as seasoned as Cain came something new, or rather the return of something old. The men-at-arms, the knight, the cavalryman had returned, or so he had thought. Instead of horses, they rode in tanks or flew through the sky in biplanes.

He fought in the air in Spain, fighting for order against those he saw as the successors to the barbarian hordes that had challenged Rome. Then he had joined those seeking to form a new, pure, warrior elite. It hadn't taken him long to realise that it was nonsense. Perhaps he had known all along. The warrior ethos they preached was mere lies, used to bolster weak and frightened men looking for something, someone to blame. By purity they meant bigotry. They confused the joy of war with their own tawdry invented mythologies. They were more delusional than the samurai and now the rest of the world was coming for them.

Then Cain started to wonder about it all. Had each and every brotherhood he ever fought with been nothing more than a death cult? He had wondered whom he was fighting, who he was raging at.

His disgust for the Nazis came to the fore when he found out about the camps. As the tank turned off the bridge and into the rubble-strewn streets of Arnhem, he realised he had been here before. This time, however, he had come with those from *Magna Germania* and they were far more barbaric than any of the tribes that had risen with the Batavian auxiliaries. Cain triggered the machine gun, sending tracers arcing out towards the surviving paratroopers staggering from the ruins of the destroyed house. He wondered why, despite choosing the wrong side, despite the disgust, he was still fighting.

After the Loss, Ubaste System

"Clone insurance? Impressive for a lowly military contractor, salary man." Some of the Rakshasa's words sounded a little slurred. He assumed it was because the feline warrior had a mouthful of implanted fangs, low-tech grafts designed to replicate those of their *felinus erectus* ancestors. A traditionalist. "I'm fighting for my home, salary man."

He wanted to tell the Rakshasa that it was a lie, an excuse. You might fight for your home, but you don't embrace technological devolution for it. That wasn't why people became warriors. He knew that now.

"Is this what you want, salary man? To hide until your systems fail, until you have drunk all your own piss, eaten your own scat and there is no more air to breathe?" The Rakshasa's voice was little more than a whisper, a low growl of menace and promise.

"What do you want?" he asked over the comms link.

"You know what I want."

"Then show yourself."

There! The Rakshasa's mech drifted in shadow out of the mouths of one of the adjoining passages, a passage that he'd thought too small for the other war machine.

With a thought he triggered the boosters, a hard burn straight at the enemy mech. The fusion lance stabbed out, illuminating the cavern. The vacuum was filled with thousands of electromagnetically driven rounds but he did not launch missiles. Even now he could feel exhilaration surging through vastly altered neurochemistry. If this were just a trap on the part of the Rakshasa, a cheap ruse, then he would be disappointed.

1968 CE, Somewhere Over Laos

8. The Huey was on loan from the Air Cavalry. The rocket pods

and miniguns mounted on either side of the helicopter drastically cut down on the amount of cargo the Huey could carry and made it handle like a wardrobe. The runs into the Hmong-held highlands were becoming more and more perilous. The Mekong River snaked away into the distance below them. The land surrounding the river was a mix of dense jungle and a desolation of bomb craters where there had once been more jungle. Many of the craters were at least partially flooded from the river's overspill. Even at night, even in the air, Cain found it impossible to get away from the humidity, from the corrupt, sweet stench of the jungle below. Right now his eyes were locked on the horizon, however. It was a wall of fire as a B-52 Arc Light mission dropped enough ordinance to make even the most fervent communist believe in hell. Watching it through the bulky night vision goggles they had been issued with for the night flights, the fire burned green. It only added to the alien feel of the place.

He had been in Indochina since 1946. For a while he served in the French Foreign Legion with other ex-members of the Waffen SS. After one-too-many close calls with Mossad agents and his erstwhile comrades starting to comment about how he wasn't aging, he had gone to work with the CIA. The intelligence agency had arranged for a new identity. He had been here for more than twenty years now and still hadn't got used to the place.

"What's that?" 'John' asked loudly over the clatter of the rotors. Cain's co-pilot's real name wasn't John. It wasn't even some covert alias. He just wasn't important enough for Cain to remember his real name, so he called him John instead. Cain turned to follow his co-pilot's gaze. The night vision goggles caused tunnel vision. Cain was about to ask him what he'd seen when he saw the flickering ghost light of muzzle flashes illuminating the jungle canopy from within. He reckoned it was a small patrol, maybe four-to-six men. The answering fire lit up a much larger part of the jungle.

"Someone's really catching it down there," John shouted. "What are you doing?" Cain had banked the chopper towards the gunfight. "We don't have any room!" His co-pilot glanced back at the bales stacked high in the cargo area.

Cain knew that it would all depend on whether or not whomever was engaged in the firefight heard their rotors over the gunfire. Then the sky lit up as a parachute flare illuminated the whole area. John screamed and yanked his NVGs off his head. Cain didn't scream, somehow his eyes had compensated for the flash. He removed the goggles however. He had always seen very well at night. It took him a moment to find the soldier who had fired the flare. He was standing on the borderline between the jungle and the desert of bomb craters, staring straight at them. Three figures ran by him, stopped, turned and fired back into the jungle. Cain guessed they were a Long Range Reconnaissance Patrol, Lurps. The flare was a ballsy move. Yes it had got Cain's attention but it also made it easier for the Pathet Lao soldiers to see where they were.

"Fucking idiot!" John snapped from the co-pilot's seat. Tracer fire was arcing up out of the jungle towards the Huey now. Cain was holding the helicopter steady, hovering in the air, searching the ground, ignoring the sound of bullets hitting the helicopter's fuselage. "What are you doing? Get us out of here! They're on the wrong side of the border!"

Cain ignored his over-excited co-pilot as he looked for a place to land. He glanced back at the Lurps. They were moving away from the jungle, two of them provided covering fire whilst the other two ran. They were laying down a lot of bullets, burning through ammunition. The Pathet Lao were pouring out of the jungle behind the Lurps and off to the patrol's right.

"Fuck this!" John snapped and reached for the joystick of the helicopter's duel controls.

"Touch that stick and I will kill you," Cain said simply. Something in his voice made John hesitate.

"Goddamned psycho!" the co-pilot snapped but he moved his hand from the stick. Cain triggered two rockets from each pod mounted on the sides of the helicopter. It was beautiful. The four rockets drew a line of fire from the chopper to the treeline. Against the reds and oranges of blossoming explosions he saw the silhouettes of broken bodies flung into the air. Cain was smiling as he shifted the chopper to the right and fired another two rockets from each of the pods.

"Okay, you've done your good deed for the day, let's get the fuck out of here!" John shouted.

Cain took the helicopter down to land on the precarious piece of ground between three craters that he'd spotted earlier.

"What the fuck are you doing?" John screamed.

Cain felt spittle fleck his cheek. The Pathet Lao had beaten them to it. Cain had to circle around the landing zone so he didn't fire into the Lurps team as they made their way from crater to crater under heavy fire. He triggered the miniguns. The six rotating barrels on each weapon fired rounds so quickly that the individual reports merged into one long buzzsaw ripping noise. Cain used the tracers as a guide to walk the rounds into the largest concentration of Pathet Lao as the communist soldiers scattered, diving for cover in craters. Those not quick enough were torn apart. He brought the Huey into hover above the LZ. He turned the chopper, firing the minigun over the head of the patrol and hopefully into the pursuing Pathet Lao, cartridge cases raining down on the craters. John was screaming something about drawing as much attention as possible to a covert operation. John didn't seem to 'get' South East Asia. Cain was finding the screaming very, very annoying.

The Lurps team had almost reached the LZ. The Huey was taking an awful lot of fire. Holes were appearing in the cockpit's windscreen, bullets penetrating the fuselage and burying themselves in the contents of the bales behind them as Cain brought the helicopter into land. Moments before he touched down on the muddy ground he looked down to see a wounded Pathet Lao soldier pushing herself along the ground, the bottom part of her leg missing. She was still clutching her rifle. Cain locked eyes with her as he brought the Huey down, landing on her.

"We can't fucking carry them!" John broke his reverie. Made him look away from her. Cain drew his sidearm and shot 'John' in the face. Then he climbed out of the chopper.

Outside the false safety of the helicopter, away from the godlike destructive power of the miniguns and the rocket pods, the humidity, the sweating corruption of the place suffused him. He was drunk on it, addicted and laughing at all the lies he'd had to tell himself in the past about why. He fired his sidearm in the general direction of the Pathet Lao, or British Paratroopers, or vigilantes, or warrior monks, hellaquins, Germanian tribesfolk, Persians, it didn't matter. Nor did it matter that in Normandy he had fought the fathers of the men who were sprinting towards him.

The Lurps were in one of the craters just below the LZ now. Involved in a vicious hand-to-hand fight too confusing for Cain to intervene in. Cain heard a moan of pain. He turned back to the Pathet Lao soldier he'd landed on. Somehow, despite most of the lower part of her body having been crushed, she was still alive. Bullets were flying into the Huey, impacting into the mud all around him, even tugging at his flight suit, creasing his helmet but Cain found himself looking down at her again, staring as she tried to bring her rifle to bear. It hadn't been his intention to land on her. He wanted to kill her because she was this year's enemy, not torture her. He knew he should put her out of her misery but he wanted to remember the beauty of this moment, the purity. Then he knelt down, drew his *ehrendolch*, his so-called honour dagger, and slit her throat. He sheathed the dagger and took her AK-47. He stood up and started firing into the still-closing dark shapes of the Pathet Lao as the Lurps team leader reached him.

"We're here, man! Get back in the Slick!" the team leader shouted. Cain sighted on a figure trying to run from one crater to another. He squeezed the AK-47's trigger, leaning into the kick. The figure slumped to the ground.

"You need to empty the chopper first," Cain said as he

looked for another target, catching the look of dismay on the camo-painted face. The team leader was shouting instructions to the rest of his team as Cain fired again. The Lurps machine gunner joined Cain, firing his weapon from the shoulder as though the M-60 was an overgrown rifle, the phosphorous light of the tracers disappearing into the dark masses of the approaching figures. The other three members were cutting the straps on the bales filled with Laotian heroin and dumping the fortune in drugs out into the mud.

The machine gunner collapsed. He'd been too good at his job, attracted too much attention. Cain was vaguely aware of getting shot himself. He staggered, tried to bring the AK-47 back to his shoulder but the stock was gone. He heard first one and then the other door gun on the Huey start up.

"We're good, man! We need to go!" the team leader screamed at him as he dragged the machine gunner back towards the chopper. Cain threw the AK-47 into the helo. The other two Lurps were manning the door guns, providing covering fire. The team leader took a round in the arm, dropped the machine gunner as he sat down hard in the mud. The helicopter was full of holes, Cain had no idea if it would fly. Another round hit him like a hammer blow. Cain stumbled forward and fell against the chopper. The team leader was up, dragging the machine gunner. One of the door guns had gone silent as its operator helped the machine gunner into the chopper. Cain couldn't breathe as he climbed back into the cockpit.

He wasn't sure about the rest of it. He remembered the Huey wasn't responding well. He remembered firing the miniguns, and the remaining rockets as the Lurps fired the two door guns. He remembered the return fire as beautiful, glowing, inverted rain rising from the jungle and the moonlike surface of the crater-pitted land. He remembered the screaming of the team leader as he fought to keep the machine gunner alive. He remembered his disappointment when it ended, when he started to breathe again, the come down as he flew into the rising sun. And he remembered glancing at 'John'. No John hadn't 'got' South East Asia. He hadn't understood war. Here they could do what they wanted. Here they lived as gods did.

After the Loss, Ubaste System

The glow of the of the Rakshasa's mech's missiles launching backlit the enemy war machine, throwing it into shadow. The stabbing light of the fusion lance turned new growth armour into liquid. His vision was filled with red, scrolling, warning sigils but he paid them no heed as he closed. The missiles plasma contrails drew lines of light from the enemy mech towards his own war machine. Red light connected his point defence lasers to the incoming missiles, detonating them and then he was caught in a storm of silent force and light that further battered the already heavily damaged mech. Then the storm broke and he was flying straight at the other war machine. He could see the puffs of powdered armour all over the cat-like machine from the impacts of hypersonic rounds fired from his arm mounted rotary assault cannon. Closer and closer, ignoring every impact, every warning sigil, the transfer heat in the mech's cramped cockpit. Then came the bone jarring impact as he hit the other war machine low on the torso. The impact was hard enough to rattle his teeth despite the gyroscope in the pilot's cradle. He felt the Rakshasa mech elbow him in the back. All he had to do was hold on just a little longer. Lock his arms around the other mech and then detonate the warhead on every missile in his back-mounted launchers.

The Loss, Just Outside San Francisco

9.   The sky was red now. It had happened as he slept. On a nearby rock someone had sprayed the words: 'The Empire never ended.' Cain could feel the magic in the air, the demon parasites that would consume or transform. Except he knew they weren't demons now. He guessed they were alien life forms of some sort, or perhaps just their tech, a weapon that infected everything.

From his position on the hill he looked down at the warped, twisted mockery of the bayside city. Even from here he could tell that the things moving in the streets weren't human any more. So far his 'curse' had managed to fight off the alien spores.

Cain checked his surroundings and brought his AK-47 up. The stock that he had carved himself fitted snugly against his shoulder. He was heading down into the city. Food had become an issue and he was hoping to be able to avoid having to eat warped human flesh, though it wouldn't be the first time, sieges are hard. He heard the distant echoing crack of gunfire from the city's steel and glass canyons. Food was at a premium but somehow there were always enough weapons and ammunition.

If the spores were tech then it went some way towards validating Cain's theory that technology was the single biggest enemy of the warrior spirit. It should be hard to kill someone, take effort. You should be close enough to smell their evacuated bowels as you violated flesh with metal, close enough to see the death in their eyes, to understand the sacrifice your enemy had made. The more removed you are from that the less the deaths seem to matter. He'd listened to recordings of attack helicopter pilots laughing as they hit civilians with cannon fire. Cain wagered that wouldn't have happened if they had to look each and every person they killed in the eye.

Cain had done his best to embrace technology. With a new identity he had become a drone operator. He wasn't sure why. He suspected that he had always felt himself inextricably connected to war, perhaps because of the nature of his original sin. Drones were merely the latest iteration of the tools of his trade. He had sat in an air conditioned bunker more then ten thousand kilometres away as the drone fed back footage of the target, a walled property in a suburb of Baghdad close to the banks of the Euphrates river. Once again it seemed that the West had come to prize the secrets of Babylon out of the East. Something had been bothering him all night. The area was familiar. Then he realised that he was looking down on Cunaxa, where he had stood with

Clearchus and the rest of the Ten Thousand. He remembered what he had felt that day in the heat and the dust. The feel of pushing iron into flesh. The look on his enemy's face. Then he had launched the missile from the drone and watched on a monitor as, half a world away, an explosion replaced the house. There was no immediacy here. The drone wasn't a weapon, it was a game; you couldn't connect with the destruction of something precious through a screen. There was no rush. That was when Cain had walked out.

As he moved though the scrub on the side of the hill, the familiar heft of the AK-47 felt comfortable. He understood the allure of the gun. Vietnam had peeled back the layers of lies he had clothed himself in, the lies he'd used to justify what he did. Vietnam had taught him to be honest with himself. There was no wrong or right, just wants and needs. Weapons were fetish items in both senses of the word. People needed to be honest about their desire for them, about why children had to die in schools, about the arousal felt in unguarded moments by those who used weapons. The drone missed the point. To some extent the AK-47 missed the point. A conservative estimate of the amount of deaths caused by the weapon since it's invention put the number at about ten million. Until the current on-going extinction event, the AK-47 had been the single most deadly weapon of mass destruction ever invented, and that was Cain's point: it was all too easy. Just like the spores. This wasn't a battle, humanity wasn't fighting a war; it was being exterminated as an afterthought.

Cain stopped as he felt the change in the air. He watched the mushroom cloud grow over the city. A last ditch attempt by humans to pretend that they had some level of control over the situation. It reminded him of a scorpion stinging at a parasite in its own flesh. He smiled and wondered if this would be enough. Then the firestorm turned him to ash.

It wasn't enough. Not for the tall obsidian-skinned man whose face Cain could never remember. This was the man who had danced with the witches when the legions came. He had whispered in Nero's ear, in Hitler's, and he had been waiting for Cain when they' pulled him from the cloning tanks on one of the few seed ships that had escaped Earth. The man with the obsidian skin wanted him to play the part of Mars again.

After the Loss, Ubaste System

10. Cain had ejected from his mech even as the plasma fire from the detonated warheads consumed both machines. The explosion had superheated parts of the cavern, turning some of the closest pressure ridges into fountains of molten rock. The plasma fire reduced much of his space suit's armour to slag, and despite the augmentations his body was battered so badly by the explosion that he lost consciousness.

Cain came to being pelted with lumps of molten rock. The Rakshasa hit him low in the torso. It was almost exactly the same place Cain's mech had tackled the feline's war machine. The wind was knocked out of him for just a moment as he slammed into the cavern wall. Cain's internal systems compensated and he could breathe again as he spun and bounced. The suit's barely functioning scanners fed back what information it could about the Rakshasa. The feline's suit had also been damaged in the explosion but a number of its weapons were still functioning. The feline had eschewed them all in favour of the powerknife in his right hand, the monomolecular blade oscillating at a frequency high enough to slip straight through the remaining armour on Cain's suit. The Rakshasa had left his visor clear. Cain could see his enemy's contorted, growling face. Warrior or not, this was one of the violent new breed Cain had heard about. He could read the madness of a tailored designer psychosis in his enemy's face. His body would be full of soft and hard augments, more machine than uplifted feline. It took every last little bit of strength that Cain had to maintain his grip on the feline's wrist, to hold the blurred blade away from his face. Now more than ever technology was narrowing the edge that experience had once provided.

Cain had left fear behind a long time ago. As he watched his latest death inch towards him, he wondered if this would be enough. Would the obsidian devil just regrow him and uplift his consciousness into the next copy? Detached, he wondered how many he had killed. He had lived for so long, fought in so many wars, he'd bombed entire worlds. Had he killed ten million, as many as the AK-47? As the blade touched his suit's helmet and he felt the vibration through his head, as he watched the tip protrude through his visor, he wondered what had made him think of that.

"No," he said quietly as he heard the air escaping from his helmet. "You've got to earn this."

It had been a mistake to fight the young warrior high on madness and his own augmentations strength to strength. He changed the direction of the force he was exerting on the feline's wrist. At the same time he jerked his head to one side. The blade skidded across the visor, making a deep score. Only one of Cain's weapon systems was still working, a last ditch close-in weapon only used during moments of desperation. He let go of the Rakshasa's wrist with both hands. The feline warrior immediately started bringing the power blade to bear again. Acid squirted out of the tube on the suit's left forearm, hitting the Rakshasa's visor. The powerful acid immediately began unravelling the molecular bonds of the visor's material. It was still too slow. Cain reached out with his right hand, still blood red beneath the gauntlet despite the cloning, and grabbed one of the still partially molten micro-asteroids and slammed it into the Rakshasa's visor, shattering it. Then he hit him again and again in the face. Exultation. Teeth bared, hissing, Cain felt the impact of the cooling rock striking the feline's face run up his arm. There was no warm splash of blood this time. The red droplets froze on contact with the vacuum.

Cain was still straddling the Rakshasa's now dead body as they floated amongst the cooling rock. His suit's self-repair systems had already fixed the breach in his helmet. He had never understood God's curse. He had always done what he had wanted to, lived as he pleased, fought, no, killed as he chose. He looked down at the frozen corpse. It was the same each and every time, regardless of gender, race, or species, in the end they all had his brother's face. He was bored of killing his brother.

Author's Note: Thanks to Yvonne Cunningham and Anthony Jones for advice on Roman Legionnaires and 16th Century Japan, respectively. The mistakes and downright fabrications remain my own.

About the Authors

Nik Abnett writes short stories, novels, computer games and comic books, often in collaboration with her partner Dan Abnett. When she's not writing, she spends her time messing about with old cameras and baking bread. Nik was runner-up for the inaugural Mslexia novel writing prize, and her first solo original novel *Savant* will be published by Solaris in 2016. She lives and works in the UK, with Dan and a small menagerie.

Amy DuBoff is the author of the *Cadicle* space opera series. She has always loved science fiction in all forms, including books, movies, shows and games. She first studied creative writing at the Vancouver School of Arts and Academics, and then received a Bachelor of Science in Psychology from Portland State University. Amy currently lives in Portland, Oregon, USA, with her husband. When she's not writing, she enjoys travel, wine tasting, binge-watching TV series, and playing epic strategy board games. Find her online at: www.amyduboff.com

Michael Brookes' passion for science fiction extends back to his youth with the discovery of Arthur C Clarke and Isaac Asimov. That love continues to the current day and into his day job as the Executive Producer for the *Elite: Dangerous* video game. As well as writing and guiding the game's fiction, he has his own range of science fiction books, including *Sun Dragon* and the Mitchell & Morton series.

Janet Edwards is the author of the Earth Girl trilogy. As a child, she read a huge amount of science fiction and fantasy. She studied Maths at Oxford, and went on to suffer years of writing unbearably complicated technical documents before deciding to write something that was fun for a change. She has a husband, a son, a lot of books, and an aversion to housework. Find out more at Janet's website: www.janetedwards.com

Una McCormack is a New York Times bestselling author of TV tie-in novels based on franchises such as Star Trek and Doctor Who. She also writes short fiction and audio dramas, and is a university lecturer in creative writing.

Christopher Nuttall was born in Edinburgh. He writes science fiction, fantasy, historical fiction and more. He wrote his first manuscript in 2005, since when he has been responsible for some forty published titles, including the best-selling *Ark Royal* and its sequels and the popular Empire's Corps series.

Mercurio D. Rivera's fiction has been nominated for the World Fantasy Award and has appeared in markets such as *Asimov's, Interzone, Lightspeed, Nature,* and *Black Static.* His collection *Across the Event Horizon* (NewCon Press, 2013) was called "weird and wonderful" with "dizzying switchbacks" by Tor.com. His stories have been published in China, Poland and the Czech Republic and taught in writing courses at university level in the USA and Venezuela. Find out more at: www.mercuriorivera.com

Adam Roberts is the BSFA Award-winning author of several score science fiction short stories and sixteen science fiction novels, most recently *The Thing Itself* (Gollancz 2015). He teaches literature and creative writing at Royal Holloway, University of London.

Robert Sharp's debut novella *The Good Shabti* (Jurassic London, 2014) was shortlisted for the Shirley Jackson Award. During the day he works for English PEN, promoting free speech and defending an author's right to break taboos, transgress cultural boundaries and speak truth to power.

Gavin Smith is the Dundee-born author of the hard-edged, action-packed SF novels *Veteran*, *War in Heaven*, *Age of Scorpio*, *A Quantum Mythology* and *The Beauty of Destruction*, as well as the short story collection *Crysis Escalation*. He has collaborated with Stephen Deas as the composite personality Gavin Deas and co-written *Elite: Wanted*, and the shared world series *Empires: Infiltration* and *Empires: Extraction*.

Allen Stroud is a writer and lecturer at Buckinghamshire New University in High Wycombe, England. He runs the BA (Hons) Creative Writing for Publication course and is studying for his Ph. D. in Creative Writing at the University of Winchester. Allen is also the editor of the British Fantasy Society Journal (www.britishfantasysociety.co.uk). He can be found online at: www.allenstroud.com

Tim C. Taylor lives with his family in an old village in England called Bromham. When he was a young and impressionable lad, between 1977 and 1978, many important things happened to him all at once: *2000AD*, *Star Wars*, *Blake's 7*, *Traveller*, and *Dungeons & Dragons*. Consequently, he now writes science fiction novels for a living. You can chat with him and discover more about the worlds of the Human Legion at www.humanlegion.com.

Tade Thompson lives and works in the United Kingdom. Along with numerous short stories, he is the author of the novel *Making Wolf* which won the Kitschies Golden Tentacle Award in 2016, and the upcoming sci-fi novel *Rosewater*.

Ian Whates is the author of eight novels (two co-written), most recently the Firefly-esque space opera jaunt *Pelquin's Comet*. Sixty-odd of his short stories have appeared in various venues, and he has edited some thirty anthologies. His most recent collection is *Dark Travellings* (Fox Spirit 2016). His work has twice been shortlisted for the BSFA Award and once for the Philip K. Dick Award. In his spare time he runs independent publisher NewCon Press, which he founded by accident in 2006.

Jo Zebedee writes science fiction and fantasy, either on the streets of her native Northern Ireland or in her space opera world of Abendau. She has three novels released to date with another two in the pipeline. She blogs regularly on writing, reading, and things to rant about in general, at jozebwrites.blogspot.uk. She also runs a consultancy, and runs after kids and pets.

Now We Are Ten

The sister volume to

Crises and Conflicts

Celebrating the first ten years of NewCon Press
With sixteen original stories written especially for this book

Available as a signed limited edition hardback,
paperback, and eBook

www.newconpress.co.uk

NEWCON
PRESS